SHE TOOK WHAT SHE WANTED
WITHOUT SAYING "PLEASE..."

"Listen to me, Longarm. It's been a long time since I've had a man I invited to my bed because I wanted to be with him. And almost from the first minute you walked through that door, I've been thinking about how fine it feels to be with a man I picked out for myself. Don't I look good to you?"

"Why, sure you do. You're a right pretty woman, Sarah."

"And I think you might be a pretty exciting man. I aim to find out! Stay around a while..."

Sarah stretched up on tiptoes, but she still had to pull Longarm's head down to kiss him. For a moment he did not return the kiss, but when her hot, moist tongue pushed between his lips and darted around, seeking his, Longarm took her into his arms and lifted her light body up so that they could do it right....

*Also in the LONGARM series
from Jove*

TABOR EVANS

LONGARM

AND THE COMANCHEROS

A JOVE BOOK

Chapter 1

Weariness mingling with reproach in his voice, Longarm asked, "Now you honestly don't expect me to ride a sorry nag like that all the way down through No Man's Land and halfway across Texas, do you, Sergeant?"

"Well, Marshal, I'll admit he ain't going to take no prizes for pretty," the remount sergeant major said, looking at the rawboned piebald gelding whose halter he was holding. "But he'll get you there."

"There, maybe," Longarm nodded. "But how about back?"

"He's a better nag than he looks like," the sergeant said.

Longarm shook his head without replying. He walked over to the rail of the paddock and lighted one of his cheroots while he studied the other horses that wandered around the enclosure. There were only eight of them, and of that number, three stood in hang-head dejection, unmoving; two more were sadly sway-backed, and another obviously had sore feet. Turning back to the sergeant major, he pointed to the two that looked to be in the best shape.

"How about one of those two, either that nice roan or the dapple?"

"I'm sorry, Marshal," the noncom replied. "They ain't army

1

stock. One of 'em belongs to the colonel's lady, and the other one's Major Carruthers' personal mount."

"If that's the best you can do, I guess I'll have to take it, then," Longarm said. "But it sure don't make me feel easier in my mind to leave for where I'm heading on such a poor-looking animal. What in hell's happened to the cavalry, any-how, not having any decent horses in the remount paddock in a big place like Fort Dodge, here?"

"Well, right now we got three troops in the field, and they had to take along some reserve horses." The sergeant major looked around and dropped his voice. "To tell you the truth, Marshal, we just don't get the kind of animals we need no more, now that all the Indians has been whipped and penned up on their reservations down in the Nation. There's none of us likes it, but I guess the officers can't do much to cure it."

"I'll take the piebald, then," Longarm told the man. "I don't say I'll be happy about it, but I guess we all got to make do with what we can get these days."

"Yessir. Well, if you'll step over to the stable with me, I'll get one of my men to saddle up for you while I write up a requisition." The sergeant looked at the saddle, saddlebags and rifle that Longarm had dropped beside the paddock fence. "That's your gear yonder, ain't it?"

Longarm nodded. The sergeant major started for the stable, with Longarm following. While the noncom was filling out the forms, Longarm said thoughtfully, "You know, I ain't been around Dodge City since the moon turned blue, but it was a rip-roaring hell-raiser back then. What's it like now?"

"It's been a pretty dead place since I got posted here about a year ago," the man said, frowning. "I hear it used to be different, when all the buffalo hunters brought their hides here to ship, but there's not all that many buffalo anymore, I guess. I'd say it's coming back to life a little bit, though. A lot of ranchers down in Texas are beginning to drive some cattle herds up to ship East. But it's sure as hell quiet right now."

"I guess there's still a few good saloons in town?"

"Oh sure. There's plenty of saloons. I don't know whether a man in your position would call any of them good or not, but you sure won't have no trouble getting a drink in Dodge."

"What I'm looking for is a saloon that might have a pretty good stock of liquor. I want to buy a bottle or so to carry with me. From what I hear, it can be a long way between saloons up in the unsettled part of Texas where I'm headed."

"If it's just whiskey you want, you can get plenty at the sutler's store right here on the fort."

"No thanks, Sergeant. I've had more'n enough of that raw, cut-down whiskey out of army sutler's barrels to last me a lifetime. More'n I can stand to think about. What I want is some good Maryland rye. Texas ain't too much for rye whiskey, I've found out, and bourbon's a mite sweet for my taste."

"Well, you might try Lonergan's place," the sergeant suggested. "Or the Long Branch, even if it ain't much more'n a hole in the wall. It's got a pretty good liquor stock, and the beer there's the best you can get in Dodge."

"Thanks." Longarm signed his name three times on the requisition forms the noncom held out to him, and returned them. "One more thing, Sergeant, and I'll be on my way. You think I might get a new map of the part of Texas I'm heading for, before I ride out? The one I'm carrying's pretty old, and it don't show too much detail north of Austin."

"You mean North Texas, Marshal?"

"Whatever they call the Llano Estacado down there. It's in the north, all right, but I ain't quite sure where."

"Ask at the engineers' office," the sergeant replied. "That Texas country's strange to me too."

"Strange to almost everybody except the Comanches, I guess," Longarm grinned. "Thanks, I'll see what the engineers say."

In the office of the Corps of Engineers, the young lieutenant shook his head when Longarm asked for a late map of North Texas. "I'm afraid not, Marshal. We've got plenty of maps of the Indian Nation, but since McKenzie whipped the Comanches back in '76, and got them penned up in the Indian Nation, we haven't had much need for maps of North Texas."

"It'd sure save me a lot of riding if I had a map that'd show me where I was at when I get down there," Longarm said regretfully. "But I'll make out without one, I guess. It won't be the first time."

"You might stop off at Fort Elliott on your way south," the lieutenant suggested. "It's up in the Texas Panhandle, just a few miles west of the Indian Nation boundary line, and—"

"I know about where it is," Longarm interrupted. "I just disremembered it was there, and I never was real close to it on any of the cases I handled in the Nation."

3

"You shouldn't have any trouble finding Elliott," the lieutenant said. "There's a pretty well-used military supply road that runs from Elliott over to Fort Supply, in the Nation. You can just follow the wheel ruts right to the fort."

"Sure. Well, thanks, Lieutenant. I'll be on my way, then."

Riding into Dodge City from the fort beside the Santa Fe right-of-way, Longarm found that the afternoon sun was now slanting low enough to glare in his eyes under the wide brim of his hat.

Old son, he told himself, *you might just as well make up your mind to stay here tonight, get a barbershop shave and supper in a cafe, and sleep in a real bed. Because it sure looks like it'll be bacon and spuds and parched corn and jerky and a blanket on the ground, once you hit that trail south.*

Riding into the thick dust of the main street, Longarm studied the saloon signs as the piebald gelding picked its way between the jagged, uneven rows of stores. Lonergan's Saloon didn't appeal to him; there were too many loafers sunning themselves on the board sidewalk in front of the place. He rode on until he saw the Long Branch sign, and even though from the outside the narrow building with its sagging batwings fitted the sergeant's description of it as a hole in the wall, Longarm decided to try it first. He pulled the piebald over to the hitch rail and dismounted.

Once inside, he decided that the sergeant's phrase had been even more aptly chosen than the Long Branch's exterior indicated. The place was barely a dozen feet wide, and perhaps three times as long. A scarred and unvarnished bar stretched the length of the interior, brass spittoons spaced along its foot rail. The floor was worn to splinters from the boots that had trodden it. There were plenty of bottles on the shelves of the backbar. Most of them were dusty, and a number of them held only an inch or so of liquor.

A stack of beer kegs stood along the back wall, beside a rear door. Tables crowded the narrow area that remained between the bar and the opposite wall. Only one of them was occupied. At it sat a solitary drinker. His back was turned to the bar, but Longarm judged by what he could see of the man's clothing that he was not a resident of Dodge City, for he wore a neat city suit over a white shirt with a high starched collar, and a derby hat was pushed far back on his head.

Longarm gave the man a casual glance and tagged him as

4

a solitary drunkard just starting on a prolonged spree. Two full bottles of whiskey stood on the table in front of him, as well as a third bottle that was almost empty.

Behind the bar stood a sleepy-eyed barkeep, his soiled apron hitched up around his chest, under his armpits. He looked up without interest when Longarm walked in, and made no move to step up and serve him.

Longarm stopped midway down the bar, in front of the barkeep. "I hope you got a bottle of Maryland rye. Tom Moore, if I got any choice."

"I'm afraid you ain't," the barkeep replied. "I got plenty of good bourbon, but I'm sold outa rye. That fellow over at the table there, he bought what was left in my last bottle of bar whiskey along with the only two other bottles off'n the backbar."

"Who in hell is he, anyhow? One of your town drunks?"

"Not that it's any of your damn business, mister, but I don't know him from Adam's off-ox. I been working here almost a year, and I never set eyes on him before."

"Looks like I'll have to ask him myself, then, if I expect to find out," Longarm commented as he turned and started toward the table. Getting closer, he could see the labels on the two bottles. One was Tom Moore, the other bore Joe Gideon's likeness, as did the bottle the stranger was just emptying into his glass. Longarm waited politely, lighting a cheroot, until the man at the table had sipped from his refilled glass.

Stepping up to where the stranger could see him, he said, "I ain't meaning to be nosy about your affairs, friend, but I was wondering if you're aiming to drink both of them bottles of rye whiskey all by yourself?"

"Sooner or later," the stranger replied, turning in his chair to face Longarm. "Why?"

"Why, I was sort of hoping you'd let me buy one of them full bottles off of you. Seeing as how you got a taste for good rye, and you got two bottles full, and I got none, I figured you might be willing to sell me that bottle of Tom Moore you got there. You see, I'm going down into Texas when I leave here, and it's mighty hard to find good rye whiskey there."

"It's damned near as hard to find good rye here in Kansas, after you get out into the little towns, mister. And I'm going to be working the little towns for a couple of weeks. I'm sorry I can't oblige you, but I'll need both bottles to see me through."

"Well, no harm in asking, I suppose," Longarm said.

"No harm. Sorry I can't oblige you."

Draining his glass, the man stood up, tucked a bottle of the rye under each arm, and started toward the batwings. Just as he reached them, the swinging doors burst open and several roughly dressed men started pushing into the saloon. The first two of them through the doors collided with the man who was going out, knocking one of the bottles from under his arm. He almost dropped the second bottle as he juggled it, catching the one that was falling just before it crashed to the floor.

"Don't be in such a hurry," he snapped at the pair who'd gotten inside the Long Branch. "You damned near made me drop my liquor."

"Well now, ain't that just too bad!" one of the newcomers snorted, as his companions outside crowded up to the still-open batwings to peer in curiously. "Suppose you just step aside now, and get outa our way while we come on in."

"I'll be glad to," the man with the whiskey said. He moved to one side as the three men still on the board sidewalk shoved into the Long Branch. The second man through glanced idly at the waiting whiskey-carrier, took another step forward, then stopped short and turned to face him.

"Well, move on, Abel!" urged the man behind him. "Let's get on up to the bar and get the ballast-dust outten our guzzles."

"Wait a minute," the man named Abel said, frowning. "I know this dude from someplace."

"I'm afraid you're mistaken." The man holding whiskey shook his head. "Even if you think you know me, I certainly don't recognize you."

"Well now, there just might be a good reason why you don't," Abel retorted. "Because I place you now. It was three years ago when I seen you last, mister. It was right here in Dodge too! You going to tell me you wasn't here then?"

"I don't lie, friend, it's not my style. Yes, I was here three years ago, and quite a few years before that, too. But I did business with a lot of men then, and I can't remember everybody I ran into."

"Well, I can't call your name either, but I never forget a face, mister," Abel said. Anger was growing in his voice as he talked. "And I sure do recall yours. I been waiting for a long time to run into you again!"

It was as obvious to Longarm as it was to the men with Abel that he was working up to a storm of anger.

One of his companions took Abel by the arm and said, "Oh, hell, Abel, pull up on that temper of yours and let's go get the drink we come in for. This fellow don't know what you're talking about, anybody can see that."

"You butt out, Smitty!" Abel snapped. "I got some unfinished business with this lying buzzard, and now's the best time I can see to wind it up!"

"Your friend's right," the man with the whiskey said soothingly. "Three years . . ." He shook his head. "I certainly don't remember having met you before, and I can't think that I've done anything to a man that'd keep him angry for that long."

"Well, I'll just dust off your memory for you," Abel said. "You're the damned cheating hide buyer that turned down the last bunch of flints I brought in here to Dodge to sell before the buffalo run out!"

"That may be true," the other man answered. "I did buy hides in Dodge for several years. And I had to turn down more than one batch of flints because whoever cured them didn't do a good job."

"You wasn't satisfied just turning mine down!" Abel shouted. "You had to go blabbing to all the other buyers that they wasn't cured proper! By God, mister, I never was able to sell them flints after you got through flapping your jaws all up and down the Santa Fe tracks! Cost me a season's take, you did! I ought've got around six thousand dollars for them flint hides!"

"Now look here," the former hide buyer said, "I'm sorry if you're still carrying a grudge against me after three years, but if I said those flint hides weren't cured properly then, I'll still stand by it. Because I never did cheat a buffalo hunter or the company I was buying for. If a man had good hides, I'd buy them at a fair price. If his hides looked like they'd go soft before they got to the tannery, I turned them down."

Taking a step forward, the fellow brushed past Abel, heading for the door. Longarm was tempted to call out to the man, to tell him that walking away from a quarrel picked by someone like Abel would not only resolve nothing, but could be downright dangerous. On second thought, he decided it was none

7

of his business and that he'd better stay out of it.

"Now, by God!" Abel snarled, "I don't take any man calling me a liar!"

Either the former hide buyer failed to catch the threat in Abel's voice, or he ignored it. He did not turn around, but kept on walking, and was outside the batwings and on the sidewalk before Abel acted. Pulling aside the rough, dusty work coat he was wearing, he began tugging at an ancient sidehammer Colt he wore in a belt holster.

Longarm had no time to reach Abel, but reacted in time to save the unsuspecting man from being backshot. Before Abel's pistol was completely out of its holster, Longarm had his own Colt out and leveled.

Abel was still bringing up his weapon, its muzzle coming up to aim at the departing man's back, when Longarm called loudly, "Abel! Drop that gun! Do it now, dammit!"

For a fraction of a second Abel hesitated while his head turned in the direction from which Longarm's shout had come. His eyes widened when he saw Longarm's Colt covering him, but anger had displaced common sense. Instead of letting his pistol fall to the floor, Abel swiveled to face Longarm, still bringing his gun's muzzle to bear, this time with Longarm as his target.

His move gave Longarm no choice. Like all veterans of many such confrontations, Longarm had learned that when facing a man with a gun aimed at you, shooting to wound can be a fatal mistake; in a second or less, even after your lead has struck, your antagonist can get off a shot that might be fatal.

Longarm fired. Abel's answering shot, triggered with his dying reflex, tore into the splintered floor of the Long Branch Saloon, ripping a streak of fresh yellow pine from its boards. A look of surprise flashed over Abel's face. The heavy side-hammer Colt seemed to pull him down as his gunhand dropped. He toppled back against the doorframe and slid silently to the floor.

In the first few seconds that ticked off after Longarm's shot, the silence that gripped the saloon seemed as thunderous as the report of the Colt had been. Longarm kept his gaze fixed on the men who'd come in with Abel, but out of the corner of his eye he could see the former hide buyer, frozen stiff in shock, staring at the group from the sidewalk.

Then the dead man's companions began stirring, surprise

8

and anger twisting their faces. Before they could move or speak, Longarm whipped his wallet out of his coat pocket and flipped it open to show his badge.

"You men hold still now," he commanded, his voice coolly level. "I ain't no gunhand. I'm a U.S. marshal, and I shot that man because he was drawing down to backshoot somebody."

"Just the same, you didn't have no right—" one of them began.

"Like hell I didn't!" Longarm said coldly. He held the men's attention with his gunmetal-blue eyes while he took out a cheroot and lighted it one-handed. None of the four men watching him moved or spoke. Longarm went on, "Your friend Abel begun that fuss. Maybe he didn't mean for things to happen like they did, but you was all standing right there watching."

Again there was silence, broken by the man called Smitty.

"I'd say the marshal's right," he told the others. "Abel was as good as being a dead man the minute he pulled out his gun."

"Now wait a minute!" one of the others protested.

Longarm cut him off short. "No, you wait a minute. I'll tell you what your friend's trying to say, if you don't see it yet. You men know better'n I do that a jury here in Dodge City wouldn't waste a minute on a man that backshot somebody who maybe didn't even have a gun on him."

Smitty nodded soberly. "That's about what I was trying to say, Marshal." He turned to the others. "If Abel had gunned that fellow out there, he'd've been dancing a jig at the end of a rope necktie before this time tomorrow."

"Smitty's right," another of the men agreed. "Abel always was a damn fool, anyhow. Never could hold back his temper, once he started gitting riled."

"It don't surprise me none, neither," said the third man. "I guess about all we can do now is see he gets put away proper."

"You do that," Longarm told them. "Now, when I write up my report, I'll explain how it all come about, so you men don't need to worry about a thing but getting your friend buried."

"Which is what we better do," Smitty said thoughtfully. He turned to his companions. "Come on. We'll get him over to old man Wilson. Maybe we can still get him planted today."

With Abel's body sagging between them, the four survivors left the saloon. The former hide buyer, still standing in a state of shock on the sidewalk outside the saloon, moved aside to let them pass. Then he looked at Longarm and said, "I owe you quite a lot, Marshal, and I don't even know your name."

"Name's Long. I work out of the Denver office, not that it makes any difference."

"I'm Carl Werner. And I give you my oath, Marshal Long, if I did turn down that man's load of hides three years ago, I don't remember it."

"Like you said, his wasn't the only hides you turned down."

"No. But nobody ever turned it into a shooting matter with me before. I didn't have any idea that that man Abel would. I'd be a dead man right now if you hadn't done what you did. I owe you quite a lot, Marshal."

"You don't owe me a thing," Longarm replied. "It took me by surprise for a minute too."

"I don't suppose I was very smart," the man said thoughtfully. "I saw enough shooting scrapes begin out of next to nothing when I was here buying hides. I should have known—"

"You ought to've been looking back," Longarm told him. "I've seen men shot over a lot less than what he was blaming you for."

"It seems to me the least I can do is—well, you wanted to buy one of these bottles of rye I've got." He held out the unopened bottle of Tom Moore. "Here. If you want the other bottle too, you're welcome to it."

"Now I wouldn't shoot a man for a bottle of whiskey, Mr. Werner," Longarm protested.

"Hell's bells, I know that!" Werner exclaimed. "But I sure do owe you something, and if I've got you sized up right, you'd take it as an insult if I offered you money."

"You're right about that," Longarm said. "I ain't even real sure I'd be doing the right thing if I was to take your whiskey."

"Nonsense!" Werner said. Then he went on, "Why don't we talk about it over a drink? I was just starting out to get some supper, but I think I need a drink more than I need food right now. How about you?"

"Well, I'll be glad to sit down and have a drink with you." Longarm turned to start back to the table.

Werner put a hand on his arm to stop him. "Not in there, Marshal. In a few minutes the Long Branch is going to be full of men wanting to rehash what happened. I don't feel like I want to be stared at by a bunch of curious strangers. Let's go

10

up to my room in the Dodge House and have our drink in peace."

For a moment Longarm was about to refuse, but it had been a long, dry day and the thought of a smooth-sharp sip of Maryland's best rye whiskey sliding down his throat changed his mind. He'd also remembered his plan to stay over in Dodge that night.

"I'll just take you up on that invitation, Mr. Werner," he said. "I guess I could use a little drink myself, about now."

Chapter 2

Longarm and Charles Werner sat in Werner's room in the Dodge House, the opened bottle of Old Joe Gideon on the small table between them, glasses in their hands. The still-untouched bottle of Tom Moore was on the bureau. In spite of Werner's urgings, Longarm hadn't yet agreed to accept the whiskey. In one corner of the sparsely furnished room, Long-arm's saddlebags leaned against the wall, his rifle in front of them. As he'd remarked to Werner when they were leaving the saloon, anybody who tempts thieves by going off and leaving his gear on an unwatched horse at a public hitch rail deserves to have it stolen.

As will most men who have just come unscathed from a period of stress, Longarm and Werner had been unwinding their taut nerves by talking about everything except the events of the immediate past.

Werner was saying, "You know, Marshal, when I take time to look back on it, I don't think I've ever seen anything that I can compare with the way the buffalo-hide trade ended a few years ago."

Longarm nodded. "I've heard it was a sort of sudden thing."

"It just happened overnight," Werner went on. "Why, the

12

last season I was buying hides here in Dodge, there were all the hides in the world, hundreds of thousands of them, stacked up along the railroad right-of-way in rows that were a couple of miles long and maybe a half-mile deep. Then, the next year, there weren't any."

"That's enough to surprise a man, all right."

"Well, it was sudden, but not exactly a surprise. In the office back East, we kept in touch with the Santa Fe for about three weeks before the buying season opened every year. They used to wire us about twice a week to let us know how many hides the hunters were bringing in to their different stations, so we'd be able to plan our buying trips. That year they kept wiring that no hides were coming in. I thought maybe it was just the Kansas depots that weren't getting any, so I started checking with other buyers, those who'd been working farther north."

"And they were getting the same story?"

"Exactly. When I found out it wasn't just the southern market that was drying up, I didn't even bother to make another trip to Dodge. That's why I haven't been here for three years."

"But you figure the hide trade's about to open up again?" Longarm asked.

Werner shook his head. "No. From what I've gathered, there just aren't any more buffalo left. Not around here, not farther south, not up in Montana or Dakota Territory. Oh, I suppose there are bound to be some buffalo left. Not many, though. And if my guess is right, they're scattered out here and there in little bunches, fifty or a hundred in one place. But nothing like the herds that would support the kind of hide trade we used to have."

"Funny, ain't it?" Longarm remarked. "Funny how they just went, all of a sudden that way. I never figured there was enough hunters to wipe out all them buffalo."

"It seems they did, though. Pity, too. There'd still be a market for hides, you know. Why, right now I'd be more than glad to pay twelve or fourteen dollars apiece for hides I used to buy for a dollar and a half."

"You're still in that line of business, then?"

"Oh yes. But I buy cattle hides now. It's not as interesting, dealing with slaughterhouse managers instead of buffalo hunters, but it's a living." Werner tipped the bottle over their glasses to refill them, and after he'd waited politely for Longarm to take the first sip and had a swallow himself, he went on, "Now I'd imagine your business is always interesting, Marshal. No two cases are ever alike, are they?"

"Not exactly," Longarm agreed. He'd never enjoyed discussing his work with those who weren't in the same line. He avoided amplifying his reply by pulling a cheroot out of his coat pocket and flicking his thumbnail across the head of a match to light it. He blew a puff of blue smoke into the gathering dimness of the hotel room.

Werner was persistent. "You said you were going down into Texas. A new case, I guess? Or is it something you can't talk about?"

"Oh, there ain't no mystery of any kind about the case I'm on," Longarm replied. "It's only that I don't know enough about it yet to do much talking. I ain't exactly sure where I'm supposed to look, or what I'm looking for. About all I got to go on is that somebody in the Indian Bureau had a hunch there's something fishy going on, so I got sent to find out."

"It sounds to me as though you've been sent out on something of a wild-goose chase, then," Werner suggested.

Longarm nodded without replying. Werner's remark had reminded him that he'd said much the same thing to his chief two days earlier, when Billy Vail had assigned him to the case.

Longarm had reported for duty that morning even later than usual. When he'd stuck his head into the chief marshal's office, Vail was reading the last of the overnight wires that had come in on the direct telegraph line between the Federal Building in Denver and Justice Department headquarters in Washington. Without looking up from the sheaf of pink flimsies, Vail motioned with a pudgy pink hand for Longarm to come in.

His suspicions about the kind of case he was going to be assigned were immediately aroused by the lack of his chief's customary remarks about deputies who didn't seem to be able to get to work on time, but Longarm said nothing. He stepped into the office and stood waiting for a moment before pulling up to a corner of Vail's desk the red morrocco-leather chair that stood against the wall. He'd barely settled down into it when Vail put down the flimsies and gazed at him across his paper-strewn desk.

"I hope you're as ready as you generally are to do a little traveling," the chief marshal said without any preliminaries.

"Where you figuring to send me this time, Billy?"

Vail ignored the question and went on, "I've got my clerk writing up your papers now. Travel vouchers, expense money, all the other stuff you'll need."

"Billy, how come you don't want to tell me where this case is at?" Longarm asked.

"Oh, I didn't mention that, did I? It's in Texas."

"Now hold on a minute! You know I ain't right popular with the Texas Rangers, Billy. If they catch me down in what they figure's their country again, they're likely to gang up on me and kick my ass clear back to Denver with them damn pointedy boots they all favor."

"You don't have to worry about the Rangers this time. There won't be any, where you're going."

"Now, Billy, you used to be a Ranger yourself. You know damned well there's no place in Texas I can go where I might not run into one."

Vail ran a hand across his shiny bald head and said nonchalantly, "Even if you did, you still wouldn't have to worry. You're in good standing with the Rangers now. At least that's what a friend of mine who's still on the force wrote me in a letter I had from him a while back."

Longarm frowned suspiciously. "You never mentioned nothing about that to me."

"I think the letter got here while you were handling that case up on the Humboldt. Or maybe I just forgot to say anything about it."

"Well, Billy, even if it was a while ago, I'd sort of like to know what made them Rangers change their minds about me being a first-class, grade-A, number-one son of a bitch."

"Chiefly, it was all the help you gave Tom Dodd when he got shot up down in Mexico. Seems that Tom spread word to just about every Ranger he talked to after he got back. But you won't have to worry about running into any Rangers where you're going, anyhow. There aren't any stationed within five hundred miles of where you'll be."

"Oh, now hold on! Five hundred miles takes in a lot of ground, Billy!"

"And I'll stand by it too," Vail answered. "There aren't any towns, there aren't any people, so there's no use in there being any Rangers stationed anywhere close by."

"Billy, the way you say that gives me the idea I'm going

to someplace like the North Pole, not to Texas."

"There'd likely be as many people there," Vail said, no sign of a smile on his florid face.

"Just where in hell is it in Texas that I'm going? I know it's a big state, but until you started talking, I figured I'd been over pretty much all of it. I sure ain't run into anyplace like you've been telling me about, though."

"Where you're going is what they call the Llano Estacado. That means the Staked Plains, and it's up in the northwest part of Texas, between the Panhandle and the Big Bend. The story is that it got its name because the first men going over the place used to drive stakes in the ground so they'd have landmarks to guide them on their way back."

"Are you real sure it's as godforsaken as you make it out to be, Billy?" Longarm asked.

"I'm sure. All you'll see is mile after mile of prairie, as flat as the top of this desk. Oh, there's a lot of gullies you don't see until your horse is about to step off into one, and a couple of pretty good-sized canyons where there's a stream or maybe a puddle of water and a few trees. But mostly it's about as bare as a baby's butt."

"You talk like you seen it for yourself at one time or another."

The chief marshal's eyes narrowed under his bushy black eyebrows. "I have. When I was with the Rangers, I rode over that Llano Estacado a couple of times. It was still Comanche country then, so I didn't waste much time looking at the scenery. I got through it as fast as I could, just going by the compass."

"You sure don't make it sound pretty."

"It's not what you'd call pretty, and there's no farms on it yet, nothing but a few old-time sheep ranches on the far west side, along the border of New Mexico Territory. And as I said a minute ago, no towns."

"What in hell am I supposed to do there, Billy? You said it used to be Comanche country, but I had an idea that all the Comanches is settled down in the Indian Nation by now."

"They're supposed to be."

Something in the chief marshal's voice struck a false note in Longarm's ears. He said suspiciously, "Now wait a minute. I ain't going down there to do the army's work, am I? Rounding

16

up a bunch of Indians that's jumped the reservation? If I am, I say let the army do it."

"I'd say the same thing, Longarm. The army did it once, a few years back, when McKenzie whipped the Comanches and had his men shoot all their horses and mules, then marched them to the Indian Nation and tucked them in. But this isn't an army job or an Indian Bureau job. It's ours."

"Don't you think it's about time you told me what the case is about, instead of keeping on beating around the bush?" Longarm suggested.

Vail flipped through the sheaf of telegrams he'd been studying when Longarm entered. He found the pink flimsy he was looking for, glanced at it, and said, "It seems that somebody in the Indian Bureau's seeing ghosts under the bed. They've got a report that there's Comancheros working down there again."

"Comancheros!" Longarm exploded. "There ain't no such thing anymore!"

"You know what they are, then?"

"Why, sure! At least what they used to be. They was outlaw traders that swapped guns and ammunition and pepper-whiskey to the redskins to ransom prisoners the Indians took off emigrant wagons and homesteads. They'd trade for horses and mules, and I guess for whatever jewelry and gold and other loot they'd managed to get their hands on. But that all begun a long time ago, when most of Texas was Indian country."

Vail nodded. "I thought the same thing you did, that the Comancheros faded away when the Comanches were shut up on their reservation in the Nation. But that might turn out to be what everybody was thinking, and the facts of the matter could be real different, so you'd better go find out what the truth is."

"Billy, are you certain this ain't going to be just a big wild-goose chase?" Longarm asked. "Anybody that's got any brains at all knows the Comancheros can't do business unless they got Comanches to trade with."

"Sure. Even the people at the Indian Bureau are smart enough to know that. But there've been more Commanches than usual jumping the reservation lately, and the word's spreading that the Comancheros are back, so that's why the Indian Bureau people are getting worried. They don't want the Indians getting their

17

hands on guns and ammunition again."

"Can't say I blame 'em for that." Longarm dropped the butt of his cheroot into the spittoon that stood by Vail's desk. "I don't guess you can tell me anything more about what to look for when I get down to Texas, can you?"

"There's not much left to tell. Just go look, and if you find the Comanchero trade's started up again, do whatever you've got to do to stop it."

"I guess I'm ready to go, then. Look for me back when you see me."

Carl Werner stood up, and his companion's movement brought Longarm's mind snapping back to the room in the Dodge House. Werner stepped over to the bureau. He picked up the bottle of Tom Moore and put it on the table beside the bottle of Gideon.

"I'm not going to let you say no any longer, Marshal," he told Longarm. "You've got the look on your face of a man who's thinking about a job that's facing him, and if you're going to be in Texas for any length of time, you'll need this a lot worse than I do. Now tuck it away in your saddlebag, and let's go get a bite of supper."

"Tell you what, Mr. Werner. I'll buy that bottle off of you, but I won't take it as a reward or nothing like that."

"I'll sell it to you, then. My price is two bits, not a penny more or less."

"Now dammit, that's just the same as giving it to me. A quart of Tom Moore costs a dollar and a quarter most places I've bought it."

"Take it or leave it, Marshal."

"I reckon I'll have to take it, then. Because I'm just fresh out of drinking whiskey, and I've got a long ways to go."

By midafternoon of the next day, Longarm was realizing just how far he did have to go. He'd ridden out of Dodge City in the gray dawn, angling southwest. Sometime around noon, he figured he'd crossed the southern border of Kansas and entered the strip of the Indian Nation that was called No Man's Land, a finger of land that was as yet unallocated to any of the Indian tribes.

As best he could judge, he might get into Texas by sundown, but with no landmarks to go by, there wasn't any real way of being sure. The piebald had turned out to be a better horse than it appeared. It had a hard mouth, and its gait wasn't all that smooth, but it plodded along at a fast walk and the uneven terrain over which they were traveling didn't seem to bother the animal a bit.

It was rolling country that Longarm was crossing, the land gently slanting downward to the east. The distances between the long symmetrical humps, too low to be called hills, that rose and fell at intervals to break the general flatness of the terrain, might have been laid out by a surveyor, they were spaced so evenly. The earth under the piebald's hooves was solid, and the horse's shoes left no tracks in the drying grass. There was little vegetation to be seen; the grassy sides of the humps were dotted here and there with clumps of thin-stemmed soapweed, and in the broad, curving valleys between the humps grew sparse stands of low pinoaks or twisted mesquite brush.

Most of the valleys between the little hillocks were lined along their bottoms with raw rocks and pebbles where small streams had once coursed. The piebald had splashed across two or three tiny rivulets, no more than fetlock-deep, and once Longarm had let the reins go slack, giving the horse its head, letting it pick its way cautiously across a fairly sizeable river.

Throughout the day the only signs of life he'd seen had been one small herd of antelope, their white tails like signal flags as they put a safe distance between themselves and the intruder, and he'd gotten two or three fleeting glimpses of coyotes, their bushy tan-gray tails extended straight and tense from their thin bodies, their bellies hugging the earth, slinking to take cover but finding none in the short grasses that so sparsely covered the ground.

Several times in the course of the morning, Longarm had passed the bleached skeletons of buffalo, starkly white against the gray-green grasses. The skulls were missing from almost all of the skeletons. They'd been left lying where some hide-hunter's bullets had dropped them, in staggered, strung-out lines, their spinal columns sagging between bowed ribcages.

As the afternoon wore on, the character of the land changed. The humps began to flatten out, their tops widened. The grass grew thinner and in spots the ground seemed bare. Not until he reached these bare-looking spots and was riding over them did he observe that the bareness was an illusion caused by a change in the type of grass. Here it no longer grew in clumps with spreading roots on the surface, but each blade sprang up directly from the soil. The earth was no longer rich and brown. Wide swaths of dark yellow cut it into stripes, and as he moved on, the brown loam gave way almost completely to the light grayish hue of a rockier, less fertile soil.

Before the pink of sunset tinged the sky, Longarm could see that in the distance ahead of him the land was becoming broken into a gullied maze. Even in the softer light he saw the ridges that marked sharp shelves where steep-sided cliffs cut through the suddenly uneven surface of the land. He reached the chopped-up area and was soon guiding the piebald around the wider gullies, making long detours off the almost straight line in which he'd been traveling.

Old son, he told himself, *this ain't no place to get caught in after dark. What you better do is get down into the first one of them gullies that ain't got real steep sides, and stop till it gets light in the morning. Maybe if you're lucky you'll find one that's wide enough across the bottom to hold you and the nag without crowding too bad, and if you're real lucky, you might find one that's got a little crick running along the bottom.*

Another mile fell behind him, and ahead Longarm saw a wider crack in the surface of the soil, and as he drew closer he saw also that its sides slanted gently to a troughed bottom where a thin shallow stream threaded its course. For a half-dozen yards back from the water, its banks were covered with a thick growth of lush green grasses. Oaks and a few bois d'arc trees grew on the bottom of the canyon. He let the piebald soft-foot down the canyon's sloping side, and reined in by the creek.

Longarm tossed his saddlebags to the ground, unsaddled the piebald and hobbled it, and unrolled his blankets beside the stream. He opened the bottle of Tom Moore and had a heartening swallow from it before digging out his ration packet from the saddlebags and making a supper of jerky and parched corn. He sat by the creek long enough to smoke a cheroot and take a nightcap sip of the rye, then crawled into his bedroll and in two minutes was asleep.

Sunrise found Longarm in the saddle once more, pushing steadily south. After he'd gotten out of the area of broken ground that extended beyond the creek, the land became smooth and level. It was broken only by the occasional faint, thin trace of an old buffalo trail, a narrow, almost invisible thread of hard-beaten line at the roots of the short grass.

In midmorning he began watching for the wagon road that the lieutenant he'd talked to at Fort Dodge had told him ran between Fort Elliott and Fort Supply. While the sun slowly climbed the bright, cloudless sky, Longarm kept his eyes ahead, scanning the terrain on both sides of his course, looking for the ruts that he knew the heavy army wagons would have cut in the prairie soil. He was still looking, concentrating on the landscape in front of him, when he became aware of a change in the piebald's gait. The horse was no longer maintaining its steady, even pace, but was favoring its off-hind leg.

"Well, dammit, now!" Longarm said aloud. "This sure as hell ain't the time or place for a horse to go lame, a million miles from no place and a long day still ahead!"

Reining in, he dismounted and hunkered down beside the piebald's hindquarters and took a close look at the animal's leg. A small swelling showed just above the fetlock. He lifted the leg and felt the swollen spot. It was warmer than the areas above and below it, and when he tightened his hand around the swelling he felt it pulsing gently.

"Must've pulled a tendon climbing out of that canyon this morning," Longarm muttered, lowering the ailing leg. The horse's haunch muscles quivered as the leg took its weight, and the piebald let the leg go limp, its hoof just touching the ground.

He took a cheroot from his pocket and squatted in the scanty shade the horse's body cast while he smoked the long thin cigar down to a stub. On his feet again, he bent over the ailing leg and ran his hands once more over the swollen area. It felt just about as he'd expected, warmer than the flesh above and below it, and throbbing gently.

Well, staying here sure ain't going to cut the mustard, Longarm told himself. *Seems like a shame to hurt a horse any more'n it's hurting already, but horses was made to ride, and I damn sure don't aim to go the rest of the way shank's mare.*

He swung back into the saddle. The piebald's flanks quivered a bit when it felt Longarm's weight, but it moved ahead without protesting when he nudged its flank with his boot toe, though it still favored the lame leg.

Longarm kept the animal moving slowly, its lurching gait making him more uncomfortable the longer he rode. He covered a distance of two or three miles before stopping to rest the horse again, and when he started off after the rest, its progress

21

was noticeably slower and its limp obviously worse. When the horse's haunches started quivering and it began to toss its head, Longarm heeded the signs of its distress and pulled up once more. He let the beast rest a bit longer this time, but when he resumed the trip, the horse's gait grew progressively rougher.

Engrossed in the piebald's predicament, which was of course his as well, Longarm almost missed the road he was looking for. He didn't know how long he'd been riding parallel to the ruts when he saw them, but they were a welcome sight indeed.

He moved on, stopped for almost a full hour at noon, and somehow coaxed the piebald to keep hobbling on through the long, stretched-out hours of the afternoon. The pastel-blue hues of dusk were creeping in from the east when at last he saw a few faint spots of light on the horizon in front of him.

Reining in, he let the horse rest for a last time, then he mounted and let the crippled horse limp on slowly but steadily as the sky darkened and the lights of Fort Elliott grew progressively brighter.

Chapter 3

"Well, I don't know, Marshal," the corporal on duty at the stables said after he'd examined the piebald's swollen leg by the light of a flickering lantern. "It could be just a sprain, or it could be worse, a real bad pulled tendon."

"Think you can fix it up so I can push on tomorrow?" Longarm asked.

"Depends on whether it's a tendon or a sprain," the corporal replied. "I won't be able to tell that until tomorrow morning."

"I wasn't meaning to stop here more than an hour or so," Longarm frowned. "Just long enough to see if I could get a map of the country south of here. Can't you fix up the critter one way or another?"

"If it's just a sprain, I guess I can. If it's a pulled leg tendon, that might be another story. You wouldn't be able to go on for maybe a week, if it's a tendon."

"Well, I'd appreciate it a lot if you can get him so I can ride out in the morning."

"I'll sure try," the corporal promised. "Trouble is, we ran out of horse liniment three weeks ago, and our requisition for more hasn't been filled yet. I've been making do with pure grain alcohol, though, and if it works on our horses, it ought to work on yours. You'll just have to ride him easy for a day or so."

"Well, do the best you can," Longarm said. "Now, who had I better see about getting those maps? And maybe some hot supper and a place to sleep tonight?"

"Try the orderly room, Marshal. It's in the headquarters building. Just bear to the left across the parade; it's the door with a flagstaff in front of it, right in the middle. Whoever's on duty tonight will take care of you."

Like so many temporary outposts on the arid Western frontier, Fort Elliott had been built of blocks of sod, stacked together to form two long, narrow buildings partitioned off into separate rooms. The two buildings were connected together at each end by walls of thicker sods, to make an enclosed rectangle. The stable and paddock stood at one end of the enclosure.

Carrying his saddlebags over one shoulder and his Winchester in one hand, Longarm angled across the small parade ground toward the flagstaff, barely visible against the star-bright sky. Immediately behind the staff, an open door spilled light out into the night. Longarm went into the orderly room; an elderly lieutenant sat beside a very young corporal at a long, battered table, going over a duty roster. Both looked up, questions on their faces, when they saw him come in.

Longarm said to the lieutenant, "I take it you're the officer of the day?"

"Yes, sir. Are you looking for somebody?"

"Looking for you, Lieutenant, if you've got the duty," Longarm said. "Name's Long. Deputy U.S. Marshal out of Denver."

"I'm Hastings, Marshal. What can I do for you?"

"Two or three things, I guess. Maybe it'll be best if I give 'em all to you at the same time."

Hastings nodded and said, "Fire away."

"I requisitioned a horse off of the Fort Dodge remount station the day before yesterday, and it went lame on me back up the trail a ways. I stopped here to see if your men could fix it up. If they can't, I'll want to swap it for one of your spare nags. I was aiming to stop anyway, to see if maybe you could let me have a map of the Llano Estacado country, which is where I'm heading."

"I don't think it'll be too much trouble for our ordnance officer to dig you out a map or two, Marshal," Hastings replied.

24

"I can't guarantee anything about your horse, of course. There's no veterinarian on the post, but I'm sure our boys will do all they can for it. Anything else?"

"Well, it looks like I'm going to have to stay overnight, so if you've got a little grub left over in the kitchen, I could use some supper, and a bed to sleep on."

"I haven't had my own supper yet, but I'll be through here in a few minutes," Hastings said. "If you don't mind antelope stew, just sit down and eat with me. It'll be a pleasure to have somebody new to talk with. And we're undermanned, so we've got plenty of beds to spare. If you don't have to leave before six o'clock in the morning, stay for breakfast too."

"That's real nice of you, Lieutenant. I'll say yes to all three."

As small as Fort Elliott was, army protocol was strictly observed; there were separate mess halls and kitchens for officers and enlisted men. Longarm sat down with Lieutenant Hastings in the small officer's mess hall off the orderly room, where one of the kitchen workers served them bowls of antelope stew, biscuits, and coffee.

"We're a little bit short on rations right now, Marshal," Hastings apologized as they ate. "We usually get some civilized rations from Fort Supply, but the wagons are running late this month. They're almost a week overdue, and we're a little short of almost everything."

"Sounds like the army," Longarm nodded. Then he added, "I hope there's not any trouble busted out, over in the Nation."

"Nothing out of the ordinary that we've heard about here, or we'd be on alert right now." Hastings stirred sugar into his coffee. "At least there's nothing stirring up in the Cherokee Outlet, where Fort Supply's located. Of course, there's always a certain amount of trouble in the Nation, and most of it seems to spring up in the reservations that are nearest us."

Longarm dug into his memory of the cases he'd handled in the Indian territory to recall the location of the areas assigned to the different tribes. He said, "That'd be the Cheyenne and Arapaho, I suppose. And maybe the Comanches."

"And the Kiowas and Apaches," Hastings added. "The Indian Bureau made some bad mistakes when they were allotting the Indians their reservations over there, Marshal."

"Oh?" Longarm finished his coffee and lighted a cheroot. "How's that?"

"Why, they bunched all the so-called civilized tribes on the

25

east side of the Nation, instead of putting them in the middle of it where they'd keep the wild tribes separated. Damn it, the bureau saw far enough ahead to reserve that big section in the northeast for the Cherokees, even back in '52. It'd have been just as easy then for them to have given the Cherokees one big reservation right in the middle of the Nation."

"I guess it never occurred to anybody back in Washington then that the wild tribes would have to have land too."

"No, I suppose it didn't," Hastings agreed. "But if they'd just held back some of the eastern land and settled the Comanches and Kiowas and Apaches where they were separated by the civilized tribes, the Cherokees and Osages and Seminoles might have had a restraining influence on their red brothers."

"That makes sense." Longarm nodded thoughtfully. "The way things worked out, you got the troublemakers all bunched up together right across the line from you here."

"And they do make trouble too," Hastings said. "They keep us pretty busy, sending out patrols to chase down little bunches of Comanche or Cheyenne or Apache reservation-jumpers and herd them back where they belong."

"Have they been making a lot of trouble hereabouts?"

"Oh, nothing big. There hasn't been any really big fighting since Quanah Parker took the Comanches and Cheyennes over to run that bunch of buffalo hunters away from the new trading post they'd built at Adobe Walls."

"That was quite a spell ago, wasn't it?" Longarm asked. "In '75 or '76?"

"Before that," Hastings replied. "It must've been '74, because Fort Elliott was built about a year after that fracas. I didn't draw my tour here until the place was a couple of years old, and I've been at Elliott nearly two years now."

Longarm took a few moments to sip his coffee and puff on his cheroot before he asked, "Does it seem to you that maybe there's been more of 'em busting loose lately, Lieutenant? I've heard there's been a real rash of Comanches breaking out during the last few months."

"Come to think of it, we have been busier than usual lately. How did you know that, Marshal?" Hastings asked.

"It just happens that's the reason I was sent to Texas. The Indian Bureau back in Washington's got a suspicion there's Comancheros at work again, down on the Llano Estacado."

Hastings smiled. "Now that's the biggest piece of damned

foolishness I've heard come out of Washington in a long time."

"I don't put much stock in it myself," Longarm said.

Hastings went on, "Why, there haven't been any Comancheros since McKenzie started his first campaign against the Comanches, and that's more than ten years ago. He kept them too busy to raid and trade, and the Comancheros just faded away."

"That's what I always heard," Longarm said. "But the Indian Bureau spun a good enough yarn to get my chief believing 'em, so he's sent me to find out if it's true or not."

Hastings pulled out a pipe, already filled, and lighted it. He refilled his coffee cup and looked through a haze of smoke at Longarm, then said slowly, "It's not my place to tell you how to handle your work, Marshal Long, but while you're here, you might want to ask a few people around here some questions. If you get answers to them, you might be saving yourself a lot of work when you get down on the south plains."

"Sounds like you got somebody in mind," Longarm said.

"Yes, I have. Quanah Parker's one man you ought to talk to while you're up here."

Longarm nodded. "I heard something about him before. He's a white man's Indian, ain't he?"

"Pretty much so, Marshal. At least he gets along well enough with the cattlemen down in Greer County. They've worked out some kind of arrangement with him to graze their herds on the wild tribes' reservation land."

"You think if there's really a bunch of Comancheros working on the Llano Estacado, that Quanah Parker'd know about it?"

"I'm sure he would. Quanah has a way of finding out what just about every member of the Comanche tribe's doing, Marshal. If some of them are jumping the reservation to go down south and dicker with Comancheros, he'd know it."

"Question that pops into my mind is, would he tell me?"

"That'd depend pretty much on how you hit it off with him."

"Well, I reckon I wouldn't lose anything by trying," Longarm said, more to himself than to Hastings. "All right. I'll figure on going to the Comanche reservation and talking to him."

"There's one other person you might want to see before you pay a visit to Quanah Parker," the lieutenant said.

"Oh? Who's he?"

"He's a she, Marshal." The lieutenant hesitated, then said, "Her name's Sarah Renfro, and she's a lot closer to where we're sitting right now than Quanah Parker is. She lives in Mobeetie, which is only about four miles south of the fort. But in your line of work, you're pretty sure to've heard about Mobeetie."

"I've heard about it, how rough and tough a place it is, but I wasn't ever sure just where it was at," Longarm replied.

"Well, you know now. It's about like Tascosa, used to be a buffalo hunter's hangout, which brought the sure-thing gamblers and quite a few outlaws. It's pretty well cleaned up now."

"Suppose you tell me about this Sarah Renfro," Longarm suggested. "How do you figure she can help me out?"

Again Hastings hesitated before saying, "Sarah's a breed, half Apache. If there's anything going on in this part of Texas that involves Indians, she knows about it."

"But she don't live on the reservation?"

"No. You'd have to ask her why. She helps us out with tips about reservation-jumpers sometimes. I—well, you ought to talk to her before you ride over to see Quanah Parker."

"If my horse can carry me, I was figuring I'd ride over and talk to him tomorrow. Seeing as how this Sarah Renfro lives so close, maybe I ought to see her tonight. You think I could get the loan of an animal for a few hours?"

"Take mine, Marshal," Hastings offered. "My tour as officer of the day doesn't end until six o'clock tomorrow evening, so I won't need it."

"You're sure?"

"Marshal Long, the colonel wouldn't relieve one of his men from desk duty if every wild tribe in the Indian Nation broke out and started a new war with us. He'd send the stablemen and the cooks, but regulations say there's got to be a commissioned officer on duty as officer of the day, and that's where I'd be."

"If that's the case, I'll be real obliged if you'll lend me your horse for a while, Lieutenant." Longarm stood up. "And it ain't getting any earlier, so I better think about starting out."

"Whatever you say. I'll walk over to the stable with you and arrange for the horse, then."

A full moon had risen while Longarm and Hastings were eating and talking, and the flat landscape over which Longarm traveled

28

during the short ride to Mobeetie was as bright as day. The road between Fort Elliott and the town was well traveled, but Longarm needed neither the road nor any directions to guide him to his destination, for within a few minutes after riding through the sallyport, he could see the town's lights across the level prairie that surrounded him.

Mobeetie was a mixture of sod and frame houses, sprawled with little apparent order along the north bank of the Canadian River. At its heart was a cluster of a half-dozen saloons and stores, all of them showing lighted interiors at this early hour of the evening. Riders outnumbered pedestrians on the higgledy-piggledy streets in the center of the small town, and Longarm kept to the edge of the busy area. Following Lieutenant Hastings' directions, he zigzagged between the houses to the river and followed its bank until he reached a small frame house that stood off by itself, as though its occupant wanted to be close to the settlement, but not part of it.

Lights gleaming through shuttered windows told him the house was occupied. He reined in at its front steps, swung out of the saddle, and knocked on the door.

"Yes? Who is it?" a woman's voice called.

"Miz Renfro?" he asked, raising his voice.

"Yes. Who are you?"

"You wouldn't know me, ma'am, but my name's Long. Lieutenant Hastings out at Fort Elliott sent me."

A pattering of footsteps sounded from inside the house. The door swung open, and a woman stood silhouetted against the lamplight. Longarm saw her only in outline—a small woman, her head reaching barely to the middle of his chest, her body slim. Her face was completely shadowed; all that he could see was a nimbus of gold around her head.

"What is it you want, Mr. Long? Or do you just have a message for me from Wilford?"

"Excuse me, ma'am, but who's Wilford?"

"Lieutenant Hastings, of course."

"Oh." Longarm understood now the hesitancy the lieutenant had shown when he'd first begun talking about Sarah Renfro. He said, "It ain't rightly a message, Miz Renfro—"

"Please don't call me that! It's *Miss* Renfro, and if you don't mind, I'd rather you'd just call me Sarah."

"Whatever you say, ma'am. As for why I come to see you, I'm a deputy U.S. marshal passing through here on a case, and

29

the lieutenant said I ought to talk to you before I head over to the Comanche reservation tomorrow to talk to Quanah Parker."

"Is Quanah in trouble with the law?"

"Not as far as I'm concerned. I just want to talk to him, same as I'd like to talk with you."

"I see." It was evident from Sarah Renfro's tone that she didn't see. She went on, "Well, if Wilford sent you, I guess it's all right. Come in, Mr. Long. But if you've got anything of value in your saddlebags, you'd better bring them inside."

"I don't aim to be here very long, ma'am—"

"Marshal, here in Mobeetie you don't have to leave a horse unwatched for more than a few minutes to lose your saddlebags, possibly your saddle, and maybe the horse as well."

"Lots of thievery going on here, is there?"

"Constantly. I moved out here because right in town—well, so far, I've been left alone, and you're not here to talk about the town. Fetch your saddlebags and rifle and come in."

Longarm blinked in the brightness of the small parlor, and as his eyes adjusted from the relative darkness of the moonlit night, he got his first clear look at Sarah Renfro.

She stood by a small round table in the center of the room, looking at him expectantly. She was even smaller than he'd judged her to be from her silhouette; her stature was small, her arms and waist were thin, but full breasts and swelling hips that filled out the bright coral robe she wore proclaimed the grown woman inside the girlish body.

Sarah's hair was yellow-gold and her complexion fair, but her half-Apache ancestry was given away by her midnight-black eyes and high cheekbones, the wide nostrils of her small nose, and the square heaviness of her chin. Her lips, too, had the fullness that betrayed her Apache blood; like small, elongated red pillows, they swelled over her large white teeth.

"Well, do I pass your inspection, Marshal Long?" she asked.

"Excuse me, Miz Ren—"

"Sarah!" she broke in, her voice snappish. "I detest titles and any other kind of formality!"

"If you feel that way, maybe you better quit calling me 'Marshal,' then," Longarm suggested.

"I'd be glad to, Mr. Long. What's your given name?"

"That wasn't quite what I had in mind. I got a sort of nickname my friends call me. Longarm. Seems only right for you to call me by it, if I'm going to call you Sarah."

"Fine. Now suppose we sit down. Would you like a drink? I find that most men talk a bit more comfortably with a glass in their hand."

"I'd relish a sip or two of Maryland rye whiskey," Longarm began, and when he saw Sarah begin to shake her head, he went on, "And it just happens I got a bottle here in my saddlebag."

"Good. You drink it, then. I'll stick to brandy."

Sarah moved over to a china cabinet with a curved front that stood against one wall of the parlor and held bottles and glasses. Longarm took the bottle of Tom Moore out of his saddlebags, and placed the bags and his rifle against the wall, out of the way. Then, while Sarah still had her back to him, he took advantage of the opportunity to study the room.

A white-shaded Aladdin lamp sat on a round table in the center of the small parlor. Two chairs, one an easy chair, the other a side chair, and a small sofa, all upholstered in red velvet, were the only other pieces of furniture in the room, except for the cabinet. Red and blue predominated in the colors of the Brussels carpet that covered the floor. There were red drapes at the windows, but no pictures adorned the walls, nor were there any other ornaments or personal knickknacks on display.

Sarah placed the glasses and a bottle of Otard brandy on the table. "Would you like for me to pour for you, Marshal?" she asked. "It's the only gesture I can make as a hostess, since you're furnishing your own liquor."

"That'd be fine, Sarah."

Longarm put the bottle of rye on the table, waited until she'd poured his drink, then her own, and sat down in the easy chair to which she gestured. She settled onto the sofa.

"Now," she suggested, "suppose you tell me why Wilford sent you here to talk to me."

Longarm quickly sketched the case he was working on, and his reason for wanting to talk to her and to Quanah Parker. When he'd finished, Sarah shook her head.

"Quanah may be able to tell you something, but I certainly can't," she said. "Most of my"—she paused for a moment before going on—"my father's people don't have a great deal to do with me now. I suppose some of them even consider me their enemy since I began my"—Sarah paused a second time— "my close association with the army."

Puzzled, Longarm said, "Lieutenant Hastings told me you heard a lot of gossip and talk from the reservations. If it hadn't been for that, I wouldn't have bothered you."

"There was a time when I did hear about almost everything that happened, especially among the Apaches and Comanches and Kiowas," she nodded. "That's what led to my present situation."

"You'll excuse me, Sarah, but I guess I don't know enough about what you call your present situation to understand what you're getting at."

"Wilford didn't explain to you?"

"He didn't explain a thing except he told me I ought to talk to you before I went over to see Quanah."

"Have you ever met Quanah Parker?" she asked. When Longarm shook his head, she smiled. "I can tell you a great deal about him, if that interests you."

"I got a feeling that everything I know about him might help me when I visit with him."

Sarah got up and held out a hand for Longarm's glass. She moved to the table and refilled it as well as her own. While she was still standing with her face half turned away from him, she went on talking.

"Well, the first thing you want to remember is that Quanah's like I am, we're both only half Indian. That keeps us out of either of the two worlds we might want to belong to, and means that we don't have any real rules to live by. If we feel like it, we can conveniently ignore what other whites or Indians consider proper, because in our hearts, we know that neither race is going to accept us completely."

"That sounds sort of complicated to me," Longarm said. He took the glass Sarah held out for him and watched her with a puzzled frown while she went back to the sofa.

"It is and it's not," Sarah smiled. "What I'm really saying is that since we're half white, we don't feel bound to honor any of the Indian tribal traditions or customs we feel like ignoring, and since we're half Indian, we can ignore white society's conventions without feeling guilty."

Longarm nodded. "Which means you can act like Indians when you're with your tribe, and like white folks when you're in town, if you feel like it. Or the other way around," he added.

"You put it quite well, Longarm. Take Quanah, for instance. Before the Comanches were beaten and put on the reservation, he very often took more than his share of loot from the raids the Comanches made, claiming that as their war chief he had a right to it. Now I don't know whether you know it or not, but it's a Comanche tradition for each man to keep whatever loot he's taken himself, and anything that's left over is divided equally among all the men who'd taken part in the raid."

"I can see where that'd rile the other ones pretty bad."

"It did. And after the tribe got settled down on the reservation, Quanah made his men build six houses, one for each of his wives. Now, Comanche law has always been that every man takes care of his own family, and he and his wives all live together."

"Sounds to me like Quanah Parker sort of cracks a big whip."

"He does. He acts like white people think an Indian chief ought to act. But that's not important compared to Quanah selling out his own people—excuse me, selling out the Comanches—to the white ranchers down in Greer County."

"I guess you better explain that," he told Sarah. "The lieutenant mentioned Greer County, but it didn't mean much."

"Well, if you don't know this part of Texas," Sarah went on, "Greer County's to the south, where the Indian Nation and Texas come together at the Red River. The government claims the Nation extends to whatever map line it is, latitude, I suppose, south of the river, but Texas insists the border *is* the river."

"That'd make it a sort of No Man's Land, like the strip between Texas and Kansas up north?"

"Exactly. Well, the Greer County ranchers were grazing their herds north of the Red River before the reservations' lines were set up, and they still do. The Comanches don't like it, but Quanah says they can't do anything about it until Texas and the federals agree on a boundary line. What's really happening is that the ranchers are paying Quanah to say that."

"In plain English, he's being a white man to the cattlemen and an Indian to the Comanches," Longarm said.

"I see you understand," Sarah smiled. "You catch on pretty fast, Longarm. Are you sure you're not part Indian yourself?"

"Not that I know of. But in my business you learn how to catch on quick, or you don't last long."

"It's the same way in my business too," Sarah said.

"Oh? Lieutenant Hastings didn't mention you was in any

33

kind of trade. What do you do, Sarah?"

"I can't believe that Wilford didn't tell you."

"I already told you what he said to me."

"Yes, I know you did. I thought you were just being polite."

"You'll have to excuse me if I ain't following you, Sarah."

"Wilford didn't tell you that I'm—" Once more she hesitated and then went on, "Well, if you wanted to be very polite, you'd call me a hostess, since all the officers at Fort Elliott support me and I entertain all of them. If you were just being normally polite, you'd say I'm a kept woman. But if you wanted to be ugly, or maybe just honest, you'd call me a whore."

Chapter 4

Longarm's experience in questioning assorted prisoners, suspects, and witnesses served him well when Sarah burst her bombshell. He kept his face impassive and his voice level as he told her, "From what I seen of you so far, Sarah, I'd just say you're a nice, obliging lady."

"Thank you, Longarm. If it's a compliment, that is."

"How else did you think I meant it?"

Sarah started to reply, but before she could say anything, she gazed at Longarm's expression for a moment and shook her head.

"No," she said. "You aren't a man who'd stoop to using that kind of subtle insult."

"Hold on a minute now!" Longarm protested. "How you could take what I just said to be an insult's beyond me. I sure didn't mean it to be."

"I know you didn't. But when somebody who's mealymouthed says a woman's obliging, they sometimes mean that she's a fancy lady who obliges men by going to bed with them, and I—" She shrugged, then said hurriedly, "Now I'm being insulting. I didn't mean you're one of the mealymouthed kind, Longarm. Please forget what I said." She stood up quickly,

35

adding, "I'll just refresh our drinks and we'll start again."

Sarah took their glasses to the table and refilled them. In spite of his initial surprise, Longarm felt easier now. He'd seen similar situations, where the officers in a fort had joined in setting up a woman or two in their own houses, to avoid the common whorehouses where they might run into enlisted men. He lighted a cheroot, and after Sarah gave him his refilled glass, he took a sip of whiskey while she was going back to the sofa.

When she was facing him again, Sarah said with a wry smile, "I guess I made a fool of myself, didn't I?"

"Now I wouldn't say that. Nobody ever made a fool out of theirselves by being honest."

"I suppose you know now what I thought you came here for?"

"It's pretty easy to figure out. Except Lieutenant Hastings didn't tell me your situation."

Sarah shook her head. "Wilford's a nice man, better than most, but he's a fool in a lot of ways. He was a bit embarrassed at first, when the other officers explained my position to him, and he still acts a bit uneasy sometimes, when it's his turn to visit me."

"How'd this all come about, Sarah? If you don't mind talking about it, that is."

"I don't mind a bit. It'd probably do me good to talk about it with somebody who's not in the army. There was a very handsome lieutenant in the company of New Mexico Dragoons that was putting the Jicarilla Apaches on the reservation. I was quite a lot younger then, so I fell in love with him, or thought I did. We were going to be married, but first he sent me to the Cherokee Female Seminary at Talequah, to get an education so I wouldn't embarrass his family."

Sarah fell silent, a faraway expression on her face. Longarm said quietly, "But it didn't work out that way?"

She shook her head. "No. I only saw him twice during the three years I was at the seminary, and when I went back to Santa Fe, I found him already married to a woman of his own kind."

To fill the awkward pause when Sarah stopped again, Longarm said, "I've noticed quite a few men change their minds about a certain woman when they ain't around her for a while. And it's the same thing with women too, sometimes."

Sarah nodded and went on, "All I could think of was going back to the Apaches, and at that time Alsate and Victorio were still fighting in southern New Mexico and Arizona, holding out against being put on the reservation, just like Geronimo still is. But to find out where they were, and how to get to them, I had to start in the Nation, on the Apache reservation."

"So you come to these parts and never got no further?"

"Oh, I tried to leave. I started out with a few outlaw Apaches who jumped the reservation to go join Victorio over in Arizona, but by then Fort Elliott was here. We ran into a patrol and got caught." Sarah paused again, caught up in memories, then continued, "The officers asked me a lot of questions, of course, and I answered them as best I could, even if none of the Apache full-bloods would talk. After all, I am half white. Nobody could blame me for that, could they?"

"Not in my book," Longarm replied. "You just did what you felt was best."

Sarah sighed and nodded. "When they found out I spoke good English, they offered to pay me to bring them information about what the wild tribes were up to. They got me a room here in Mobeetie, where I could stay when I came in to report. Then one of the captains took a fancy to me, and I decided that letting him keep me was better than going back to the Nation. And—well, I guess he found he couldn't afford me on a captain's pay, and suggested that his officer friends at the fort would like to share me. So that's how it was."

Longarm could see that telling her story had put a strain on her. He waited for her to sip her brandy before remarking, "I've found out you can't keep many things private in a little place like this. Did the Apaches quit telling you things after you worked out your arrangement with the officers from the fort?"

"Oh yes," she replied wearily. "The Apaches don't have a great deal to do with me now. None of them ever did accuse me of being an army spy, but they just stopped telling me much about what the tribes are doing. Of course, by then it didn't matter, I was already set up here as the officers' private whore."

"Don't go running yourself down, Sarah," Longarm cautioned. When she made no reply, he added, "It looks like it wouldn't do much good for me to ask you about what I come to find out."

"I'm sorry I couldn't help you more, Longarm."

37

"Oh, you helped considerable." He stood up and stretched. "I do thank you for telling me about Quanah Parker, it'll come in handy when I ride over and talk to him." He started to pick up his rifle and saddlebags.

Sarah asked, "You're not leaving, are you?"

"Why, sure. I got to get back to Fort Elliott. I'll want to start out early tomorrow, if my horse is cured up."

Sarah stood up and moved to his side, and he was aware of the heady scent of her perfume. Her voice dropping almost to a whisper, she said, "You don't have to go, you know. I'm not expecting any visitors tonight."

"Now look here, Sarah, you don't have to—" he began.

Sarah interrupted him. "I know I don't have to, but I want to. Listen to me, Longarm. It's been a long time since I've had a man I invited to my bed because I wanted to be with him, and almost from the first minute you walked through that door, I've been thinking about how fine it feels to be with a man I picked out for myself. Don't I look good to you?"

"Why, sure you do. You're a right pretty woman, Sarah."

"And I think you might be a really exciting man. I want to find out! Please don't go just yet!"

Sarah stretched up on tiptoes, but she still had to pull Longarm's head down to kiss him. For a moment he did not return the kiss, but when her hot, moist tongue pushed between his lips and darted around, seeking his, Longarm took her into his arms and lifted her light body up so that they could prolong the embrace without straining.

While he was still holding her in midair, Sarah released an arm from around his neck and slid her hand between them, down to his crotch. She fingered him gently, her full lips working under the pressure of his, her tongue twisting and coiling in his mouth, and Longarm felt himself beginning to grow erect. Sarah twisted her head away to break their kiss.

"My God!" she gasped. "I thought you might be exciting, but I didn't expect to find anything like this! Why, you'll be huge when you get really hard, Longarm! I'm not going to let you go now, not after feeling of you!"

"When you feel of me that way, I don't think I want to leave," Longarm answered.

"That door over there leads to my bedroom," she said. "Do you want to carry me in?"

Longarm did not reply to her question, but carried her for

the few steps required to cross the small parlor and go through the door she'd indicated. The bedroom was unlighted, but enough light spilled into it from the parlor lamp to illuminate it.

He lowered Sarah to her feet. She helped him slip out of his coat and hung it on a hook behind the door. Longarm used the moment while she was doing this to slide his derringer into the same pocket of his vest where his watch rested, and hung the vest on the headboard of the bed. He hung his gunbelt over the vest and was reaching for the buttons of his trousers when Sarah returned.

"There's a bootjack by the bed," she said. "I'll get your shirt off while you're taking off your boots."

Her fingers flicked lightly down Longarm's chest while he levered off his stovepipe cavalry boots, and before he'd slid the boots free, she had not only unbuttoned his shirt, but the top buttons of his balbriggans. She buried her face in the thick curls of his chest and sighed gustily.

"I like the feel of a man's chest hair on my face," she said in a half whisper. "Hurry and get the rest of your clothes off, Longarm. I want to see if what I felt is real."

Longarm peeled off his skintight twill trousers and his balbriggans at the same time. Sarah backed away from him, holding him at arm's length, and looked at him.

"You're still not hard yet!" she said, a hint of disappointment in her voice. "But I can cure that fast enough."

Dropping to her knees, she began caressing him with her lips and tongue. Longarm began to swell, and when she took him into her mouth it took only a few moments for him to become fully erect.

Putting his hands on Sarah's pulsing cheeks, he said, "You don't have to keep that up any longer, Sarah. I'm good and hard by now."

She pulled her head back away from him long enough to ask, "Don't you like having a woman love you this way?"

"Why, sure I do. I guess most men do."

"Then just stand still and let me finish."

Longarm did not try to hold himself back from the pleasure of Sarah's caresses. He stood quietly, feeling himself build to his climax, and when his body began to twist, Sarah grasped one of his slim hips in each hand to keep his involuntary jerking from pulling him away from her. She held him in her mouth until his last pulsations faded, then rose to her feet. When she glanced down and saw that Longarm was still firmly erect, she smiled.

"Now you can take me to bed," she told him. "Most women enjoy loving a man that way, and I'm one who does. It just makes me readier for what comes next, and I see you're still just as ready as I am."

Sarah was fumbling at the neck of her robe as she spoke, and now she twisted her body suddenly. Her robe slid down and fell in a heap at her feet, leaving her naked except for her low-heeled pumps.

Longarm gazed at her admiringly. Sarah was a perfect Venus in miniature. Her breasts were fully rounded, the dark rosettes at the center of the firm mounds puckered, the tips pointed, inviting Longarm's lips. Her waist drew in sharply, to flare out at once into shapely hips, and her thighs swept down in rounded columns on either side of her dark pubic hair. She stepped out of the circle of crumpled cloth and held out her arms.

"Well?" she asked. "Do you like what you see?"

"I sure do! You're a beautiful woman, Sarah!"

Longarm picked her up and lifted her to the bed. He ran the palms of his callused hands over her erect nipples before following them with his lips. Sarah shuddered when the bristles of his mustache prickled against her soft skin, and her hand reached out to encircle Longarm's erection again. He moved above her, and she brought up her knees, guiding him between them. He felt the moist, warm touch of her curls around his tip, then thought of her small size. For a moment he hesitated, wondering if he might hurt her.

Sarah understood his hesitancy. "Go on, Longarm. Big as you are, I'm not worrying that you'll hurt me."

Longarm plunged into her then, her hands on his hips pulling urgently. Wet heat engulfed him as he penetrated deeper, and he forgot to worry. He lunged hard, went into her full length, and for a moment held himself there without moving.

"Hurry!" Sarah gasped. "Hurry up, Longarm! I got so hot while I was loving you that I'm almost ready to come! Don't just tease me! Let me feel you pumping into me!"

Longarm began stroking. Sarah's body twisted snakelike under his quick thrusts, her face buried now in the matted curls on his chest as she rubbed her cheeks against him. He felt her breath fanning hotly on his breastbone, and speeded up.

Sarah's hips writhed, meeting his thrusts as he pounded into her again and again, until she gave a sharp animal scream and her body began jerking beneath him. Her hips rose and fell convulsively, cry after cry burst from her throat. Longarm slowed the rhythm of his lunges. He still went into her deeply, and pressed hard against her at the end of each long thrust until he felt her final shudders fade away and her small body relax. Then he stopped, his hips still pressed firmly against her.

Sarah lay quiet until her breathing settled down to normal again. Her face was still buried in Longarm's chest. She turned it to free her mouth and said in a voice just louder than a whisper, "Oh, you don't know what you've done for me, Longarm!"

"I'm glad I pleasured you, Sarah."

"Not just pleasured, though you certainly did do that. But what I'm trying to say is that you made me feel good because you wanted me the way a man ought to want a woman. Not just as a convenience, but for herself."

"I've still got some wanting left, you know," Longarm said. "That first time, you just took off my edge."

"Yes. I know that. I had an edge that needed to be taken off too, and you've just done that. Now that we've helped each other, we can both enjoy the next time. I know there'll be a next time, because I can feel you're still hard, and I don't want you to go soft. So I'm ready to start again, whenever you are."

"If you've rested enough—" Longarm began, but Sarah broke in on his suggestion.

"I don't need any rest when I'm with a man like you," she said. "Start right now, if that's how you feel. Unless you'd like for me to get on top this time."

"Was I too heavy on you?"

"Of course not. But I enjoy having a man's hands on me, and I'm so small that you can't reach me unless I'm on top."

"We'll change, then."

They shifted quickly, rolling over on the wide bed without breaking the fleshy bond connecting them. Sarah brought up her knees and lifted her hips slowly, leaning forward. Longarm strained upward, trying to reach her lips with his, but her torso was too short. He could not reach her full, swaying breasts with his mouth, either. After trying and failing, he contented

41

himself with rubbing his hard hands over her ribs and grasping the firm, protruding tips of her bouncing breasts between his fingers.

Feeling his hands on her breasts seemed to drive Sarah into a frenzy of delight. She'd moved slowly when they first began, lowering and raising herself slowly, with her eyes closed and a satisfied smile on her full lips. When his fingers touched her nipples, she began rearing up furiously, rotating her hips as she let herself fall, impaled on his rigid shaft. Longarm was far from ready yet. He let his arms fall, leaving Sarah to set her own tempo, and she slowed down to an easier pace.

Longarm could tell when she began to tire. He did not ask, but held Sarah's hips firmly in his strong hands while he reversed their positions. On top again, he began to set their tempo, driving into her as deeply as he had before, but with a more deliberate penetration. He slowed even that more leisurely tempo, or stopped and simply held himself inside her, when he felt the first tremors of an orgasm begin to seize her body.

Each time he waited after a period of such gentle stroking, Sarah's tremors lessened and faded away, and she stopped straining so urgently against him. Longarm kept varying the speed of his lunges until he felt his own orgasm building. Then, positive that Sarah would reach her climax with him, he forgot everything and let his own body's needs dictate the tempo of his no longer gentle strokes.

Sarah started quivering almost at once. Her shivering grew in intensity with each of Longarm's driving lunges, until she was gyrating her hips furiously, wildly, thrusting against him so fiercely that their bodies met with a thud.

"I hope you're almost ready to come," she said jerkily. "Because I'm getting there fast."

"I'll be ready," he promised. "Let go when you want to."

Almost at once, Sarah's small, sharp screams of ecstasy began filling the dimly lighted room. Longarm reached the point of no return just as her cries rose in a vibrating crescendo and died away. He let go at last, and then relaxed on her small, soft body until he was totally drained.

"You know, Longarm," Sarah sighed as they moved apart after a long silence broken only by the gusting of their breathing, "I wish I had you in a bigger town. I'd put you out at stud with all the widows and unsatisfied wives who need a man, and we'd both get rich."

"Now, whatever gave you an idea like that?" he asked.

"Oh, it's occurred to me several times, after I learned that a woman can feel just as randy as any man does, but women don't have whores to work their feelings off on."

"I don't think I'd take to that kind of life, Sarah. If I stay too long in one place, I get spooked after a while."

"Are you sure you're not a breed too, Longarm?"

"Sure as any man can be, I guess. Why?"

"Because Indians get spooked too, especially those from the wild tribes, when they're shut up on a reservation."

Longarm thought for a minute, then nodded slowly. "I reckon I can see that, Sarah. But so far nobody's come up with a better answer. Maybe they will, someday." He stirred restlessly. The turn of their conversation had reminded him that he had work to do, work connected with the wild tribes. He rolled off the bed and began separating his balbriggans from his trousers.

Sarah moved to the edge of the bed and sat up, watching him. She asked, "You're not leaving so soon, are you?"

"It ain't that I want to, Sarah, but I got to. It's pretty late by now, and I got to be moving before daybreak again."

"I was hoping you'd stay here for the night."

"There ain't a thing I'd like better, Sarah, but there's too many things for me to do. And after I get finished here, I still got a long way to ride to get to where my real case is at."

"You never did tell me what your real case is," she reminded him. "I've guessed it's got something to do with the wild tribes, because you were so interested in finding out about Quanah Parker, but I still don't know why."

"Oh, the Indian Bureau's got some fool idea there's Comancheros at work again down on the Llano Estacado. They're afraid the wild tribes are going to be able to get their hands on guns again, and maybe rise up and all jump the reservation at the same time. What I've got to do is find out if the yarn's true."

A frown had been growing on Sarah's face while Longarm was explaining his assignment. She shook her head. "It wouldn't make any sense for Comancheros to be working that far from the Indian Nation, Longarm. They'd be more likely to operate out of someplace like No Man's Land, up north. And I haven't heard anything about Comancheros for years."

"Maybe Quanah Parker has." Longarm was fully dressed by now, except for his coat and hat. He took a cheroot out of his coat pocket and lighted it before donning the coat. Sarah stood up and pulled her robe on.

"Don't you want a drink for the road?"

"I wouldn't turn one down. But as soon as I put it away, I'll have to ride."

"Will you be back?"

"I'll try to. It'll depend a lot on what I find out over in the Nation. But in my job, a man can't figure on being anyplace where a case he's on don't take him."

Midmorning found Longarm riding east from Fort Elliott. The piebald's hoof seemed to be cured, after the alcohol treatment given it by the stableman. When he'd saddled up to leave, the soldier had given Longarm a quart bottle of the alcohol, saying, "I think I've got him fixed, Marshal, but if he starts limping again, you just heat up some of this and rub it on his leg. Don't breathe in the fumes, though, or you'll feel like you've been drinking popskull."

Longarm had set a fast, distance-eating walk as its pace, and the animal had no trouble maintaining it. In his saddlebags, in addition to the quart of alcohol, he now had two military sketch maps. One covered the Texas Panhandle from Palo Duro Creek, just below its northern border, to the Prairie Dog Fork of the Red River. The second took in the Llano Estacado, which began at the Red River and extended south more than a hundred miles to the headwaters of the Brazos, where the Panhandle officially began.

In the breast pocket of his coat, Longarm had a third map, hastily drawn by the orderly room corporal during the night. It showed the salient features of the southwestern corner of the Indian Nation, from the Texas border to the eastern boundary of the wild tribes' reservations.

"Although if you're as good at reading trail sign as I'd imagine you to be, you won't really need a map of the Nation," Lieutenant Hastings had explained while they ate breakfast. "Just ride east until you hit the wagon road between Fort Supply and Fort Sill. There's no mistaking it, of course. Then follow

44

the road south to Sill. Anybody there can tell you where to find Quanah Parker."

Hastings had asked no questions about Longarm's visit with Sarah Renfro, and Longarm had volunteered no details except to remark that she'd been helpful. Longarm had finished his business at Fort Elliott as quickly as possible, and taken the trail to the east.

There were no boundary markers, of course, to tell him when he'd left Texas and entered the Indian Nation, but Longarm judged he was well inside the territory's borders when he heard the distant booming of what was unmistakably a Sharps buffalo gun.

He was crossing a patch of broken country, cut by the dry beds of small creeks that ran in gullies between walls of orange-hued earth, when he heard the first shot. Ahead of him the land rose in a gentle slope along a curving line that marked the bed of some long-dry river, or perhaps an inlet of a lake that had dried up centuries ago. The shot he heard came from the south, and the broken terrain sharply limited Longarm's line of sight. He could see only a few miles to the east, and very little farther to the north and south. As he rode up the slope to its top, he heard a second shot, again the booming crack that only the .50-caliber Sharps could produce.

Flicking the reins, Longarm turned the piebald in the direction from which the shots had sounded.

Chapter 5

Longarm reached the top of the slope and reined in. He looked all around, but saw nothing. For perhaps a mile ahead the land ran level, to what he could see was another wide, shallow depression much like the one he'd just crossed. He scanned the landscape ahead of him, but there was no sign of life except a flop-eared jackrabbit, its long hind legs pumping, fleeing from the rider who'd appeared so suddenly. All that was visible was a straggly line of thin mesquite brush and a few clumps of ocotillo.

Lighting a cheroot, Longarm waited patiently. The cheroot was half smoked before another shot sounded, the same heavy boom of a Sharps .50. This time the report seemed to have come from a more southerly angle. Longarm turned the piebald's head and started in that direction, nudging the horse into an easy lope and hoping that its leg was as sound as he'd judged it to be.

Before he'd gotten across the flat, he heard a fourth report from the southeast, and corrected his course by its reverberating echoes. The flat debouched into another wide, shallow valley, and Longarm rode across it to the top of its upslope, and there he saw yet one more long flat stretching ahead.

No more shots had sounded. Longarm kept the piebald moving steadily, and as he'd expected it would, the flat that he was crossing gave way to another valley. He'd started down-slope before he saw the dead buffalo. The beast lay almost in the center of the valley, on its side, its forelegs thrust straight out and at a slight upward angle, its thin hindquarters sloping down to merge with the bare earth and become almost invisible against the dun-colored soil.

Not until he was within a quarter-mile of the carcass did he see the second dead animal, several hundred yards beyond the first one. Then the valley or sink curved, and if there were still other buffalo ahead, the slope of the land hid them from sight. Longarm reached the first carcass and pulled the piebald to a stop. He looked at the downed buffalo, its massive head twisted upward, its tongue lolling out of its half-open mouth. A thin trail of blood had run from its mouth and nostrils and congealed as it puddled along the lolling tongue, indicating that the animal had been lung-shot.

Whoever shot that critter knew just what he was doing, Longarm mused as he gazed at the carcass. *And it's dollars to doughnuts that you're going to find the one laying on ahead was shot the same way. And you better hurry and catch up with whoever's doing the shooting, because if any Indians hear them shots and get to 'em first, you're going to have a whole bunch of trouble on your hands. Maybe more'n you'd feel like you wanted to handle.*

When he rode up abreast of the second buffalo carcass, Longarm found that his prediction had been accurate. This animal, too, had been dispatched with the same favorite shot of the professional hide hunter, a bullet that entered the body just behind the buffalo's massive ribcage and slanted forward through the creature's lungs.

Buffalo shot this way did not snort and run and alarm others in the herd, but stood quietly, blatting softly. Depending on the buffalo's size and the path taken by the big chunk of lead from a large-caliber rifle, an animal might stand motionless for as long as a half hour, until blood from the tissues and veins torn by the heavy slug seeped into its lungs and filled them.

Suffocated by its own blood, a buffalo that had been lung-shot simply toppled over and died quietly without the rest of the herd noticing there was anything wrong. A skilled hunter with an accurate long-range rifle like a .50-caliber Sharps could stay a quarter-mile or more from a herd of buffalo, and if he'd chosen a spot flanking the animals and slightly behind them, he could wipe out the herd one at a time before the buffalo were aware they were in any danger.

Not only was the manner in which the buffalo had been shot an earmark of the professional hide hunter; the fact that their carcasses had been left unskinned fitted the professional's pattern of operation. They invariably waited until all the shooting had been done and the herd had moved out of the vicinity of the carcasses before removing the hides.

Looks to me like whoever's doing this is following a bunch of buffalo up the canyon, Longarm concluded. *And judging from how fresh the blood was out of that last carcass, they ain't too far ahead of me.*

Longarm set the piebald on a course that took him down the center of the wide valley's floor. As he rode farther, the floor narrowed, the depression deepened, its walls grew steeper, and wide, sharp-edged fissures started to appear on both sides. Its curvature became more pronounced, and it began to narrow down.

He'd ridden only a half-mile or so when Longarm saw a third buffalo down, dead or dying; still another lay a short distance ahead of it. He did not stop to examine these animals closely, for it was apparent at a glance that they had been shot in the same fashion as the first two he'd seen.

By the time he passed the last of the dead buffalo, the once-wide and shallow depression had become a deep canyon, with high, fissured walls rising on both sides of a floor that had narrowed to a width of only a few hundred yards. On the barren and narrow floor of the valley, Longarm could see fresh buffalo dung in dark wet circles on the ground.

Four shots, four buffalo, Longarm muttered as he scanned the canyon's walls, which were beginning to close in around him. *That hunter ain't too far ahead, and he's likely hustling to keep even with what's left of that herd of buffalo, if there is any. He'd want to get a lead on 'em, if I still remember anything about how a buffalo hunter works. He sure ain't had much to shoot at for a while, or I'd have heard that old Sharps booming out.*

Longarm rode on, straining his eyes up the curving canyon, looking for buffalo. He paid little attention to the canyon's

48

walls, a bit of neglect that he regretted instantly when a man's rough voice hailed him from behind.

"All right, you!" the man called. "Let go of them reins and get your hands up! And then knee your nag around so's I can see who in hell you are and so's you can see who we are!"

Longarm decided instantly that he'd better see what the odds against him were before arguing with the instructions he'd been given. He raised his hands and pressed a knee into the piebald's ribs. The horse turned readily. Longarm found himself staring into the threatening muzzle of the Sharps .50 he'd heard earlier. The barrel of the big rifle lay on a crossed-stick rest, and three roughly dressed men stood behind it.

One of the fissures that seamed the canyon walls opened directly in back of the trio; Longarm's educated guess was that the three had been hiding in the narrow gully when he rode past. The two men flanking the one holding the rifle had revolvers in their hands, and looked mean enough to be willing to use them.

"Now then," the man holding the stock of the Sharps told Longarm, "just nudge that pony over here where we can talk comfortable. And don't get no ideas, neither. This Sharps has got a set trigger and it's filed down to a hair. All I got to do is breathe on it if I wanta knock you off that horse."

Longarm had seen two men who'd taken slugs from a Sharps. One of them had nearly been beheaded when the lead tore away most of his throat, and the second had been left with a hole in his chest big enough to swallow a fist. He said nothing, but obeyed the hunter's directions.

As he rode toward them, Longarm studied the trio. The man holding the buffalo gun on him was obviously the hunter; the two others were skinners. All of them wore straggly, untended mustaches, and their chins were stubbled with a growth at least a week past shaving. They were dressed in the rough, ill-assorted clothing that buffalo hunters seemed to favor. Their hats had high, rounded crowns and overwide, floppy brims. The clothing they had on might have been pulled out of the same ragbag, it was so uniformly dirty, so wrinkled and tattered.

To a man, they wore lumpy hip-length coats over heavy woolen shirts, and greasy, dirty brown duck trousers tucked into scuffed, low-heeled, calf-length boots. Their appearance was that of three overstuffed scarecrows. It was impossible for

49

Longarm to tell whether the rifleman also carried a pistol, but the skinners had their pistol belts cinched up on the outside of their coats. Longarm was quick to notice that in spite of the sloppiness of their dress, their weapons looked well cared for.

When the piebald was within ten feet of the trio, the rifleman said, "All right, you're near enough. Hold up where you are, and tell us what your business is."

"My name's Long. I'm a deputy U.S. marshal. I'm on my way into the Nation on a case."

"How come you been tracking after us, then?" one of the others demanded. "We seen you a long time back, mister. You was heading straight east, and all of a sudden you swung south and begun following us."

"Oh, I won't say I wasn't tracking you men," Longarm replied casually. "I was figuring I better warn you that you're liable to cause a lot of trouble, shooting buffalo on land that belongs to the Indians. But I guess you know that already."

One of the men standing behind the rifleman broke in, "He's lying, Slocum! He's not no federal man! I'm betting he's a goddamned hide pirate! That's plain as day! He's trying to bluff us outa our hides, and if that don't work, he'll dog after us and steal 'em after we skin out them hulks you dropped!"

"By God, he could be a hide pirate, at that!" the man beside him agreed. "Been following us a long time, for all we know. If we fall for him bluffing us, all he'd have to do is lay low till we turn in tonight, and sneak up and haul our hides off while we're sleeping!"

"Now hold on," Longarm protested. "I won't say I wasn't following you, but all I wanted was to ask you if you knowed the best trail to Fort Sill."

"That's as unlikely a damn lie as any I ever heard!" Slocum snorted. "Mart, you and Forney get his guns and tie him up."

"Oh shit, Slocum!" the man named Forney said. "It'd be a lot easier if we just slit his throat and let him lay and go about our business!"

"That's right," Mart agreed. "We got business to tend to. No use wasting time on a hide pirate."

"We ain't sure he's a hide pirate," Slocum pointed out. "He might be a federal man, like he claims he is. We'll give him a chance to prove that later on. Right now it's like Forney says, we got business to tend to."

"If you'll just listen to me—" Longarm began.

"You shut up!" Slocum commanded as his companions moved toward Longarm. "We'll give you a say later on. Right now, we ain't got time to waste palavering. There's four hulks gettin' cold back down the canyon, and Mart and Forney's got to skin 'em out while they're fresh enough so's the hides'll slip off easy. And I got to go on up canyon to see if there ain't a few more."

Longarm had already decided that the buffalo hunters were on edge, and were not in a mood to argue with him. He was also very much aware of the threatening muzzle of the Sharps, which Slocum kept trained on him. He said nothing and made no effort to resist when they took his Colt out of its holster and slid the Winchester from the saddle scabbard. He had no intention of giving the keyed-up, hostile men an excuse to shoot him.

"All right," Forney ordered him. "Get down off that horse while we tie you up."

Longarm dismounted and stood quietly. He hoped they'd search his pockets when they relieved him of his weapons, because then they'd find his wallet with his badge and federal ID, but when they took leather thongs from the pockets of their coats and began to tie him up, he decided to try speaking again.

"If you men'll just listen to me, I can save you a lot of trouble," he began. "If you'll just—"

"Goddammit, I told you to hush up!" Slocum snapped. "Mart, you better put a gag in that bastard's mouth. There might be somebody with him, waiting for him to holler at 'em."

"Maybe we better not be in such a hurry," Forney suggested. "This horse he's riding's got a cavl'ry brand on it."

"Son of a bitch prob'ly stole it," Slocum retorted. "Go on, dammit, Forney! You and Mart do what I said! I'm gettin' outa patience. I got some hunting left to do!"

At that point, looking down the muzzle of the Sharps, Longarm decided it was better to endure the indignity of being tied up than to make an immediate effort to get the three to listen to anything he might tell them. Later, when they'd had a chance to cool down, there'd be time for persuasion.

He stayed as relaxed as possible, neither resisting nor cooperating, while the two skinners tied his hands behind him with rawhide thongs and gagged him with a bandanna.

"That's good enough to hold him till we get back, I guess," Slocum said when Mart and Forney marched Longarm up to

51

him. "Put him in that gully we was hiding in and tie his legs good. Put that sorry-looking nag he's riding in there with him. Then go get the horses and skin them hulks out while I go on up ahead and see if there ain't some more buffalo to knock over."

Longarm allowed his captors to march him into the gully, and sat down to allow them to lash his ankles together. He noticed that the knots they used were tied with skilled speed, and that the men knew how to apply pressure in the right places to keep the thongs from slipping. The two skinners left him without a backward look.

Their departure was the beginning of what to Longarm was one of the longest mornings he could recall. From where he'd been left lying, he could see only a small area of the canyon into which the gully opened. The section that was visible to him had no vegetation except a few patches of sparse grass; there were no trees or bushes, no boulders, nothing that cast a shadow by which he could judge the movement of the sun.

He knew that time was passing by three signals his body was sending him. He had a growing desire to urinate, the gag had caused a parched feeling to grow in his mouth and throat, and his stomach had never seemed so empty. He had no way, though, of telling how long he lay bound and gagged before boots grated on the coarse soil outside the gully and Slocum's bulky figure loomed in its mouth.

"Well, looks to me like Mart and Forney did a pretty fair job with you," the hunter commented, "seeing as how you ain't busted loose." Belatedly realizing that Longarm was unable to reply because of the gag, Slocum came into the gully and freed the bandanna that he'd ordered put on. He said gruffly, "It ain't much use talking to a man that can't answer back."

For a moment all that Longarm could do was breathe hard and try to swallow, to get his mouth moist enough to reply. The waiting gave him a moment to let his anger at the sight of the buffalo hunter subside and to think about what he ought to say. When he could speak, he told Slocum, "If you hadn't been so damn feisty about having your skinners put that gag on me, I could've saved you the trouble of doing it."

"Meaning what?" Slocum asked.

"Meaning that I'm just what I tried to tell you I am, a U.S. deputy marshal. If you'll reach inside my coat you'll feel a

52

leather wallet. Take it out and look at it. You'll see a badge and an ID with my name on it."

Slocum grinned. "Don't try to shit an old hand like me," he said. "You just wanta get me up close enough for you to reach me. For all I know, you might've got your hands free and be trying to fool me right now." He put the tip of a grimy forefinger on his lower eyelid and pulled it down. "See any green in there?"

"Maybe you ain't a greenhorn, Slocum, but you're sure acting like one. Go on, take out that wallet and look at it."

For a moment Slocum hesitated, then he stepped up and bent over Longarm's recumbent form, found the wallet, and took it out. He flipped it open and his eyes widened.

"By God!" he gasped. "If this damn badge is real, I guess you really are a U.S. marshal!"

"It's real enough, all right. And I could arrest all three of you men for interfering with a federal officer trying to do his job, but I'll guarantee you that I'll overlook this whole damn messup if you'll get me untied without wasting any more time jawing."

After a moment of thoughtful silence the hunter said, "I don't see there'd be any harm in me letting your hands free."

"If you're going to untie my hands, you might as well loosen my legs too," Longarm suggested. "You know your men took my guns, and I'd imagine you got a pistol on, under your coat."

"Sure I have. I don't need it to handle you, though. But I don't guess you need to be tied up no more." Slocum took out a sheath knife and sliced expertly through the leather thongs that secured Longarm's hands and feet.

For a moment Longarm said nothing. Slocum handed back the wallet, and Longarm took it and replaced it in his pocket. He rubbed his wrists and waited until the prickles had stopped bothering his legs before saying to Slocum, "Now just give me a minute to piss, and we can talk sensible."

While he relieved himself against the gully wall, Longarm took out a cheroot and flicked a match into flame with his thumbnail to light it. He was conscious of Slocum watching him, but gave the hunter no attention until he turned to face him. Keeping his anger in check, he asked, "What in hell ever got into you, Slocum, that you'd pull a fool trick like you did, grabbing me and tying me up that way?"

"Hell, Marshal, all I could think about was them buffalo. Do you know, it's been two years and more I've hunted without seeing none? All I could think about was hurrying on up the canyon to see if they was maybe stragglers that belonged to a herd deeper in the canyon somewheres."

"I don't suppose you found any more, though?"

"Not in this canyon. But there's bound to be some more, real close by." Slocum tried to force confidence into his voice, but failed. "All the buffalo can't be done for!"

"Don't be too certain. A few days ago, when I was up in Dodge City, I heard the buffalo herds was gone and all of you hunters had give up."

"Well, you heard right," the rifleman replied. "Sure as shit stinks, there ain't no buffalo herds around. But there's still a few of us that goes out looking. And by God, we found us some buffalo this time!"

"Damned few," Longarm commented. "Unless you shot more'n those four I seen."

"I didn't today, but—" Slocum stopped short and cocked his head, listening. Longarm heard the sound of horses' hooves on the ground outside the gully. Slocum went on, "That'll be Forney and Mart coming back with the hides."

In a moment the two skinners came in, their unwashed hands still streaked with red, and the smell of fresh blood on their boots. They stopped in the mouth of the gully, staring. Longarm noticed with a flash of anger that his Colt was in Mart's holster. He smothered his anger and waited for them to speak.

It was Slocum who broke the silence. "Well, don't stand there like ninnies!" Slocum told them. "If you're worrying about this man here, you can get over it. Turns out he's a real U.S. marshal, just like he said he was. Maybe you better give him back his guns."

Instinctively, Mart covered Longarm's Colt with his hand. Longarm ignored the move. He wanted to end his trouble with them as quickly as possible and be on his way.

"I'll get the guns," Mart said quickly. He wasted no time, but went out immediately. Forney said, "I guess we was wrong about him being a hide pirate, then." Turning to Longarm, he went on, "I hope you ain't mad at us, Marshal. We just made an honest mistake, and you can't blame a man for that, can you?"

Longarm was saved from replying by Mart's return. He was

carrying Longarm's Colt and Winchester, and Longarm saw that the skinner had replaced his own weapon in the holster. Mart held out the Winchester and Colt, saying, "No hard feelings, I hope, Marshal. I'll be the first to say I'm sorry, but like Forney told you, it was all a mistake."

"Just hand me my guns," Longarm replied in a brittle voice. "Don't bother to offer to clean 'em. I'll do that myself."

He kept his eyes fixed on Mart's until the skinner came to him and handed over the rifle and pistol. Longarm checked the Colt's cylinder before holstering it, and looked at the magazine of the Winchester, then tucked the rifle into the crook of his elbow.

Slocum went back to what he'd been saying. "Like I was telling you, Marshal, I didn't find but only four buff today, but I aim to keep lookin'. There's lots of sign in this canyon, and some of it ain't too old. It's a bigger canyon than you think, too. Goes on for forty for fifty miles. I got a hunch there's a good-sized herd in it somewheres."

"I sure hope you're right," Forney said. "Skinning out the ones we got today makes me think about how it used to be."

"Oh, there'll be more where them four come from," Slocum insisted. "And there damn well better not be nobody try to stop me from huntin' 'em!"

"If you can find 'em, there ain't any law I know of to keep you from shooting and skinning 'em," Longarm told him.

Mart said, "Shit, Marshal, anybody that's smart enough to git elected to make up laws is going to be too smart to pass a law that'll try to keep a man from going out and shootin' whatever critters God put on earth for us to use."

"No, I guess there won't ever be laws like that," Longarm agreed. "But that don't give you the right to shoot anything on land the government's give to the Indians."

"Now, goddammit, a critter belongs to whoever shoots it, and it don't make no difference whose land it's on!" Slocum was almost shouting.

"That ain't the way the Comanches and Cheyennes and Kiowas and Apaches feel about it," Longarm reminded him. "A bunch of any of them could jump you while you was hunting on their reservation, and the Indian Bureau would have to be on their side. That is, if the Indians didn't just cut you up into little chunks instead of bothering to complain to their agent."

"They'd sure have to do some powerful jumpin', then,"

55

Slocum said, his unshaven chin outthrust belligerently. "Because I got my Sharps and my pistol—"

"And me and Mart got guns too!" Forney broke in. "Anybody that feels like jumping us can try it, but if they do we'll give 'em a good dose of hot lead!"

"But you'd still be in a heap of trouble."

"Mebbe," Slocum grunted. "Only I ain't heard about no cases yet when a white man ever stood trial for shooting a murderin', scalpin' Indian in self-defense!"

"Tell you what I'm willing to do, Slocum," Longarm offered. "I'll forget how you held me at gunpoint and had your men tie me up, if you'll skedaddle off Indian land and do your buffalo hunting someplace else."

Slocum stared at Longarm for a moment, as though he could not believe what he'd heard. Forney and Mart were watching their employer, waiting to hear his reply.

"You got any right to tell us to get off this land, Marshal?" Slocum finally asked. "Even if you are a federal officer, and the gov'mint give it to the redskins?"

"I don't know of any federal law that would," Longarm admitted quickly. "I could put you in protective custody, to keep you from getting scalped if a bunch of Comanches or Cheyennes caught you, or I could march you off it at gunpoint, even if there wasn't a law that'd give me the right. But I'm hoping it won't come down to that. Which it won't, if you men got good sense."

"You just let us worry about keeping our hair on, Marshal," the buffalo hunter said. "We can take care of any trouble we might get into."

"Damn right!" Mart agreed.

Forney nodded, and Slocum went on, "Dammit, we run onto buffalo today for the first time in two years! We sure as hell ain't about to knock off hunting now, and I'd say the same thing, irregardless of whoever said it's their land we're hunting on!"

Before Longarm could reply, rapid hoofbeats drummed on the ground outside the gully, and a burst of war cries split the air. The cries were followed by a light volley of shots. A half-dozen bullets sang into the gully, but all of the lead buried itself harmlessly in the dirt walls.

Longarm was as fast as the buffalo hunters in hitting the ground. He saw the three men drawing their pistols, but his

Winchester was already in his hands, covering them.

"Leave them guns holstered!" he commanded.

"Dammit, them's Indians shooting at us!" Slocum snapped.

"Sure as hell," Longarm agreed. "And we might have a fight on our hands, no matter what. But before we get ourselves killed, I'm going to try to get 'em to call off the fight. And I'll shoot the first one of you that gets in my way!"

Chapter 6

Outside the mouth of the gully, the din of shouts, hoofbeats, and rifle shots was renewed as the Indians swept past it on their ponies for a second time. The buffalo hunters had drawn their hands away from their gun butts when Longarm made his threat, but when the second volley of shots sounded and lead whistled into the gully above the heads of the men sprawled on its floor, they moved to draw their revolvers once more.

"Damn you, leave them pistols holstered!" Longarm ordered, threatening them again with the muzzle of the Winchester.

"You can go plumb to hell, Marshal!" Slocum snarled. He drew his revolver and let off an unaimed shot through the mouth of the gully, disregarding the fact that the Indian attackers had already galloped by the opening and were no longer visible.

Longarm did not want to cripple Slocum. He rolled to his feet in a single swift move as the buffalo hunter was leveling his pistol, and lashed out with his booted foot. The boot's toe cracked into Slocum's gunhand, sending the revolver flying to the far side of the narrow cleft. Slocum flopped down on his back, staring up at Longarm, his left hand cradling his bruised right fist.

"I won't let you off so easy next time, Slocum," Longarm warned. "Next time I'll *shoot* the damn gun out of your hand." He swiveled to bring the rifle muzzle to bear on Mart and Forney, who'd taken advantage of the byplay between Longarm and Slocum to draw their revolvers. "And that goes for you two as well," he said sternly. "If either one of you pulls a trigger, you'll wind up with a hole in your gunhand!"

"We got to defend ourselves, dammit!" Slocum rasped. "You don't act like any white man I ever seen before, standing up for them bastard redskins instead of helping your own kind! Just what in hell are you trying to do?"

Outside in the canyon, the yells of the attackers and the hoofbeats of their mounts grew louder again as the Indians began their third sweep past the defenders' position. Longarm dropped back to the gully floor and flattened himself out before the galloping riders reached the point where they could begin firing into the mouth of the cleft. The spatter of flying lead made the whites duck their heads between hunched shoulders and try to press lower on the ground, but the Indian bullets were no more effective this time than they'd been in the two earlier sorties.

Longarm had been listening carefully to the reports of the Indians' guns. He told the hunters, "Sounds like they got eight, maybe ten rifles. And they'll likely have a few pistols they ain't used yet."

"Old guns, mostly," Slocum broke in. "You can tell that from the way they sound. And two to one ain't bad odds."

"I'll grant you that," Longarm agreed. "But there's more'n any eight or ten horses out there. If you was listening close, like I was, you could've told that."

"I was listening, all right," Slocum said soberly. He added reluctantly, "It sounded to me like about twenty."

"That's how I figured," Longarm agreed. "And the ones that ain't got guns will have knives and tomahawks. They're going to get tired of just parading past and wasting lead in a minute or so. Then they'll start thinking, and they'll know they ain't getting at us. If I know Indians, they'll figure out real fast that they can send a bunch up on the bluff and make a sneak to the edge of this gully. If eight or ten of 'em jump us from up there, we ain't got a chance to stop all of 'em, and we'll be up shit crick without a paddle."

Apparently the thought of an attack from the rim of the

59

gully hadn't yet occurred to the others. Slocum, Mart, and Forney gazed up at the strip of open sky that gaped between the steep walls above their heads.

"Now you just stay where you are and don't use them guns," Longarm told them. "I'm going to see if I can talk 'em into a parley before things get too hot for us."

Taking out the blue bandanna that had been used to gag him, Longarm knotted a corner of it on the muzzle of his Winchester. He belly-crawled to the mouth of the gully, stuck the barrel of the rifle out, and began waving it to and fro as the hooves of the approaching Indian ponies signaled that another sweep was beginning.

This time the Indians yelled defiantly as they galloped past the gully, but fired no shots. The tempo of their ponies' hoofbeats changed as they reined in beyond the cleft where Longarm was still waving his bandanna. What seemed to the men in the gully to be a long time passed before one of the Indians replied to the bandanna's signal.

"What you want?" one of them called; the voice sounded guttural even at a distance.

"Talk!" Longarm shouted back. "Parley!"

"You give up," the reply came. "Then we talk!"

"We talk first!" Longarm answered. "Make peace!"

Several minutes passed before the Indian responded. "We talk!" he called.

Handing his rifle back to Slocum, Longarm said, "Don't use it, Slocum. Not unless they cut me down." Getting to his feet, he walked out of the opening to face the Indians.

Advancing toward the attackers, who had drawn up in a semicircle a hundred yards from the gully's mouth, Longarm made a quick count. There were eighteen in the Indian band. About half of them carried rifles, two wore pistol belts, three of them held lances, the others were armed with bows and arrows. Most of them wore the coarsely woven trousers issued by the Indian Bureau to its charges, but a few had stripped down to breechclouts. He could not tell to which tribe they belonged, for none of them had on warpaint.

Longarm took this as an encouraging sign. It was evidence that the group had been hastily assembled when word of the presence of Slocum and his skinners reached the Indians. Had their faces and bodies been painted, that would have meant the attack had been ordered after a tribal decision to fight had been made at a council of the head chiefs. Killing the whites would then have been a matter of pride to the entire tribe. No peace talk would have been possible without the approval of the same council that had ordered the attack.

Halfway between the gully and the semicircle of warriors, Longarm stopped and lighted a cheroot. He stood impassively, his posture relaxed, to show he was in no hurry to talk. Had he gone farther than halfway, the Indians would have taken it as evidence of weakness; he would have lost face, which would have encouraged their spokesman to be adamant in demanding surrender.

Bargaining from a position of at least minimal strength, Longarm was sure he could arrange a truce with the Indian band. He stood puffing his cheroot, holding his attitude of patient waiting, and after he had waited several minutes, one of the men at the center of the semicircle kneed his pony and walked the animal slowly forward. He stopped ten feet from Longarm.

"Chi-Ko-Be," the Indian said, tapping his chest with his forefinger.

"Long," Longarm replied, imitating the Indian's gesture.

In giving his name, the Indian had also given Longarm his first clue to the band's tribal origin. He recognized both the name and the intonation of Chi-Ko-Be's voice as being Uto-Aztec and not Shoshonean. This identified him as being either Comanche or Kiowa, as the Cheyenne language was a Shoshonean-based tongue. Since the Comanches on the reservation far outnumbered the Kiowas, he assumed that Chi-Ko-Be was a Comanche.

Reaching into his breast pocket, Longarm took out the wallet containing his badge. He flipped the fold open and held the badge where it would catch the early afternoon sun.

"Government," he said.

Chi-Ko-Be leaned forward, his brows drawing together. Longarm moved closer to the Indian so he could see more clearly. Chi-Ko-Be studied the badge and the federal identification card behind a celluloid window in the wallet's opposite fold.

"You are Long?" the Indian asked. "From Washington?"

"I am Long," Longarm repeated, positive that the man knew a lot more English than he was willing to display. He put the wallet back in his pocket and drew out a cheroot, which he held out to Chi-Ko-Be. "Will we smoke as friends, Chi-Ko-Be?"

Chi-Ko-Be looked longingly at the cigar, but made no move to accept it. After a moment of silence he said, "Not friends. The buffalo you killed belong to the Comanche, Long. For this we should kill you. In the Shining Times we would not even have talked, and you would be dead by now."

Longarm interpreted Chi-Ko-Be's reply to mean that killing the buffalo could be settled, but at a high cost to Slocum and his crew. Then he told himself that he owed Slocum nothing beyond getting him out of trouble. Whatever the Comanches asked would be little enough for the buffalo hunter to pay.

"I didn't kill your buffalo, Chi-Ko-Be. Those other men done that. I reckon they'd be willing to save trouble by paying for 'em, though, if we can dicker a price."

"Who can put a price on the last buffalo?" Chi-Ko-Be asked. "Three were cows, one a bull. They would have made a herd, if you had not shot them."

"I told you, I didn't shoot your buffalo, Chi-ko-be. It was them other fellows, they're the hunters, not me. All I want to do is get this settled. Now how much do you want?"

Chi-Ko-Be shook his head. "I cannot say that, Long."

"How come? Ain't you one of the chiefs of the Comanche?"

"This is a true thing. But the buffalo belonged to *all* the Comanche. Only a council can say how much they were worth."

"What about one of your main chiefs? Maybe one like Quanah Parker, who can settle it by himself?"

"It is a true thing too, that Quanah is one of our chiefs. But even he cannot settle this by himself. There must be a council," Chi-Ko-Be said stubbornly.

"I guess I don't follow you, Chi-Ko-Be."

"Quanah is war chief, same as me. At council there will be a peace chief and a medicine chief, and we must all agree on the price your friends have to pay for our buffalo."

"Sounds to me like you Comanches got as many chiefs as we got in Washington," Longarm smiled. He could see the price that Slocum would pay going higher every time Chi-Ko-Be spoke. "We better get a council together, then. How do we go about it?"

"We go to the Elk Creek settlement. That is where we rode out from. There will be chiefs there to make a council."

"How far away is it?"

Chi-Ko-Be raised his hand directly above his head and swept it down until it was below the western horizon. "A long half-day. We can reach it tonight."

"If that's the way of it, then we better start out. You'll tell your men the fight's over, and I'll get the hunters started, if that's all right with you."

Chi-Ko-Be nodded. "It is done. Now I will smoke the cigar you offered me, Long."

Dusk was turning the surface of the slow-moving Washita River into a softly gleaming leaden sheet when Longarm saw the twinkling lights of Anadarko reflected beyond the bend he'd just rounded. His eyelids felt as leaden as the river looked, after his long, sleepless night with Sarah and an even longer, equally sleepless night with the Comanche tribal council. The sunset also marked the end of his sixth long day spent in the saddle.

He'd ridden out of the Elk Creek Comanche settlement as soon as the council had ended, in the first pink flush of dawn. On the whole, the council had not been too harsh on Slocum and his two skinners. After a lot of palaver, the trio of chiefs had agreed to let the three buffalo hunters off for a price of ten dollars for each of the buffalo they'd shot, with the provision that the meat and hides of the animals also be given to the Comanches. Slocum had sworn that the verdict of the council was reducing him to poverty, but he'd paid it.

Longarm let the piebald amble along the riverbank while he took out a cheroot and lighted it, then twisted in his saddle to reach into the saddlebags for the bottle of Tom Moore. From the description he'd gotten before leaving Elk Creek of the location of Quanah Parker's multiple residences in Anadarko, he couldn't be too far from his destination, and he was hoping he could have his talk with the Comanche leader, get a full night's sleep, and start early the next morning for the Llano Estacado. He took a satisfying swallow of the smooth-sharp rye and restored the bottle to his saddlebags. Quanah was supposed to have a taste for whiskey, and Longarm didn't plan to share his scanty supply of rye.

Just ahead of him were the first houses that straggled along the riverbank. He kept his eyes peeled for the group of six frame dwellings in a close cluster where Quanah made his

63

home, one house for each of the wives he'd acquired, with Quanah dividing his time among them.

For a moment Longarm wondered what it would be like to have six wives, then dismissed his thought with a chuckle when it occurred to him that he'd never had even one. He didn't have time to start wondering how he'd get along, married, for just then he saw what must be the group of six houses for which he'd been looking. They stood a few yards off the road, away from the riverbank where most of the other houses had been built, in a neat semicircle.

Longarm twitched the piebald's reins and rode over to them. A single hitch rail stood in the middle of the arc formed by the houses. For a moment he studied the almost identical facades. Lights shone through the windows of all six of the houses, and he looked from one to the other, wondering which one Quanah might be visiting that evening. He still hadn't decided which house he'd try first when he dismounted and wrapped the reins around the hitch rail. Finally, with a mental shrug, Longarm mounted the steps leading up to the door of the center house and knocked.

"Quanah Parker?" he asked the woman who opened the door.

She was short of stature and dressed in the old-style Comanche fashion, in a long deerskin dress that fell straight from her shoulders to her ankles. Her hair was parted in the center and fell unbound down over her breast. Her face was wide, her nose broad and flat. She looked at Longarm for a moment, shook her head, and pointed to the house on her right.

"Quanah there," she told Longarm, then closed the door abruptly.

Longarm went to the house she'd pointed to and tapped on the doorjamb. This time a much younger woman appeared when the door swung open, though she had on the same type of dress and wore her hair in the same fashion as had the other woman.

"Quanah Parker?" Longarm asked a second time.

She nodded, and indicated with a gesture of her open hand that he was to come inside. The room into which the door opened could have been any room in any house in this part of the country, except for the buffalo hide that served as a rug. It was small and sparsely furnished. A sofa stood along one wall, two chairs and a table in the center. Several cardboard-mounted photographs and two or three sketches of scenes in Indian camps had been tacked on the walls. Quanah's wife acted as though Longarm had not come in; she kept her face turned away from him, closed the door, and disappeared through another door across the room.

His hat in his hand, Longarm waited where Quanah's wife had left him for a full three minutes before the room's inner door opened and Quanah Parker came in. The war chief was a stocky man; he lacked half a head of being as tall as Longarm. His body was sturdy, though, deep in the chest and wide in the waist and hips, as were most of the men of his tribe. His legs were short, and even in the full-cut black serge trousers he was wearing, Longarm could see that they were horseman's legs, slightly bowed. His white linen shirt was collarless, but a gold collar button shone in the neckband. Even though he had on no collar, Quanah wore a gray double-breasted vest with shiny pearl buttons.

Quanah Parker might have been any age from thirty to fifty, but there were no strands of gray in the traditional Comanche braids he wore, one hanging down on each side. The braids reached to his waist, but for all their length his hair grew sparsely on top of his pate, in a thin layer that seemed barely to cover his scalp. The braids were without ornament, secured at their tips with small bows of narrow black ribbon. The Indian chief's brow was surprisingly high, his hairline so high on his forehead that he brought his braids down to his shoulders behind his ears rather than over them.

It was mainly Quanah's eyes that gave away the heritage of white blood he'd gotten from his mother. Most Comanche men had very sparse eyebrows and short eyelashes that were almost invisible, but his were thick and long. Instead of being deepset, his obsidian-black eyes protruded slightly. His nose was a bit narrower than the flat, broad nostrils usually seen on full-blooded Comanches, another indication of his mixed blood. His lips were thick, and he was clean-shaven.

For a moment Quanah looked at Longarm with a frown that indicated he was trying to place his visitor's face and could not do so. Finally he said, "I am Quanah Parker. What is it you have come to see me about?"

Longarm did not reply for several seconds; he was surprised by the ease and fluency with which the Comanche chief spoke. He replied, "My name's Long, Mr. Parker. Deputy U.S. marshal out of Denver. I come to see if you can help me with a case I'm on."

"I am always ready to help if my brothers are in trouble, Marshal Long." Quanah motioned for Longarm to sit down. The two men sat across the table from one another, and he asked, "How does your case concern the People?"

Quanah's application of the phrase to the Comanche tribe did not surprise Longarm; the Navajo, Blackfoot, and two or three tribes besides the Comanches called themselves "the People."

"Well, it might not concern the Comanches in a real direct way," Longarm said. "Then, on the other hand, it might. It'd all depend."

"Depend on what?"

"On what you can tell me, I suppose."

"You don't seem to be quite sure what you expect me to tell you, Marshal. Perhaps you'd better explain why you're here."

Longarm took out a cheroot and lighted it. When it was drawing well, he said, "My chief in Denver got a wire from somebody in the Indian Bureau. There's a story going around that the Comancheros are trading again down south, on the Llano Estacado. Everybody I talked to over in Texas said if anybody'd know the truth of things, it'd be Quanah Parker. That's why I rode over here to talk to you."

Quanah Parker sat silently for a long while, his eyes veiled as he looked into the past. He exhaled a deep breath that was almost a sigh. He said, "Pardon me, Marshal. I was thinking of my younger days, when I spent much time on the Llano Estacado, trading with the Comancheros. You know how young men are. They look for excitement and danger, trouble to get into. Of course, that's what I did too, like any other young man from my tribe. I might even have been a little more reckless than most, because as the son of Chief Nocona, I had to seem braver than anybody."

"I'd imagine so," Longarm answered, his voice expressionless. "What I want to know is, have you heard anything about your young Comanche men acting right now like you used to then?"

"In my position I hear many things, Marshal Long. I hear some of our young men talk about the Shining Times and our old ways, but most of them are too young to have seen battles.

66

They talk of the Comanchero trade because they have heard the old men speaking of it."

"But you ain't heard of any of 'em jumping the reservation and going down there looking for guns?"

"I think all our young men are restless, Marshal. They hear us, who saw the Shining Times, talking of the days when we ruled the prairie, and think that such times will return."

"And you don't think so?"

Quanah shook his head. "I did when I was younger, even when I led the war party against the buffalo killers at the place you call Adobe Walls. But my education has been great, since then."

Longarm took time to puff his cheroot before he asked, "And you're certain some of your reckless young braves ain't jumped the reservation to do some gun-trading?"

"Our young men are restless. I was restless too, when I first came to the Nation. The Shining Times were still close behind us then. I left the reservation several times."

Longarm said patiently, "Sure. I heard about you being one of them that took on the buffalo hunters at Adobe Walls. But you ain't quite answered what I asked you about gun-trading."

Quanah shook his head. "I have heard boasts, but with my own eyes I have seen no guns brought by my young men to the reservation."

"There was a war party of your people that jumped some buffalo hunters over east yesterday. They had guns. I know that's a fact, because I was there and seen 'em."

"You're talking about Chi-Ko-Be's punishment of the hunters who came on our lands to kill our buffalo," Quanah said.

Longarm stared at the Comanche. He'd heard of the way that Indians many miles from a battle seemed to learn of it within a few hours, but this was his first encounter with the phenomenon.

Seeing Longarm's surprise, Quanah smiled. "News does travel quickly among our people. I heard that a federal official was at that little fight, but when you came in, I didn't realize it was you. It's a long ride from Sweetwater Canyon, Marshal. You can travel almost as fast as we Comanche do, I see."

"I reckon I can take that as a compliment, Mr. Parker."

"Yes," Quanah said. His voice was quite serious. "I meant it that way." He paused briefly, then went on with a frown, "I can understand why the Indian Bureau would be worried if my people were trading with the Comancheros again. When we were free, we got most of our rifles from them. And bad whiskey, which made cowards brave and foolish and made brave men reckless."

Longarm nodded. "So I've heard."

Quanah went on, "The bureau would take it as a sign that those who were trading with the Comancheros were planning to go back to old ways which all but a few of us have given up."

"But not all of your people are satisfied on the reservation here," Longarm observed. "And from what you said a minute ago, about hearing talk, I take that to mean there's a chance the stories that got all the way back to Washington might be right."

Parker shook his head. "No, Marshal. I think they're the same stories I've heard, which aren't anything but talk. I don't think the Comanchero trade has started again. Not unless it's with Geronimo's Apaches. His Chiricahuas and some of the Jicarillas in the north are the only ones left of our race who are still fighting your people."

"I know about the Jicarilla country, Mr. Parker. And from what little I've heard about Geronimo, his bunch spends most of their time in Mexico. They wouldn't need Comancheros to get what supplies they got to have. Besides, if they was trading with a bunch of Comancheros, they wouldn't travel all the way east to Texas to do it."

"That's true, of course," Quanah agreed. "But in the Shining Times, we Comanches traveled a long way to get to the trading grounds." He added thoughtfully, "The Comanchero trade is a very old one, Marshal. It was going on long before I was born, when we Kwahidi Comanches claimed the country all the way south to the forks of the Brazos as our own range. When I was a boy, the Texas Rangers had already driven us north of the Red River, and the Comancheros had followed us to the Llano Estacado."

Longarm was not really comfortable listening to Quanah Parker's reminiscences of early Comanche life. He'd sat with as much patience as he could muster, but by now he saw he was going to get no useful information from the war chief. He picked up his hat from the table and stood up.

"Well, I'm grateful for your time, Mr. Parker. I guess I'll just have to ride on down to the Llano Estacado and see for myself what there is to those rumors."

Quanah did not rise. He looked up at Longarm, his face impassive, and said, "I'm sorry I couldn't tell you very much, Marshal. In my position, I do try to give my white friends all the help I can. But I've just thought of something that might interest you."

"Oh? I'd be real pleased to hear it."

"Before you start south, you might stop in at Tascosa."

"I've heard the place mentioned, but I never have been there. Is it a pretty good piece from here?"

"Three days, if you have a good horse. Just ride straight west until you get to the Canadian River, and follow the river to the town."

"What'd I be looking for, was I to go there?" Longarm asked.

"Tascosa was settled by New Mexicans, Marshal. Many Comancheros lived there when the trade was very big. Some of them must still be there, and if the Comancheros are trading again, they'd know about it."

"That sounds like a shrewd idea. I'll just have to do that. Well, I'll bid you good night, Mr. Parker, and thanks for the help you've given me."

Chapter 7

On his way to Tascosa, Longarm put temptation firmly aside and rode in a beeline. Mobeetie was a bare half-day's ride from the route he'd selected after studying the map of the Panhandle that he'd been given by Lieutenant Hastings, but as much as he knew he'd enjoy another night with Sarah Renfro, he did not turn off the direct path he'd set out to follow.

Riding in a straight line was easy on the featureless, level prairie he came to after he'd crossed the North Fork of the Red River. There were no hills except small peakless humps that rose gently in almost perfect circles. There were only a few earth-walled canyons, and most of these were narrow enough to jump, while even the widest of them required him to swerve only a mile or less from the straight line he rode.

More often than not, Longarm's detours from the straight line he'd set himself to ride were made to skirt buffalo wallows. He encountered these by the dozens, and though he'd ridden over the buffalo-thick prairie in the days before the big bison vanished, he'd never seen as many wallows before. They ranged in size from depressions only a few yards wide to huge, deep saucers that were a mile or more across. Even though the short rainy season had ended months ago, many of the biggest

70

wallows still held water, and others had a deep layer of mud on their bottoms; he was forced to skirt those that were still wet.

These craters had been formed when the buffalo herds numbered in the millions. They'd begun as small dimples in which rainwater collected. During the late spring, when the buffalo began to shed, big patches of their bare tender skin became exposed to the bites of stinging gnats and flies. Until their new coats grew out, the big animals wallowed in the dimples to cover themselves with a protective coat of mud.

When they left after they'd finished wallowing, each buffalo carried away a small amount of soil from the dimple, clinging to its hide. After unnumbered centuries of use by uncounted millions of buffalo, the wallows where the biggest herds had gathered were excavated into great circular depressions, which collected water when the rains came. The biggest of the wallows, as large as ponds or small lakes, stayed filled through most of the summer, and a few held water the year round. Often the wallows were a more dependable source of water than the scarce, small streams of the arid plain, which frequently dried up in summer.

Keeping steadily to the straight line he'd set himself to follow, riding from first light to twilight, never hurrying but never wasting time, Longarm reached the brakes of the Canadian River shortly after noon of the third day. The piebald's ailing leg had apparently been completely cured. Though he did not push the animal, it gave no sign of limping in spite of the steady pace he kept it on.

As he got farther west and entered the brakes, the going got rougher. There were bluffs where the ground dropped suddenly away without warning, as well as big areas of broken ground cut by ravines that marked the beds of long-dry streams, and few of these were narrow enough to jump. After so many long hours in the saddle, Longarm soon grew impatient with the zigzag patterns in which he was forced to ride. When he saw the glint of green water ahead, he sighed with relief and celebrated by reining in long enough to take a sturdy swallow of rye from his nearly empty bottle. While he was stopped, he took out his map and looked at it again.

Well, old son, that's got to be the Canadian River, because there ain't another one of any size for fifty miles north or south, so that means you ain't got much further to go, he told himself as he measured miles with his thumbnail as a ruler. *That river's maybe three or four miles away yet, then another twenty and you ought to hit Tascosa. Looks like tonight you'll be setting down for a hot supper, if there's a decent place to eat in the town.*

Longarm did not reach the river as quickly as he'd thought he would. When at last he came to the stream, he slacked up on the reins and let the piebald soft-foot down the gently sloping bank to the water's edge, and while the animal drank, he lighted a cheroot. He looked upstream and down; there was a clear view to the east, but to the west his vision was blocked by a high undercut where the river curved sharply. He let the horse finish drinking, then turned its head upstream and toed it into motion, following the Canadian's twisting curves.

A low rise led up to the place where the river changed its course in a long, wide sweep. The piebald mounted the rise, and ahead of him Longarm could see that the river widened and grew shallower. He looked along its course and blinked; the slanting sun glinted into his eyes off the surface of the stream, blinding him for a moment. Shielding his eyes with one hand, Longarm broke the glare by looking between outspread fingers. Only then did he see the rider in midstream.

It's about time you was seeing some signs of life, he thought. *Maybe that cowhand yonder knows the country hereabouts. He might be able to tell you how far you still are from Tascosa.* He kicked the piebald into a faster walk.

Perhaps a half-mile separated Longarm from the rider, and he had covered half the distance before realizing that the rider was not moving, that the horse was not drinking, which would have been the only reason for a midstream stop. Almost at the same time that he could see this, Longarm also saw that the horse's neck was twisting, its head tossing, and that its rider was fighting the reins.

Digging his heels into the piebald's flanks and slapping the reins across its shoulders, Longarm urged the animal to a gallop. As he drew closer he could see that the horse in the middle of the wide expanse of water was standing at an abnormal angle. Its forequarters were slanting downward, and the rider was having to lean back in the saddle to keep from being pitched off over its neck. By now the rider had seen Longarm and was making frantic gestures, obviously calling for help.

Longarm turned the piebald into the river, heading on a long slant toward the foundering horse. The river was very shallow, the bottom slanted so gently that the piebald was far out into the stream before the water reached its knees. The new angle at which Longarm was riding took the sun's glare out of his eyes, and for the first time he could see that the rider who was in trouble was not a cowhand, as he'd supposed, but a woman. He still could not see her except in silhouette, but no cowhand who'd ever forked a horse on any range had swelling breasts and wide hips and rode sidesaddle.

When he got close enough for his voice to carry, Longarm called, "Just sit tight, ma'am. I'll get your horse out of whatever he's tangled up in, soon as I can get to you!"

"No!" she called back. "Don't come too close! I'm caught in quicksand, and if you come too near, it'll get you too!"

Longarm checked the piebald at once. He was still almost a hundred yards from the woman, and after a moment's thought he decided that he could safely get closer. He toed his horse forward again, this time at a cautious walk, ready to pull back hard on the reins the instant he felt the piebald balk when its front feet touched a soft spot on the bottom.

"Don't get too close to me!" the woman called again. "It won't help either of us if you get in this quicksand too!"

"Now don't worry," Longarm replied. "I ain't about to get myself bogged down. Just set as still as you can, and keep your horse from churning around. He'll sink in deeper if you let him start thrashing his legs."

"I've got him under control," she said. "He's not sinking as fast as he did at first."

Longarm asked, "How far away are you from where you hit the sinkhole, ma'am?"

"Oh—" she looked around, studying the riverbank, and went on, "Not more than eight or ten feet. I pulled up as soon as I felt the horse starting to sink."

"Chances are he won't bog down real fast, then," Longarm reassured her. He was within fifteen or twenty feet of the bogged horse by now, and he reined in. "Now let's see what I can do about getting you out of there."

"Throw me your lariat," she suggested. "Then you can back your horse out and mine will be able to follow you."

"That's the trouble," Longarm replied. "I ain't carrying a rope with me."

"Well, what the hell kind of cowboy are you, anyhow! I

73

thought all you men carried lassoes!"

"I don't, because I ain't a hand," Longarm told her. "But don't worry, I'll figure out something we can use instead."

Since he'd first heard the word "quicksand," Longarm had been trying to think of something that he could use in place of a rope. The only substitute that had occurred to him was his bedroll. The pair of heavy wool blankets and the canvas tarpaulin in which they were rolled up would reach the woman if he knotted them corner-to-corner, but he wasn't sure the improvised rope would be strong enough to handle the weight of the bogged horse and its rider.

"I'm going to use my bedroll to make a rope," he told her, forcing into his voice more confidence than he felt. His own McClellan saddle had no horn, as did the Texan-style saddle on the woman's horse, and while he worked, Longarm was racking his brain to figure out a way to anchor his end of the blanket-rope.

"What I'm rigging up here won't be much for stout," he called to her. "It ought to do the job, though."

Twisting in his saddle, Longarm untied the rawhide thongs that held the bedroll to the cantle. He draped the rectangular canvas groundcloth over his saddle horn while he unrolled the blankets. Working with the heavy woolen fabric, trying to fold the blankets diagonally without a flat surface on which to spread them, was a frustrating and time-consuming job. Finally he got the blankets folded the way he wanted them and dropped their corners into the water to soak them for a moment.

"You're wasting a lot of time!" the woman said, watching his careful manipulations of the unwieldy blankets. An edge of fear crept into her voice as she added, "My horse is sinking faster. It got stirred up when you rode up."

"Sit tight, ma'am," Longarm replied. "Wet blankets hold a knot better'n dry ones. Once we get lashed together, I don't want nothing to slip."

Working with deliberation, but with all the speed he felt he could afford, Longarm joined the blanket corners with a double square knot, then added the canvas groundcloth to one end of his improvised rope. He tested the knots, trying to pull them apart, and though he wasn't sure how the fabric would stand up, he decided he'd done the best he could.

He looked at the woman; she was being forced now to lean far back in the saddle, her feet pushing the stirrups high, her

74

boots almost touching the surface of the water. The horse's chest was only an inch or so above the river now, and the whites of the animal's eyes were showing as it felt itself sinking deeper.

Longarm could see its muscles trembling as the horse tried to swim. He knew it was reaching the point of panic, and that within a very few minutes it would begin to thrash its legs wildly as it redoubled its efforts to follow the instinct that told it to churn the water with its legs and swim to safety.

Keeping his voice heartily confident, he masked his worry and told the woman, "Now, I'm going to toss one end of this lashup over to you. Be careful not to try to reach out if it falls short, because if you move too sudden you might fall out of your saddle."

"If you can throw it far enough, I can catch it," she said. Her voice was tart, but Longarm caught the undertone of growing fear in it.

Longarm made a loop of the clumsy blanket-rope and whirled it once, then tossed it across the stretch of green water that separated them. The loop unrolled sluggishly and almost fell into the river, but by stretching and leaning out, the woman got her hand on the end at the last possible moment.

"What do I do now?" she asked.

Longarm did not reply at once. He had raised himself in his stirrups and was winding the end of the rolled blanket around his thighs. He settled back into his saddle and tested the lashup with a few hard tugs. When he was reasonably sure he could hold himself in the saddle against the pull of her horse, he said, "Tie the end to your saddle horn," Longarm told her. "I sure hope you know how to make a knot that'll hold!"

"I grew up on sailboats," she retorted. "My knot will hold, don't worry about that! I only hope you've tied yours as tight as mine will be!"

Longarm watched anxiously as she began lashing the end of the blanket to her saddle horn. He breathed a bit easier when he saw she hadn't been boasting idly. Her fingers moved with quick precision in spite of the clumsy fabric she was handling, as she took a double turn around the saddle horn and secured it with a jam knot that would tighten the fabric against the leather when it began to take a strain.

"All right!" she said when she'd pulled the knot tight. "What shall I do now?"

"Just hang on to your saddle horn with one hand. Keep the reins in your other hand. Don't let that knot slip off the saddle horn, and talk to your horse, try to gentle it so it don't start thrashing around when I begin to pull."

"You can start whenever you're ready," she said. "It won't be a minute too soon for me!"

Slowly and gently, Longarm turned the piebald until its body was quartering the horse mired in the quicksand. He prodded a boot toe into the animal's belly and nudged gently. The piebald took a step forward, felt the strain that had been added to its saddle, and stopped. Longarm nudged again, and the horse took a hesitant step ahead. The blankets grew taut around his thighs as he felt the knots settling into place and he braced himself to hold his seat in spite of the strain.

"Step on, boy," Longarm told the horse, his voice firm and even. He accompanied the urging with a firm pressure of his toes in the piebald's ribs. The horse tried another step forward, but started to balk when the strain increased. Longarm kept the pressure of his toe against the beast's body, his calves and thighs clinging to the animal's sides. The piebald whinneyed and pulled, and finally gained a step, then another.

A thrashing in the water behind him caught Longarm's ears. He turned to look. The mired horse was churning with its hind legs, the water around it becoming dark with bottom-silt. The woman was hanging on to the saddle horn with one hand, the blanket with the other. Her face showed her worry, but Longarm could see that her jaws were set with determination.

"Easy does it, ma'am," he called over his shoulder. "Don't let your horse get all worked up, just try to keep him quiet. Soon as his legs get free of the quicksand, you better hang on, because this rope's going to drag him sideways till he can get his forefeet on solid bottom!"

"I'm doing all right so far," she called back. The anxiety had gone out of her voice, he noted, now that rescue seemed a bit closer.

Bit by bit, Longarm increased the tension on the blanket-rope. He heard a few twangs as an overstressed thread or two in the fabric snapped, but his inspection showed no signs that the blankets were beginning to rip. The piebald was straining hard now, its forefeet slipping on the riverbed as it tried to get a solid footing. Longarm kept urging it ahead, and the horse kept up its efforts.

Longarm could not tell exactly when the battle was won. In one instant the horse was exerting itself to the utmost, and the blankets were as taut as the strings of a violin.

Looking over his shoulder, Longarm saw that the woman on the mired horse was sitting erect in her saddle now, but fighting at the same time to keep her seat on her wildly shaking mount.

Then, suddenly, the horse's knees broke water. It reared up on its hind legs, almost unseating its rider, as the rope of blankets swung it to follow the piebald. Its forefeet plunged down into the water and it found solid footing. After that, it was clear sailing. Longarm stopped nudging the piebald and let the blanket-rope slacken as the woman's horse, freed from the quicksand and with firm bottom under its hooves, tossed its head and stepped out briskly. The woman reined in when the horse came abreast of the piebald.

"For a minute I didn't think those blankets were going to hold," she said. Though she made a valiant effort, she could not keep a quiver of dying fear out of her voice. "But it was lucky for me that you came along with you did."

"I was of a mind with you, ma'am," Longarm said. "I wasn't sure those blankets would hold either. But let's head for shore now, and talk later. These horses need to rest a spell."

"Yes, of course. And I need a little while to pull myself together, too. I don't suppose I need to say this, but I'm very grateful to you, Mr.—" She paused inquiringly.

Longarm doffed his hat. "My name's Long, ma'am."

"Mr. Long," she finished. "I'm Ellen Briscoe." She leaned toward him and extended her hand. Longarm grasped it in a brief but firm handshake. "You're right about us needing to get on dry land," she went on. "I can feel my horse trembling."

They started toward the bank, and Longarm got his first really good look at her. Ellen Briscoe was younger than he'd taken her to be when he'd first seen her at a distance. Then, all he'd been able to make out was her mature figure. Later, when he'd gotten closer, he'd been too preoccupied with getting her out of the quicksand to pay much attention to her appearance.

She had yet to reach thirty, he judged. She was a tall woman, and generously built; her shoulders were wide, her breasts full. Her waist was uncorseted, and wide in proportion to her hips. Her hands were large, and looked capable. She was wearing

77

a pink-checked gingham shirt under a light riding jacket, and a riding skirt and black boots. The boots, like the wide-brimmed grey Stetson that hid her hair, looked store-new. From her full, dark eyebrows and brown eyes, Longarm imagined that her hair was dark. He was aware, as he studied her covertly, that she in turn was studying him.

They reached the shore and rode a short distance away from the edge of the stream, to a small patch of fine-sprigged grama grass that covered the ocher soil. Longarm swung from his saddle and held his cupped hands for her boot while she dismounted. She stretched, sighing.

"Solid ground feels good," she said, smiling ruefully. "For a few minutes there, I wasn't sure I'd ever feel it under my feet again. And now that I'm standing up, my legs are trembling so that I'd better sit down." She folded her legs and sat down on the fine, springy grass. Longarm sat down facing her.

Ellen Briscoe said, "I don't really know how to thank you, Mr. Long. If it hadn't been for you—"

"Now you don't need to feel like I done anything special, ma'am," he replied. "Anybody that was riding past and seen you in trouble would've done the same thing."

"Only perhaps not as quickly or efficiently," she commented.

"Not that it's any of my business, but how'd you happen to get into a fix like that?" Longarm asked.

"It was my own fault," she replied. "And I can understand now why you people out here call strangers 'tenderfeet.' The men at the ranch warned me about trying to cross that river anyplace where there weren't tracks or a path showing that others had crossed there before. They said the river was full of quicksand."

"Excuse me for saying so, Miz Briscoe, but I don't see how even a tenderfoot could forget something like that."

"Oh, I didn't forget. I took a chance because I was anxious to get back. And got into trouble, as you saw."

"As long as it ended all right, I don't guess there's much harm done. Just be careful the next time."

"There won't be many next times, Mr. Long. I don't have a lot longer to stay."

"You wouldn't be staying in Tascosa, would you? Because I'm heading there, and if you are too, we can ride in together."

"No. Not Tascosa. I'm visiting at the LX Ranch. One of

my uncles in Boston owns some stock in the company that bought it a short while ago. But the ranch house isn't too far from Tascosa, not by the way you measure distances out here."

"They are liable to be a little bit far, as I remember the East. But I been out here so long that I'm used to 'em." Longarm took a cheroot from his pocket and was about to strike a match when he remembered that some Eastern women objected to having men smoke in their presence. He asked Ellen, "You don't mind if I light up, do you, ma'am?"

"Not at all. In fact—" She stopped short and looked at him as though trying to make up her mind whether or not to go on, then said, "In fact, if you have one of those thin cigars to spare, and it wouldn't shock you too much, I wouldn't mind smoking one myself."

"I got more'n enough for you to have one, if you'd like."

"I'd like to very much, Mr. Long. Usually I smoke cigarettes when I'm at home alone, or with close friends, but I left my case at the ranch today." She looked at him narrowly and asked, "You don't object to women smoking, I hope?"

"Ma'am, I don't object to ladies doing anything they got a mind to," Longarm replied. He took another cheroot from his pocket and handed it to her, rasped his horn-hard thumbnail over the head of a match, and lighted the two cigars. They puffed in relaxed silence for a few moments, then Longarm began, "Miz Briscoe—"

Ellen interrupted to say, "Mr. Long, would you do me another favor?"

"I always try to oblige a lady, Miz Briscoe."

"Then please don't go on calling me 'ma'am.' It makes me feel old. And I'm not really fond of being called Mrs. Briscoe, either. I didn't go back to using my maiden name after my husband died a few years ago, but the name doesn't seem to fit now. Please, just call me Ellen."

"If that's what you want me to do."

"Thank you. And if you're going to be informal, so will I. Do you have a first name you don't mind my using?"

"Well, I got one, but I don't cotton to it much. But I got a sort of nickname my friends use. Longarm."

"Then, if you don't object—"

"Not a bit, Miz . . . Ellen, that is."

They smoked without talking for a moment, then Ellen asked, "Are you going to Tascosa on business, Longarm?"

"In a manner of speaking. You see, I'm a deputy U.S. marshal, work out of the Denver office. I'm down here in Texas on a case."

"How exciting! It—" Ellen hesitated. "It's not something you can tell me about, I suppose?"

"Well, I don't guess you'd call it a secret, but it's a pretty long story—"

"Longarm," Ellen broke in, her eyes shining, "I've got an idea. Why don't you ride over to the ranch house with me, and stay for supper? You won't get to Tascosa until quite a while after dark, it's still a long way, the ranch house is closer."

"Well, now—" Longarm began.

Ellen interrupted him again, bubbling, "It's not much out of your way, unless you're in a terrible hurry to get to Tascosa, and Bob Adams—he's the manager—seems to be so glad to see everybody who stops by that I know you'd be welcome. I'm sure your case would interest me—everything about this part of the country's so different from what I'm used to back in Boston—and I'd love to hear about it."

Longarm glanced at the sun; it had dropped close to the horizon. The time spent in rescuing Ellen, and their talking since then, had eaten up a lot more of the afternoon than he'd realized. And unless the LX Ranch was an exception to what he'd found to be a general rule about isolated cattle spreads, he'd not only be welcomed, but would get a better supper there than any restaurant in Tascosa was likely to provide. He made up his mind quickly.

"Well, now, I guess I don't have to be in too much of a hurry. I'll just accept your invitation, Ellen."

Chapter 8

There was no mistaking the genuineness of the welcome given Longarm by Bob Adams, the manager of the LX Ranch, and his wife, Annie, when he and Ellen rode up to the sprawling headquarters house an hour later. Adams was tall and sapling-thin, a man with a weatherbeaten face, a catching grin, and a thick shock of white hair that contrasted sharply with his springy step and light, youthful voice and manners. Annie was a short, plump woman with a face almost as tanned as her husband's.

"You're sure you weren't really heading for the LX, Marshal, instead of Tascosa?" Adams joked after they'd been introduced, waving Longarm to a chair in the low-ceilinged main room of the ranch house. "We've got some pretty rough characters working for us here, and it wouldn't surprise me if you were looking for a few of them."

"Now, Bob, Marshal Long doesn't know your reputation for joking," Annie chided him lightly. "He might think you're serious."

"If you got any wanted men, just tell 'em not to get in my way, then," Longarm said, his voice mock-sober. "I got enough on my mind with the case I'm down here on, without having to worry about arresting your hands."

"I've invited Longarm to stay for supper, Annie," Ellen told Mrs. Adams. "I didn't think you'd mind."

"I'd have minded more if you hadn't," Annie replied. "I hope he'll stay the night with us."

"Hold on, now!" Longarm protested. "That wasn't in the invite Ellen give me."

"Even if it wasn't, I'm inviting you now," Adams told him. "We've got plenty of room here in the main house, and there's not much use in your pushing on to Tascosa tonight, unless your business there's right pressing."

"Yes indeed," Annie seconded. "Bob and I know how good it is to see a new face, and I think Ellen's learned that too, since she's been here."

"It certainly did me good to see Longarm's face when I was thinking I'd never get out of that quicksand," she smiled. Then, to Longarm, she added, "But I've been here long enough to find out they're right about it being lonesome. I don't know whether you're any more familiar with the Texas Panhandle than I was two months ago, Longarm, but everyplace is so far from everyplace else that ranching's a lonely business."

"Well, the Denver office I work out of takes in a lot of territory, and I get around to quite a few ranches," Longarm said. "Most of 'em do get a mite lonesome at times."

"Traveling the way you do, your job must be lonesome too," Annie suggested.

"You could call it that, I guess. But I've got used to it."

"There's another reason for you to stay, Marshal," Adams told Longarm. "If you don't, I'll think you're angry because Ellen put you to so much trouble." He turned to her again and asked, "Haven't all of us warned you to be careful about crossing the Canadian?"

"Dozens of times," she replied. "Honestly, Bob, I don't know what got into me. I just wanted to get back quickly, so I didn't stop to think before I turned Copper to cross the river."

Longarm had been considering the ranch manager's invitation while the others were talking. He'd learned that a good manager of a ranch the size of the LX had to keep informed about the happenings and gossip of a sizeable area, so there was a chance that Adams might be able to pass on some helpful information. There was an added attraction in the thought of a night in one of the comfortable beds he knew a ranch the size of the LX provided. Weighing both items against the miles he'd still have to ride if he wanted to reach Tascosa, he made up his mind unhesitatingly. When Adams repeated the invitation, he nodded.

"I guess another night won't make much difference right now. Tascosa's still going to be there tomorrow, if I don't get there tonight."

Annie Adams glanced at the big Vienna chime clock that hung on the wall and said, "It's already getting on for suppertime. I'll go put another plate on the table. When Bob and I are the only ones in the house here, we eat in the kitchen, but since Ellen's been visiting, we've been having our supper in the dining room."

"I'll go with you, if I can help," Ellen volunteered.

"I'll show the marshal to his room while you ladies take care of the table, Annie," Adams said. "Come on, Marshal Long. I'd guess you'll want to wash up before we sit down."

Longarm followed Adams out of the room. The manager led the way down a corridor onto which several bedrooms opened, most of their doors standing ajar. Adams waved to them and said, "Pick out any one that pleases you."

"I guess this one here's as good as any of them," Longarm said. "But I'd better get my saddlebags before supper."

"Of course. Just go out that door at the end of the hall and turn left, you'll see the hitch rail. While you're doing that, I'll get you some water from the kitchen; you'll want to freshen up before supper. Don't worry about your horse, I'll get one of the hands to take care of him."

Longarm found that the main house was a sprawling structure built in a U-shape, with the main room across its front, and wings extending out from it at both ends. He guessed that the kitchen, dining room, and manager's quarters occupied one wing, while the other was kept for guests and the owners of the operating company when they visited from the East. He got his saddlebags and returned to the room he'd chosen, where he found that Adams had already put a bucket of water just inside the door. As hungry as he was, Longarm wasted little time over his ablutions. He found his way back to the main room, where Ellen was waiting to show him to the dining room.

As Longarm had suspected it would be, supper was a sumptuous meal. There were steaks from prime beef, mashed potatoes with rich brown gravy, a big bowl of tomatoes that had been heated with onions and shredded red peppers to make a dish that lay between a stew and a sauce. Dessert was a bowl of peaches, pears, and maraschino cherries heated in a brandy sauce.

"That was a real fine supper, Mrs. Adams," Longarm told his hostess as they left the dining room. "A lot better'n I'd have got if I'd had to eat at a restaurant in Tascosa."

"Well, if it hadn't been for airtights, it would've been a lot skimpier," she said. "My Lord, Marshal Long, when I was a girl, we never did have tomatoes or fruit the year 'round! I just wish somebody would find out how to put up other things in airtights. It'd certainly make housekeeping easier."

As the group sat over coffee after dinner, Longarm initiated little of the casual conversation except to ask a question now and then about some detail that might help him not only in the Panhandle country through which he'd be traveling, but in the Llano Estacado, where he was heading.

"I guess that country down south of the Red River, what you folks call the Llano Estacado, is filling up pretty good with ranches by now, like it is up here?" he asked the ranch manager at one point.

Adams shook his head. "After you get below the Red River, you won't find many ranches west of the Cross Timbers. That part of Texas is short of water and good grass. There's barely enough grass to run sheep on. About all you'll find down there are a few of the old Spanish plazas right along the Texas–New Mexico border; they claim range in both states, and they're still sheepherding."

"Come to think of it, I ain't seen any sheep hereabouts," Longarm said thoughtfully.

"You won't, either," Annie Adams told him. "This is all cattle country."

"It hasn't always been, of course," Adams put in. "The old Mexican *hacendados* used to run sheep and cattle both, here in the Panhandle. But Annie's right. It's cattle country now, and the way things seem to be going, it'll stay that way, with all the new money that's coming in from the East and from England."

"Like the company that owns the LX now," Ellen said. "I don't think Uncle Lucius or any of his friends back in Boston would've invested in a sheep ranch."

"Neither would the Englishmen," Adams smiled. "But they're sure falling all over themselves to buy up ranches in the Panhandle right now. Every time I talk to one of my friends, I hear about some kind of offers they've had. A lot of them are listening, too. I understand at least two of our neighbors, George Littlefield and Tom Bugbee, are about ready to sell out."

"It don't seem to me that the towns are coming along, though," Longarm frowned. "Mobeetie, now, it's just a little place. How about Tascosa? Is it getting big?"

"Not so's you'd notice," Adams replied. "We've still got to get a lot of our supplies out of Fort Worth. But there's a railroad talking about coming through Tascosa, so maybe it'll grow."

"I hear it used to be a pretty rough place, back in the Comanchero days," Longarm said. "Wasn't there a lot of outlaws and rough characters there, then?"

"Well, not any more than there were in Dodge City or Abilene or anyplace else. I've heard there are still a few of the Mexicans who used to be Comancheros living there yet."

"You wouldn't be able to name me some names, would you?"

Adams shook his head. "If I heard any names, it's been so long ago I've forgotten them. That's not the kind of past that folks like to talk about, Marshal, and whatever I heard when I first got here were likely rumors, anyhow."

"Too bad," Longarm commented, keeping his voice casual. "I got a hunch some of them old-timers might help me in this case that I've got down south."

"I'll tell you who might be able to help you," Adams volunteered. "When you get to Tascosa, go in and see Jim McMasters at his store. Give him regards from Annie and me, and tell him I told you to call on him."

"Well, thanks, I'll do that. Might be he could help."

"Jim's been a real friend to me. He put in a good word for me to stay on as manager when Ellen's uncle and his friends took over the spread." Adams shook his head. "I suppose if things keep booming here, there'll be some outfit from the East coming in to buy out fellows like Jim too, and put in fancy stores. Yes, sir, old John Adair really set off a boom when he tied in with Charley Goodnight to set up the JA."

"I heard a lot about this Colonel Goodnight," Longarm said. "Is he as much of a man as folks say?"

"Well, Charley's able to hold his own anyplace he hangs

85

his hat," Adams replied. "He deserves all the credit for making a go of the JA, even if the brand is in John Adair's name. Of course, Goodnight's an equal partner with Adair in the spread."

"Ain't his place south of the Red River?" Longarm asked.

"Most of it is. The JA's got quite a lot of range north of the river, though. And Goodnight keeps jumping over other spreads to add new range, because by now he's pretty well boxed in. Northwest of his range there's Lee Dyer's T-Anchor spread, then the Baby Doll's on the east, and the Mill Iron on the south. Over to the west and southwest, the JA borders on the Spur and the Matador range."

"How about up here along the Canadian?"

"Oh, we're getting boxed in here at the LX, too. We've got Tom Bugbee's Quarter-Circle T just north of us, and the LIT—that's Littlefield's outfit—on the northeast. And nobody's quite sure yet exactly how big the LIT's going to be. Every time I hear anybody mention it, the size of the range that syndicate swapped with the state for putting up the capital gets bigger. I'd say it's getting downright crowded around here."

"It's still a big, beautiful place, though, and I've come to love it," Ellen said. "I can't wait to get back to Boston and tell Uncle Lucius what he's missing by not coming out here, even if it's just for a little visit."

"You mean your uncle and his friends bought this place without even looking at it?" Longarm asked.

"Oh, two or three of them came out for a few days, I think. But most of them are too set in their ways to get any farther from home than the Union Club."

"People are like that everywhere," Annie reminded her. "I grew up in Kansas, and when Bob and I moved west right after we got married, nobody could understand it. They said Kansas was as far west as any sensible person wanted to go."

"As a matter of fact, Ellen, the men associated with your uncle did look over the LX before they bought it," Adams said. "And at least one or two of them make a trip out here every year to make sure I'm doing my job right."

"But if I owned a place like this, or any part of it, I'd want to live here!" she exclaimed.

"It's like the old man said when he kissed the heifer, I guess," Longarm told her. "There ain't no accounting for taste."

"Just the same, I like it here better than in Boston," she said stoutly. "I think if I could, I'd like to live here."

"Marry a cowhand, then," Annie smiled. "That's what I did, and I hadn't even seen where we were going to live."

"That was because we didn't *have* a place to live," her husband added. "But most of the time since then, we've had a roof to sleep under."

"Speaking of sleep, I'd imagine Marshal Long and Ellen are getting pretty tired by now, with all the riding the marshal's done lately and Ellen's excitement today," Annie Adams said. "It seems to me we'd better call it bedtime."

Closing the door of his bedroom, Longarm automatically felt below the knob for a key, but found none. Apparently the LX was like most big spreads; providing keys would have been an unspoken suggestion that the ranch could not provide for the safety of its guests unless they were behind locked doors.

A lighted lamp stood on the bureau, another ranch custom, a subtle statement that the spread did not need to stint on coal oil. Longarm began going through his nightly routine, which did not vary whether he was sleeping in his own bed in his Denver boardinghouse or in a strange bedroom while he was in the field on a case. He emptied his coat pocket of cheroots and put them on the bureau with matches beside them, where they'd be in easy reach in the morning, then hung up his long black Prince Albert coat on one of the clothes pegs behind the door, and put his tobacco-brown Stetson on the peg that held the coat.

Unbuckling his gunbelt, he hung it on the bedpost at the head of the bed, where it would be ready at hand if he needed it in the night. Taking his watch from the lower left-hand pocket of his vest, he dropped it in the upper right-hand pocket, leaving in the lower right-hand pocket the derringer whose butt was clipped to the opposite end of his gold-washed watch chain.

He hung the vest on the bedpost opposite the one where the belt with his holstered Colt was resting. More than a few times Longarm had faced situations where his life had been saved by these meticulous preparations that kept his weapons where he could reach them without fumbling.

Only after he'd gotten down to his shirtsleeves did he take the almost-empty bottle of Tom Moore from his saddlebags and tilt it for a preliminary nightcap. Lighting a cheroot, Longarm sat on the side of the bed to lever himself out of his stovepipe cavalry boots and peel off his skin-tight twill trousers.

In deference to the ladies, he'd washed and shaved before supper and also put on the black string tie that he privately disliked, but which federal regulations required him to wear on duty. By the time he'd taken off the necktie and his gray flannel shirt and balbriggans, he'd smoked the cheroot to a stub. He finished the cigar with a few appreciative puffs while having his final nightcap, blew out the lamp, and crawled into the first real bed he'd slept in since leaving Fort Elliott. A few seconds after his head settled onto the pillow, he was asleep.

Longarm woke instantly, as he always did, cat-quick and cat-alert, when the almost inaudible whisper of metal rubbing on metal reached his ears. The room was dark, but a ghostly tinge of moonlight creeping around cracks at the edges of the drawn windowshades gave him enough light to see that the bedroom door was slowly swinging open.

Silently, Longarm slid his Colt out of the holster on the bedpost while he watched the dark crack grow wider. He kept the gun poised while the door moved until it was ajar, but when he saw who his visitor was, he exhaled the breath he'd been holding. He let the revolver's weight pull his hand down beside him onto the blanket while he waited. In another second the door closed as silently as it had opened, and he could make out the dark blurs that were Ellen Briscoe's brown eyes and full red lips, framed by her dark hair spilling down over her shoulders.

She stood silently just inside the closed door, unmoving, while her eyes adjusted to the dimness of the room. Holding his voice just louder than a whisper, Longarm said, "Hello, Ellen."

"Oh!" Ellen exclaimed. Then, her own voice losing its high, startled pitch, she went on, "I wasn't expecting you to be waiting for me. I was sure that by now you'd be asleep, that I'd have to wake you up."

"You did. I wake up real easy."

"But I was so careful not to make any noise, even if I knew that Bob and Annie are way off on the other side of the house!"

"A man in my kind of job makes enemies, Ellen. I can't afford to get caught asleep."

"You don't mind my coming in, do you?"

"Not a bit, even if I wasn't expecting company."

"I think you know why I'm here, Longarm."

"Well, a grown-up woman like you are don't come calling

like this if all she's looking for is a little conversation or maybe a cup of tea."

"You must've known I'd come to you tonight, Longarm. I think you knew from the minute I asked you to have supper at the LX what I was hoping would happen."

"No offense intended, but I didn't. I don't take a woman for granted, Ellen, not even the kind that knows her own mind. A lot of women might know what they want, but don't have enough grit to go after it. Even if it's right there waiting for 'em."

"Are you waiting for me, Longarm?"

"I wasn't before you come in, but I am now."

"Then why don't you invite me to come to bed with you?"

"This is a nice big bed I'm in, Ellen. Wouldn't you like to come try it out?"

There was a smile in her voice when she replied, "I've just been waiting for you to ask me!"

Ellen seemed to float across the room, her bare feet noiseless on the Brussels carpet. During the few seconds she took moving across the room, Longarm holstered his Colt with the same sure speed he'd shown when drawing it, and flipped the blanket back. Ellen sat down on the bed. Close to Longarm, with the blanket removed, she could see for the first time that he wore no night clothing. She touched his chest, drawing her warm fingers through its matted curls.

"I'm glad you sleep naked, too," she breathed. "While I was lying in bed waiting for it to get late enough to come to you, I wondered if you might not."

She stood up and whipped her nightgown off, and let it fall to the floor. Then she sighed and stretched out beside Longarm, holding her face turned toward him, waiting for his first kiss.

Longarm bent to meet her lips and felt Ellen's body quiver as their tongues met exploringly. Her arms went around his ribcage to pull her closer to him, and he felt the soft fullness of her breasts flatten against his chest. Her hand slipped down to his groin, and she found him still soft. She broke the kiss.

"What's wrong, Longarm? Don't I please you?"

"Why, sure you do, Ellen. If you mean why ain't I hard yet, it takes a minute or two for me to get charged up. But you just keep on feeling of me a little while longer, and you won't be disappointed too much."

When their lips met in another kiss, Ellen began to stroke

89

Longarm gently, her hand soft and warm as it curled around and grasped him. She began to pump her hand up and down in slow, deliberate caresses. Longarm trailed his hand down her hips and ran the tips of his callused fingers through her generous pubic curls. She opened her thighs to let his fingers slip between them, and he found her wet and ready, the tender bud nestled between her nether lips firm and pulsing. When he touched it she began to shudder so vigorously that he moved his hand away before he aroused her to a point beyond control. Touching her, feeling her body responding, speeded Longarm's progress to a full erection. They finally broke their kiss and Ellen sighed happily.

Her breath warm on his cheek, she whispered, "When I first saw you this afternoon, I knew you were a lot of man, Longarm, but I didn't expect quite so much. Get into me fast, please! I've been waiting for an hour or more, thinking about you, and I can't wait much longer. I'm about ready to explode right now!"

Longarm raised his body over hers. Ellen did not release him as she moved under him and parted her legs. She positioned him quickly and lifted her hips to bring him into her, and squeezed him as a signal that she was ready for his plunge. Longarm thrust. Ellen gasped, a deep, full inhalation that stiffened her whole body as she rocked her hips up to accept him.

Locking her calves around his waist, she pulled her hips up, clinging to him, while Longarm lunged into her with long, swift strokes. He drove into her hard and deeply, and much sooner than he'd expected, she began gasping and shaking, her body writhing in an orgiastic spasm that shook her with its tremors, and her shuddering faded away only to begin again and bring her to a second climax almost as soon as the first had ended.

When her second spasm had died away, Ellen remained motionless for several moments, contented only to keep her legs locked around him while he continued to thrust into her. Still short of breath, she whispered in Longarm's ear, "I know you must be about ready to come, so don't wait for me."

"It'll take me a while yet," Longarm told her. "Go on and take all the pleasure you can, Ellen."

"Oh, I intend to. But I want you to have pleasure too."

"We got a long time ahead of us. We'll both enjoy it."

Ellen remained passive for only a short while as Longarm

kept up his steady, deep stroking. He felt himself growing close to the point of lost control, and speeded up. Ellen responded by gyrating her hips in rhythm with his increased tempo, and when he sighed and began to come, she rocked her hips upward a few times and shook as her own spasm seized her.

As Longarm relaxed and let his body settle down on hers, she lay silently for several minutes before saying, "I know you came, I felt you. But you're still as big and hard as ever."

"I told you it'd take me a while to finish. Unless you're too tired—"

"I'm tired, but I love the feeling of being tired out this way. Stay in me as long as you want to. I like it!"

"So do I." Longarm did not move for several minutes, then he stirred and, with a gentle, partial withdrawal and thrust, signaled that he was about to resume.

Ellen looked up at him, her eyes wide. "So soon?"

"I can wait, if you don't feel like going on right now."

"You've already served me better than any man I've ever been to bed with. Not that there've been all that many since my husband died a few years ago. But right now I feel like a virgin bride on her wedding night, when she's just learned how having a man inside you can make you feel. I'm ready if you are!"

Ellen was a tall woman, and Longarm had only to bend his head slightly to find her lips as he started stroking again. She responded to his kiss with a thrusting, busy tongue that wriggled snakelike in his mouth, curling around his tongue. Being joined by two bonds of flesh seemed to make Ellen forget her earlier orgasms. She arched her body up with a renewed fury while he continued to plunge into her with long, steady thrusts.

This time Longarm did not hold back, but let himself begin to build when she had stopped shaking after one climax, and by the time she was nearing another, he was ready too. He speeded up until the bed was shaking and Ellen was arching her back to drive her hips up in a frenzy, while the small gasping sobs that began as she drew nearer to her spasm were smothered in her throat by Longarm's clinging lips on hers.

They reached the last jarring seconds of orgasm at almost the same time, and when the weariness of their drained bodies passed, and Longarm left her to roll aside and lie supine, Ellen sighed deeply and found enough strength to get on her knees beside him and lean over to kiss his lips gently.

"You know I want to stay with you, Longarm," she whispered, "but if I lie down by you I'll go to sleep, and I'm not sure I'd wake up before Annie and Bob are up and around. But you're a man I never will forget, even if I do just tell you goodbye politely when you ride off in the morning."

"I'd stay longer if I could," he said. "You know I can't. But maybe I can stop by on the way back to Denver."

"I'll be waiting for you, if you do. And thank you, Longarm, for the best night I've never slept through."

When Ellen had slipped away, Longarm thought for a moment of getting up for another nightcap and a cheroot, but even his strong body had been drained by the unexpected finish to so many long days. He pulled the blanket over him and almost at once fell asleep.

Chapter 9

Longarm rode into Tascosa in midmorning. He'd gotten a late start from the LX. The soft bed and his exertions with Ellen had lulled him into sleeping later than was his usual habit, and by the time he was up and around, Bob Adams had already gone out to the corrals to get his men started on their day's work. Not wanting to be marked down as an unappreciative guest, Longarm had waited for Adams to get back in order to thank him for the hospitality he'd shown. Ellen Briscoe had joined him at the breakfast table, and Longarm had dallied longer than usual over what to him was ordinarily a hurried meal.

Ellen had made only one reference to their night together, and that one was oblique. When Annie Adams had left them momentarily to go to the kitchen for fresh coffee, Ellen had said in a low voice, "I'd love to ride part of the way to Tascosa with you, Longarm, or even better, all the way to wherever it is you're going. But even if I went only part of the way to Tascosa with you, Bob and Annie might get ideas about us."

"Sure," he'd nodded. "I know how it is. A woman's got to be careful."

"I'm not a bit ashamed of last night," she'd said. "Uncle Lucius is an old fussbudget where I'm concerned, though, and he keeps a tight hold on the trust fund that I live on. He'd be shocked out of his prim and proper mind, so I won't even kiss you goodbye. But don't think I've forgotten a minute of last night. And you'll stop on your way back, won't you?"

"I don't know how long it'll take me to close out my case down on the Llano Estacado, but I'll sure stop by if I can."

Annie's return to the dining room had ended any chance of further private conversation between Longarm and Ellen, and just as breakfast was ending, Bob Adams got back and sat down for a cup of coffee with them. Longarm's last look at Ellen was when she'd been standing at the hitch rail as he rode off, waving goodbye.

For most of his short journey to Tascosa, Longarm had followed the Canadian River, riding a straight line between its bends and curves. The piebald was rested, and had been well fed on the hay to which its life in army stables had accustomed it, so it stepped out briskly. It was the time of morning when range cattle sought water, and he was seldom out of sight of bunches of steers going to the river or leaving it, or simply standing with their hooves in the water drinking, or grazing lazily on the short grass that still greened most of the prairie.

Well, old son, after all you heard about it, this Tascosa ain't really such a much of a town, Longarm thought as he rode past the first houses.

Adobe houses far outnumbered all the rest of the dwellings he passed on his way into town. These were old houses, many of them badly kept, their outer layer of protective plaster needing whitewash, and on a number of the older houses, the door and window frames were cracking and darkened by the weather. Great chunks of plaster had fallen away from the walls of some of them, exposing the earthen bricks beneath.

A number of the newer houses and a substantial number of the older ones were soddies; most of these were new, the wood used in framing their windows and doors still relatively bright. There were a few frame houses to be seen as he drew closer to the town's center. The frame houses were generally small, for lumber was expensive on the treeless plains. Some of the new frame houses stood beside older adobe dwellings that had been abandoned and were crumbling away, their bricks returning to the earth from which they'd been made.

Along the town's dusty, rutted main street, Longarm saw the same hodgepodge of construction that marked its residences. Frame buildings predominated among the business establishments, and several had been covered with sheets of pressed tin, embossed to give the appearance of dressed stone. There were very few brick buildings on the main street, for like lumber, bricks had to be hauled in and were expensive.

Longarm's throat was dry after his ride in the bright morning sunshine. He saw a saloon sign and pulled the piebald over to its hitch rail. Inside, the place was dusky and cool, and smelled of stale beer, tobacco smoke, and steer manure. There were no other customers, and the barkeep was keeping himself busy washing glasses. He stopped when Longarm came in, and wiped his hands on his apron.

"What's your pleasure, friend?" he asked.

"Maryland rye, if you got such a thing."

"Well, now, we don't get a lot of calls for that kind of fancy liquor. We still got some I got stuck with when I took over this place six years ago, and hadn't found out that folks hereabouts don't cotton to much besides beer and tequila and bourbon and Taos Lightning. Let's see—"

Turning, the barkeep studied the bottles on the shelves of the backbar. He finally found what he was looking for—a square, dust-covered bottle to the rear of one of the shelves, its label gone, its shoulders covered with a thick coat of dust. He wiped the bottle and set it in front of Longarm.

"I don't need no label to remember this one," he said. "It's called Daugherty's Private Stock. Think that'll do you?" He placed a glass beside the bottle.

Longarm had already recognized the bottle by its square shape and said quickly, "That'll do me just fine." He filled the glass and sipped the pungent liquor. Lighting a cheroot, he took another sip and said casually, "If I heard right, you said you'd got stuck with quite a bit of this whiskey. Supposing you was to make me the right kind of price, I'd take a couple of bottles off your hands."

"I'll make 'em to you for a dollar and a half a bottle, a dollar and a quarter if you'll take whatever I got left in the storeroom."

Longarm finished his drink and refilled the glass before he replied. He said, "I'm traveling, friend, I can't carry but two bottles in my saddlebags."

'Too bad. It'll take me a while to dig out the case, but I guess you don't mind waiting."

"Tell you what," Longarm replied. "I got a little bit of business to look after in town. Take your time getting them two bottles out. I'll pay for 'em now, and stop in later today to pick 'em up." He put a half eagle on the bar. "Take it out of that. I'll be back after while."

Remounting the piebald, Longarm rode on down the street, looking for the store to which Bob Adams had directed him. He saw a sign on a big frame building that read "Howard & McMasters"; several horses, a buggy, and a team hitched to a deep-bodied freight wagon stood at the hitch rail. Longarm added the piebald to the assortment and went into the store. Two young clerks and an older man, whom he took to be either Howard or McMasters, were assembling orders for the half-dozen customers who stood waiting. Longarm found a spot where he'd be out of the way of both clerks and customers, and waited for the rush to end.

One of the young clerks paused as he passed by to ask, "Can I help you, mister?"

"Not right now, thanks. I'm looking for Jim McMasters."

"That's him over there." The clerk pointed to the older man, a slightly paunchy, balding individual who wore steel-rimmed spectacles that kept slipping down on his nose. "He'll be busy for a little while, but I'll tell him you're waiting."

"When you do, tell him not to hurry. What I want to talk to him about can wait till he's got some time free."

Lighting a cheroot, Longarm found a seat on an upended keg and waited until the store was clear of customers, and McMasters came over to him. "I'm Jim McMasters," the store-keeper said. "Rudy mentioned that you wanted to talk to me."

"I sure do, but I don't want to take your time away from your business. My name's Long, Mr. McMasters. Deputy U.S. marshal from the Denver office. Bob Adams out at the LX said you'd be the best man for me to ask a few questions about your town."

"I hope that what you've come here for doesn't mean the LX or Bob are in any kind of trouble," McMasters frowned.

"They sure ain't. My case hasn't got anything to do with them or the ranch. They was nice enough to feed me and put me up for the night. Seem to be real nice people."

"They are. I hope they're both doing well? It's been a while since they've been in."

"Both of 'em are fine. They said to give you their regards."

"Marshal Long, you can see I'm pretty busy right now," McMasters said, looking at two new customers who'd just come in. "It's not that I don't want to help you, but trying to talk here in the store's not easy, especially with my partner away, down in Fort Worth on a buying trip. Look here, why don't you come out to the house at noon and have dinner with me? I take a little time off in the middle of the day, when trade's slack. If you're not in a big hurry, that is."

"You sure I wouldn't be putting you to too much trouble?"

"Not a bit of trouble, Marshal. It'll save time for both of us. I'll be leaving in about a half hour. You can wait here, or if you've got some other business in town, come back and we'll go out in my buggy."

"I'd just as soon wait, if I won't be in the way."

"Don't worry about that. Make yourself at home, look around, whatever you like. I'll try to get away a little earlier than I usually do, so we'll have more time to talk."

Longarm had no trouble occupying himself during the half hour he spent waiting for McMasters. The store was a busy place, with a constant procession of customers, and when he tired of looking at new faces, Longarm walked around inspecting the merchandise on the well-stocked shelves and the tables that were set at intervals in the middle of the rambling building. Shortly before noon, the number of shoppers diminished to a trickle, and McMasters took his coat from the peg on which it hung behind the counter and came over to where Longarm was standing.

"My buggy's out in the stable behind the store, Marshal," he said. "We'll go out the back door."

"You reckon my horse and gear will be all right at your hitch rail? I've got a pretty fair Winchester in my saddle scabbard that somebody might take a fancy to."

"I wouldn't advise you to leave it there too long. We've got a few light-fingered citizens in Tascosa, like every town has. I'll drive the buggy around and you can hitch your mount to it and ride with me. It's not far to my house."

McMasters' home was a large frame building, one of several that stood off the main street at the end of town opposite that by which Longarm had entered.

"We won't have company at the table, but we won't exactly be eating bachelor-style, either," the merchant explained as he opened the door for Longarm. "My missus went to Fort Worth with Howard and his wife, but our cook doesn't need anybody looking over her shoulder to dish up a right good meal. I gave up eating in the restaurants, food's too greasy for my digestion."

Lunch, the meal that in the Texas Panhandle was commonly called "dinner," was light by local standards. There was a platter of fried catfish and another of prairie chicken, a bowl of turnips peppered heavily and slathered with freshly churned butter, and a heaping plate of pan cornbread.

"Now dig in, Marshal," McMasters urged. "If you'd like a drink before we eat, I'll be happy to pour you one. I don't take liquor in the middle of the day, though."

"What I see there on the table suits me just fine," Longarm said. "It sure looks and smells better'n cafe grub, too."

Their plates filled and the meal under way, McMasters asked, "Now, what was it you wanted to ask me about, Marshal Long?"

"Mostly about the folks here in Tascosa. It's supposed to be a wild, rough place, and when a town gets that name it generally means there's some hardcased folks living close to it, and dropping into town pretty regular."

"Oh, I know that's the reputation the town's gotten, but it tamed down quite considerably a while back. It's been about three or four years since we had any really bad men hanging out here, and the last one we had was just a boy. Being a lawman, I guess you've heard about him. His name was Bill Bonney, but everybody called him Billy the Kid."

Longarm smiled. "Don't reckon there's many that ain't heard tell of Billy the Kid," he said. "Especially with Buntline and them other jaspers all writing tall tales about his terrible deeds. I was sent down to Lincoln County one time on a case, and spent a little time chasing after a fellow was supposed to be the Kid, but I suspicion that when an owlhoot gets himself a big enough name, there's bound to be imitators out after the glory, and sometimes it gets right hard to tell who's the real article and who ain't."

"Oh, this fellow was the real goods, all right," the storekeeper said, "and he was a mean one, even if he was only sixteen years old. Fast with a gun, he was, and that drew a bunch of hardcases to him. The Kid and his bunch drove the ranchers crazy, rustling cattle and selling them over in the Indian Nation or New Mexico Territory."

"But you got rid of him, you said?"

"That's right. The ranchers finally got together and put in a sheriff that turned out to be tougher than Billy was. He took Billy to the New Mexico line and said if he ever showed up in Tascosa again, it'd be the business end of a rope without even a trial. Nobody here's seen Billy since then."

McMasters frowned. "But you're not interested in outlaws like Billy, Marshal, I can see that," he said, passing the platter of prairie chicken to Longarm. "Tell me, just what are you after?"

"First, I'll ask you not to talk to nobody about what I'm going to tell you," Longarm replied. "Not that it's much of a secret, but you never know when a word in the wrong place can be a dead giveaway."

"I've kept quiet about a lot of things. I guess I can keep from talking about whatever you don't want known."

"Sure," Longarm nodded. "Well, it's a little bit mixed up. The Indian Bureau, back in Washington, heard the Comancheros was getting busy again, down in the Llano Estacado, so they got my chief's boss to find out if it's so. I just stopped off here in Tascosa because I heard that some of the old Comancheros used to live here, or spend a lot of their time here."

"That's true enough," McMasters agreed. "But, good Lord, Marshal, the Comancheros were put out of business when McKenzie whipped the Comanches down in Palo Duro Canyon back in '73. They faded away when there weren't any more Indians to trade with."

"That's what I thought, Mr. McMasters. But there's a lot of Comanches in the Nation, and if they begin getting guns from Comancheros, like they used to, the bureau figures for them to bust out of the reservation and start to raiding again. Only it won't be wagon trains, it'll be homesteads."

"I can see why they'd worry," McMasters agreed. Then his shrewd blue eyes narrowed and he asked, "What are the Comanches going to use for trade goods to get the guns, Marshal? They've got nothing. McKenzie had his men kill their horse and mule herds, and there's no way reservation Indians can build a herd."

"I don't think the Indian Bureau give that much thought," Longarm said. "And you sure got a point. But it's still my job to investigate, so what I'd like to find out is if there's any of the old bunch of Comancheros still living here in Tascosa. All

I want to do is talk to 'em, I don't aim to arrest 'em for what they might've done years ago."

"When I first came here, I heard a lot of talk about Comancheros living in Tascosa," McMasters said thoughtfully. "The thing is, nobody ever put names to them. I always understood that most of them were from New Mexico originally, and the Spanish-speaking people hung pretty close together."

"If you heard a lot of talk, you must've heard some names," Longarm suggested He said nothing more, but watched McMasters carefully.

After a few moments the storekeeper sighed and nodded. "I heard a few names, yes. At the time I decided it was just idle talk, and most of the men they talked about then are either dead or gone from here by now. All but one. As far as I know, he's the only one still around, and he's an old man now."

"Mind telling me who he is?"

"His name's Ramon Gallegos."

"I guess you'll know where he lives?"

McMasters hesitated, then said, "Tell me something, Marshal. Are you going to have to tell anybody you got this information from me? Old Ramon stands pretty high among his people. I don't want to have the store set on fire or shot up, and I'd just as soon not lose what trade I've got among his people."

"Whatever you tell me is strictly between you and me, Mr. McMasters," Longarm assured the merchant.

"Ramon lives along the river, southwest of town. A little 'dobe house, the doors and windows used to be painted blue, and there's still enough blue paint on them so you can recognize it."

"I guess that's all I need to know, then," Longarm said. "I thank you for your help, Mr. McMasters. I'll excuse myself now. I'd imagine you'll want to rest awhile before you go back to your store."

Finding Ramon Gallegos' house was no problem. It stood between the trail south and the riverbank, a mile or so from the last houses of the town. The vestiges of blue paint were visible on its door and window frames, as McMasters had said they would be. Longarm reined in and dismounted, and knocked at the door.

"*Quién viene?*" a reedy voice called from inside.

"Mr. Gallegos?" Longarm called back. "My name's Long. I'd like to visit with you a little while, if you ain't busy."

There was a sound of stirring from within, and in a moment the door opened a crack. A bright strip of sunlight flooded through the slit between door and jamb, and Longarm saw part of an incredibly wrinkled brow, an eagle-hooked nose, and one bright brown eye.

"What you are want with Gallegos?" the man asked.

"Just to talk a minute or two."

"Talk of what?"

"Oh, a lot of things, but mostly old times."

"Why?"

"Because I want to know what they was like," Longarm said patiently.

"Who you are?"

"I told you my name. It's Long."

"De dónde viene?"

Longarm shook his head. He guessed that Ramon Gallegos had used the question in Spanish as a test to find out whether his visitor spoke and understood it. Longarm's knowledge of the language was sketchy and rusty from disuse, but he did not want to let Gallegos find out that he knew any Spanish at all, for now at least.

He said, "I don't understand."

"You come from where?" Gallegos asked.

"Denver. That's up north, in Colorado."

"Why you come to Gallegos?"

"Because somebody said you been here a long time, that you know how things used to be around Tascosa and down south of the Red River, on the Llano Estacado."

While he'd been peppering Longarm with questions, Gallegos had been scrutinizing Longarm closely. Slowly he swung the door open, just wide enough to allow Longarm to enter.

Standing just inside the door, Longarm waited until his eyes adjusted to the changed light. Slowly the interior of the dwelling and its occupant became visible. The small, one-room adobe house was neat as a pin, its creaking floor of random-width boards well swept, the covers of the narrow bed that stood along one wall drawn up and smoothed. Besides the bed, the room's furniture consisted of a table, two chairs, and a tall cabinet, richly carved, that stood near the foot of the bed. A small monkey stove was in one corner, and a domed fireplace made of the same adobe as the house yawned empty in the opposite corner.

Gallegos indicated one of the two chairs. *"Sietese,"* he said, and moved toward the second chair.

Longarm sat down. Out of habit, he took a cheroot from his pocket, and had it halfway to his lips before noticing that the old man's eyes were fixed on the cigar. He changed the direction his hand was moving and offered the cigar to Gallegos.

"Smoke?" he asked.

Gallegos took the cigar and passed it under his nose, sniffing gustily. For the first time Longarm could see that the old man's right hand had only a thumb and little finger. There were not even any stubs to show where the three central fingers had been. He took another cheroot from his pocket for himself, held a match for Gallegos, and lighted his own cigar. For several minutes the old man puffed in silent satisfaction, his gnarled face crinkled in a smile.

Suddenly, Gallegos rose and shuffled to the cabinet. He opened it and took a tin pie plate on which there were two sweet rolls. He put the plate on the table and swept his hand in an invitation.

"Siervese de un poco de alimento," he said.

Longarm shook his head after deciding Gallegos was simply lapsing into his mother language from habit. After all, he reasoned, the gesture of invitation explained itself.

"No thanks, Mr. Gallegos," Longarm replied. "I just ate a little while ago."

Gallegos nodded and resumed his seat. He said, "You wish to talk with me of the old days, no?"

"That's what I come for. I heard you know a lot about the Comancheros. I figured—" Longarm stopped abruptly when he noticed that Gallegos had stiffened when he heard the word "Comanchero," and that the corners of his mouth were drawn down forbiddingly. After a moment's silence, Longarm went on, "I ain't trying to get you in no trouble, Mr. Gallegos. Oh sure, I know folks say you was a Comanchero way back, years ago. But there ain't no more Comanchero trade, and I guess all the men you used to know in them days has moved on or died, so you wouldn't hurt them none."

Gallegos sat stubbornly silent, staring into space.

Longarm tried again. "I was talking to the Comanche chief,

Quanah Parker, over in the Indian Nation a little while back. He told me something about the old Comanchero days."

"Quanah has tell you my name?" Gallegos frowned.

Longarm had learned that often the best way to avoid lying was to answer a question with a question. He asked, "You knew Quanah back then, didn't you?"

Slowly, Gallegos nodded. *"Sí. Lo conozco bien."* He looked at Longarm and nodded a second time. His voice reluctant, he said, "Yes. Quanah I knew. And before him his father, Nocona. In the old days. What has Quanah to tell you of me?"

Again, Longarm used a careful evasion. "Quanah misses them, Mr. Gallegos. He called 'em the Shining Times."

Gallegos allowed himself a grim smile, and Longarm could see the old man's mind turning to the past. *"Las días de luz solar,"* he said, his voice low. "But only for the strong, no? For those Quanah and his people trade to us, *son las días de lágrimas, lo mismo como el puesto se llama El Valle de Lágrimas.* Is what they call the Valley of Tears, where the captive ones who have no *rescate*, no ransom, are sell to be slaves in Mexico."

"That'd be what they called the Palo Duro Canyon, I guess?"

"Sí. Sol y sombra, Señor Long. Sunshine and shadows."

"I guess them days is all over, even if Quanah might like to see 'em come back," Longarm observed.

"Is maybe not finish, the days of sunshine. Is now—" Gallegos stopped abruptly and stared through slitted, suspicious eyes at Longarm. "Who you are, *hombre*? Never you are one of us! If you are of Comanchero, you do not need the question to ask me! I theenk I talk to you no more, *señor*! I theenk is better you go now!"

Gallegos stood and shuffled to the door as rapidly as his bent and gnarled legs allowed him to move. He opened the door and waved to the outside with the imperious gesture of one who has known how to command.

"Go now!" he repeated. "You are try to treek me! I talk no more to you!"

Chapter 10

You sure done something wrong there, old son, Longarm told himself as he rode back toward Tascosa. *And the hell of it is, you don't rightly know what it was. One minute you had the old fellow starting to talk, the next minute he was acting like he wanted to slit your guzzle. Something you said or some way you acted must've tipped your hand and give him some kind of clue that just closed him up tighter'n a damn clam.*

He rode on for a few minutes, trying to recall each word of his conversation with the old Comanchero, to remember every intonation of Gallegos' voice, but the reason the old man had so suddenly become suspicious continued to escape him.

But it was when you tried to get him to talk about what's going on right now down on the Llano Estacado that he got his back up all of a sudden. And that just might be what done it. If you'd've been one of his kind like you was letting on to be, you wouldn't't've had to ask him. Or maybe he's like a lot of old hardcases, just smelled you for a lawman. But whatever's done is done, and there's no use crying over it. Anyhow, the way he shut up told you all you need to know. It looks like maybe them nervous nellies at the Indian Bureau might be seeing something worse than spooks under the bed, after all.

To help him think better, Longarm took out a cheroot and lighted it. He put a light pressure on the reins to slow the piebald's pace, and set his mind to work.

There ain't no way around it, you got to get on down to the Llano Estacado and start your nosying, his thoughts ran. *Except that when you get there you got to have a reason for staying. You act like a U.S. marshal and run into a bunch of them new Comancheros, they won't stop to listen to any palaver. They'll cut you down as fast as a hungry fox'll gobble up a rooster.*

Longarm was nearing Tascosa's commercial section now. On both sides of the road there were houses, and he could see the signs of the stores on the buildings ahead of him. He dismissed the fiasco at Gallegos' house, and began to consider his next move.

Now there ain't but one reason a man would go into that country. He'd be running from the law, or he'd be some kind of outlaw looking for a connection with a gang. Which is what the Comancheros are, a gang, so that means you'll have to act like you've got wind of 'em, and you want to join up with 'em. And if they're as smart as Gallegos, it ain't going to be easy to fool 'em. So you better do a little bit of thinking before you start, because if you get the least mite careless you'll be worse off than the washerwoman that got her left tit caught in the wringer.

Just ahead was the Howard & McMasters store. Beyond it, Longarm could see the saloon where he'd stopped when he first rode into town. The germ of an idea was beginning to form in his mind, but he decided it needed to be helped along by a small dose of his favorite brain lubricant. He let the piebald amble on past the store and reined in at the saloon. The barkeep on duty was the same one who'd been there earlier. He saw Longarm push through the scratched and splintered batwings, and by the time Longarm got up to the bar, the bottle of rye from which he'd had his drinks that morning was standing waiting.

"I guess you've come for them two bottles of that fancy rye whiskey you bought this morning," the barkeep said. "Well, I dug 'em up out of the storeroom for you."

"Just hold on to 'em till I get ready to ride out," Longarm told him, pouring his drink. "I'll be around town a little bit longer."

"Whenever you say, friend. They're yours, you paid me for them, remember."

Longarm nodded, an abstracted frown on his face. He took the bottle and his glass over to a corner table and sat down to think. Two drinks and half a cheroot later, he had the beginning of an idea. By the time he'd finished the cheroot, his scheme was in skeleton form, but there were a few details that still needed to be attended to. He took the bottle of rye back to the bar and paid for his drinks.

"Looks like I'm going to be staying here tonight," he said. "Where'll I find a clean bed and a decent supper?"

"Try the Exchange Hotel. They keep the bugs killed out of their beds pretty good. It don't make much difference where you eat. You'll get a steak cut off of the same side of beef."

Longarm rode back down the street to the Howard & McMasters store. Jim McMasters was busy writing down an order being given him by a customer. While Longarm waited for the storekeeper, he strolled over to inspect a display of saddles that stood on sawhorses along the back wall of the store. McMasters finished with the customer and came up to join Longarm.

"Did you find Gallegos, Marshal?" the merchant asked.

"Sure did. And talked to him a while. That was a good tip you give me, and I thank you for giving me a hand."

"Glad I could do it. Is there anything else I can help you with now?"

"Well, I have got one more favor to ask of you. It ain't such a much, though."

"What's that?"

"I see your store sells saddles. Is there a good saddlemaker in town that you get 'em from?"

"No. Our trade's not the kind that buys the kind of fancy saddles Lem puts out. We order factory-made saddles out of Fort Worth. But if you need some work done on your gear, Lem Edwards is as good a man as you'll find anywhere. His shop's in the back of Mickey McCormick's livery stable. You must've see the livery sign, just catty-corner across from the store."

"You think this Edwards is the kind of man that'd keep his mouth closed if I had him do a little job I got in mind?"

"I'd say so. Lem's like most men who're good with their hands, he doesn't have much to say to anybody, anytime. Tell him I sent you, Marshal. He'll take care of just about any kind of job you give him to do."

"Thanks for all your help," Longarm said. "I'll be back in afterwhile to buy a little grub. I'll be riding out early tomorrow morning."

"We're open until nine, and I always come back to the store after supper and stay till we close. Be glad to fix you up."

Lem Edwards' shop behind the livery stable was small; its floor was littered with scraps of freshly cut leather, and the pungent smell of the leather combined with the fainter scents of harness oil and beeswax to give the workroom its own individual aroma. A heap of saddles awaiting repairs filled most of one wall and contributed the animal smell of horse sweat to the air. A bony man with a thin, intent face sat at a cobbler's bench, stripping a saddle pommel to replace a broken horn. He greeted Longarm with a nod, scarcely looking up from his work.

"You'd be Lem Edwards, I reckon?" Longarm asked.

"Yep."

Edwards' voice sounded strange to Longarm, after so many years of hearing the drawling, leisurely speech and soft elisions of the far West. The saddler spoke with the nasal twang that marked him as a transplanted New Englander.

"My name's Long. Deputy U.S. marshal out of Denver."

"I guess you've got a broken saddle, or you wouldn't be in here. Well, what's the trouble, Marshal?"

"It ain't trouble, exactly. Jim McMasters tells me you got a real touch with leather, especially saddles."

"Does he? It's more than he's told me to my face. Well, what d'you need, Marshal?"

"I reckon you've heard of a saddle being fixed up with a hidey-hole, where a man can cache money or whatever?"

"A-yeh. Pokeholes, we call them in the trade. I make one every now and again, for travelers going through risky country."

"Think you can fix me up with one?"

"Depends."

"On what?"

"On how big a pokehole you'd want and the saddle it goes in, Marshal," Edwards said. "If it's a Mexican saddle, there's not much room for any kind of a cache. West Texas cowhand saddles, now, plenty of space in them."

"I got a plain old McClellan, like the cavalry uses."

"That's the easiest kind to work with, if you don't plan to be pushing your horse too hard. Here, I'll show you."

Edwards motioned for Longarm to follow him. He walked over to the pile of saddles awaiting repairs and burrowed into the heap until he found a McClellan cavalry model. He put a finger on the ventilation gap between the arch of the hornless pommel and the curved tree below it, which rested on the horse's withers.

"I guess you know what that opening's meant for, but if you don't, it's to keep the horse's back cool on a long forced march. Now that place is just made for a pokehole. I stitch up a pocket that'll slide right in there, tack it to the tree, and put a strap so you can open it. Unless somebody's looking for you to have a cache, it'll never be noticed."

"That's just what I need," Longarm said. "Think you can fix me one in a hurry?"

"A-yeh. Depending on what you call a hurry. I can have it for you in about a week."

"I need it fixed tonight, so I can ride out early tomorrow morning," Longarm said.

Edwards shook his head. "I've got too much work on hand to get to it that quick."

"Not even if it's for official U.S. government business?" Longarm asked. "And if I make it worth your while to put in a little extra time tonight to accommodate me?"

"Well," the saddlemaker frowned, "you wouldn't ask for a rush job if you didn't need it, I s'pose. Since Jim McMasters sent you over, and he's a good customer—oh, hell, Marshal, bring your saddle in. I'll get right on it, and it'll be ready for you by midnight or a little after."

Leaving his saddle with Edwards and his horse at the livery stable, Longarm walked up Tascosa's main street to the Exchange Hotel and registered. He leaned his Winchester in the corner of the room next to the bed, opened his saddlebags, and took out the bottle of Tom Moore. There was barely enough whiskey left in it to make a single swallow. Having emptied the bottle, Longarm went in search of a restaurant, and found one between the hotel and the Howard & McMasters store.

After polishing off an uninspired but adequate steak and his usual fried potatoes, Longarm sat over his second cup of black coffee, puffing a cheroot until his supper settled, then he headed for the store. McMasters was in the place Longarm had learned by now to expect him to be, behind the long main counter.

"Come to get those supplies you said you'd need, Marshal?" the merchant asked.

"That's right, Mr. McMasters. The army map I got at Fort Elliott don't show a single town after I cross the South Fork of the Red River. I figure if I can't buy grub down there, I better take some with me."

"There certainly aren't many towns down there," McMasters agreed. "Aside from that little town of Quitaque on the South Fork, there's not anything."

"I'll want some cured sausage, then," Longarm said. "And a hunk of bacon, and maybe some kind of cheese that won't go moldy on me. And soda crackers, and a few spuds. Enough to hold me for a week or so. I'll leave it up to you—I guess you've made up grub packs for a lot of men going down there."

"Some. Not too many." McMasters pulled a flour sack from beneath the counter and began moving from one shelf to another as he filled it. He said, "I guess you've got a big canteen and all the ammunition you'll need."

"I guess. I ain't looking to pass up any water holes or get into any shooting scrapes."

"If you've traveled in dry country much, you'll know to be on the lookout for alkali water."

"I've had cases in desert country," Longarm said.

McMasters finished stowing the items he'd selected into the flour sack. He put the sack on the counter in front of Longarm. "Well, here you are, Marshal," he said. "I guess you're riding out tomorrow morning?"

"Soon as its light enough to see. Now then, how much does my order come to?"

"Why, there's not enough there to charge you for. Take it as a gift to Uncle Sam, with my compliments, Marshal."

"No, sir," Longarm replied firmly. "The government ain't no different from any other customer you got. Not meaning to single you out, Mr. McMasters, but whenever a man gives the government something, he's got a way of figuring the government owes him something back. And that ain't good for him or Uncle Sam."

"Well, if that's the way you feel about it, you've got two dollars and fifteen cents worth of grub in that bag. Say you pay me two dollars, and we'll call it square."

"If it strikes you as fair, I won't argue." Longarm fished a pair of cartwheels out of his pocket and put them on the counter. He added a third and said, "And you seen the kind of cigars I smoke. I better stock up on them before I leave, too, even if I'd be better off doing without 'em."

McMasters reached along the counter to the cigar case and filled a paper sack with cheroots. He put them beside the flour sack and shoved the silver dollar back to Longarm. "Now I won't argue with you over the cigars, Marshal Long. I think all of us owe lawmen something for protecting us, and this is my way of thanking you."

"So far, I ain't done much for you, but I won't argue about the smokes. I'll just say thank you."

Detouring by the hotel, Longarm left his supplies in his room before going to the saloon for the whiskey he'd bought. It was still early in the evening, and the only customers other than Longarm were four men playing stud poker at a table near the end of the bar. Longarm glanced at them as he cleared the batwings and made his way to the middle of the bar. There was a new barkeep on duty, not the one who'd sold him the whiskey.

"Where's the man who was here this morning?" Longarm asked.

"Home pounding his ear, I guess," the new barkeep said. "A man can't work day and night. What's your pleasure, friend?"

"Well, I come in for a couple of bottles of some whiskey I bought off that fellow who was here earlier, but I'll take a drink out of your bar bottle as long as I'm here." When the bartender turned and reached for the unlabeled bar whiskey on the backbar, Longarm said quickly, "Hold on. That ain't the kind of bar whiskey I was talking about. Someplace back there you got a square bottle of Maryland rye without no label on it. That's the bottle I want my drink poured out of."

The barkeep frowned. "You sure about that?"

"Sure, I'm sure. And there's two more bottles just like it, except they got labels. They're the ones I bought this morning."

"How come you know so much about what we got in stock?"

Longarm was getting nettled. He said, "I don't know what you got in stock, and I don't much care. All I'm interested in is the kind of whiskey I drink. Now if you don't feel like looking for that bottle of bar whiskey, I'll just take the two I bought and call it a day."

"Don't get riled, friend. I'll see what I can find."

Turning to the backbar again, the barkeep looked along its shelves and in a moment exclaimed, "I guess I owe you one, friend. Is this the bottle you're talking about?" He set the unlabeled bottle of Daugherty's in front of Longarm.

"That's it. And you'll find two more just like it someplace back there, only they'll be labeled. Daugherty's Private Stock, it's called. Them's the two I bought and paid for when I was in here earlier."

After he'd placed a glass beside the unlabeled bottle, the barkeep began looking along the backbar again while Longarm poured himself a drink and lighted a cheroot. In the silence he heard one of the poker players say, "By God, Snore, the cards sure ain't falling your way tonight."

Another of the men chuckled loudly and chimed in, "Snore, if you don't play better poker pretty soon, you won't have nothing left of that money you sweated for down on the Llano Estacado."

"Shut up and deal the cards!" snarled the man they were addressing. "I ain't broke yet!"

Hearing the Llano Estacado and work mentioned in the same conversation drew Longarm's attention at once. While he sipped his drink, he watched the poker players covertly.

At a glance, a casual observer might have taken the four men to be any quartet of range-dirty cowhands, stopping for a drink and a friendly game after a hard day in the saddle. After he'd watched them for a moment or two, though, Longarm's finely tuned instincts, as well as his experienced eyes, told him they were not mere cowhands.

To him, the signs were clear. He noticed first that their pistols, holsters, and gunbelts were well cared for; cowhands, who used their revolvers only rarely, were inclined to neglect them. Nor were the hands of three of the poker players cowboys' hands. Unlike the fourth member of the group, their fingers were all straight and intact. Any cowhand as old as the players would likely be shy a fingertip or two, and some of his fingers would be twisted from having been broken when caught between lariat and saddlehorn, when the sudden unexpected lunging of a roped steer tightened the rope before the man who'd tossed the loop could pull them free.

There were other small things about the four that, to Longarm, took them out of the category of ordinary cowhands. For one thing, their shirts bore too few ineradicable sweat stains.

For another, only one of the four had on a neckerchief, and no cowhand prodding cattle in dusty country would have left the bunkhouse without a fresh bandanna knotted around his throat, to pull up over his mouth when he had to ride behind even a small herd.

Longarm had almost forgotten the barkeep, who returned from his search just then, carrying the two bottles of Daugherty's. He said, "You're right again, friend. Here they are, just like you told me they'd be."

Longarm reached into his pocket and took out most of the coins he carried in it. He said, "I already paid for the two bottles, but I owe you for this drink I'm working on." Clumsily he dropped the handful of money on the bar. The jingle of the gold and silver coins cascading on the bar drew the attention of the poker players. They watched Longarm scoop up the money, leaving a single cartwheel, which he shoved over to the barkeep.

"Your money's no good for this round, friend," the man told him. "The drinks are on me for arguing with you."

"Put those two fresh bottles on the bar, then," Longarm said. He picked up the unlabeled bottle and added, "If you're buying, I'll just top off this drink I'm working on."

Refilling his almost empty glass, Longarm edged along the bar closer to the poker game, and watched the dealer flipping out the cards. The quick, covert exchange of glances among the four players would have escaped most, but Longarm saw it. He wasn't surprised when one of the men looked up as though noticing him for the first time.

One of the players then looked up openly at Longarm and said to the others, "Dammit, four-hand poker's not a real game. How about inviting the stranger here to sit in, if he feels like it?"

Now the other three looked up and stared for a moment at Longarm. One of them said, "It's all right with me, Lefty, if you and Snore and Perez don't mind."

"Five makes a better game, that's for sure. Snore, you or Perez have any objections?"

Quickly the other players shook their heads. Lefty looked back at Longarm and said, "It's just a little friendly game. Table stakes, two-bit ante. Joker's in the deck, but the dealer don't call wild cards. High card takes shit hands, and round-the-corner straights don't count. Nobody plays the pot short, either. You want to sit in for a few hands?"

"I don't mind if I do," Longarm replied, after hesitating just long enough to make plausible the part he'd decided to play. He pulled a chair over from an adjoining table, and the four men shuffled theirs to make room for him.

"I'm Lefty," said the man who'd invited Longarm to join the game. He pointed to the others in turn, saying, "That's Morris, the one next to him's Perez, and this other one's called Snore because he sleeps so loud."

Longarm stuck to the literal truth, in spite of his distaste for his given name. "Name's Custis," he announced, after another almost imperceptible pause. He pulled a fistful of coins from his pocket, dropped them on the table, and sat down. "Go ahead and deal me in."

For the first few hands the cards ran low and betting was light. The players were like boxers in a five-way match, sparring as they tried to learn the new man's style. The deal passed around once without a pot of any size, then began to settle down.

Perez won a middling pot with two pair, and Longarm took the next, winning about the same amount with three tens. Lefty followed with queens faceup against Snore's hole-card paired eights, Snore folding when the second queen fell on the fourth card dealt. Morris filled an eight-high straight with his last card to win the next, and took the one following with three treys. Snore stayed with the deal on each hand until he saw himself beaten, and then folded in disgust. The pile of coins in front of him was steadily diminishing.

Longarm was sitting between Morris and Perez, with Snore and Lefty across the table from him. He folded with a pair of tens when Lefty dealt himself two queens side by side on the first two up-cards of the next deal, and stayed in against Perez's pair of eights and Snore's pair of jacks until the fourth card broke the ten-high straight he'd been building.

Morris was dealing. He flipped Perez a third eight, the card that would have gone to Longarm. Snore grunted in disgust when he saw the eight, and when Morris tossed him a ten and then gave Lefty the jack that would have given Snore a three-jack winning hand, Snore angrily shoved the losing cards across the table to Longarm.

"By God, Custis, I hope you do better by me than these friends of mine has been doing. I'm getting right tired of drawing busted hands," he said.

Perez stopped raking in the pot long enough to nudge Snore,

and said, "*Cómo quiero, amigo!* We are good *compañeros*, and you weel make plenty more next week, when we go south again."

"That don't make me feel no better right now," Snore shot back. "Dammit, I ain't pulled down but one little pot since we begun playing!"

"Sometimes that's the way the cards falls," Longarm said as he finished shuffling and put the cards down for Lefty to cut. "If a man won every hand, poker wouldn't be worth playing." He glanced at the pot to make sure that everyone had anted, and began dealing.

From the third card around, the pot was hotly contested. Perez was betting a pair of sixes up with such casualness that it was apparent he had a third in the hole. Snore's high card was a queen, but he had a pair of deuces beside it, and he stayed in, betting with grim intensity. Lefty bet a possible low straight until a king broke his run on the fourth card dealt, and Morris's fourth card was a diamond trey, matching the diamond ace and ten that lay in front of him. Until he dealt himself the fourth card, Longarm showed a possible straight flush in spades, with the nine and ten face up, but the fourth card was the spade king, which reduced almost to zero the odds on his filling the hand.

In spite of that, he called Perez's last raise and started dealing the final card. Perez got a third six and smiled. Snore watched Longarm's hands intently and a quick smirk twisted his lips when the card dropped was a queen that paired the one he had showing, giving him two pair. Lefty had folded when his straight was broken. Longarm dealt Morris the four of diamonds. He dropped his own last card faceup beside the nine, ten, and king of spades; it was the spade jack. Without speaking, he laid the remaining cards aside and looked across the table at Snore.

"Your two pairs bets," he said.

Snore nodded abstractedly. He was counting the money that remained on the table in front of him. He pushed his last half eagle and all but a few of his silver dollars into the pot. "My two pairs is good for fifteen," he announced.

Morris folded. Longarm met Snore's bet. Perez raised ten dollars. Snore barely met the raise. Longarm called. Perez looked at the three cartwheels that still lay in front of Snore, and shrugged. He followed Longarm's example and called.

"This might be the only pot I'll take tonight, but it'll be a good one!" Snore crowed. He turned up his hole card to show the spade queen. "You two sure as hell didn't think I'd be fool enough to push two pair!"

Longarm turned over the joker he had in the hole and slid it between the jack and king. He said, "Too bad, Snore. I figure I got your full house and Perez's four sixes both beat."

Perez shrugged and smiled, but Snore exploded.

"Goddammit, you can't fill out your flush with that joker! I got the damn spade queen in my own hand!"

"That ain't the way the rules run," Longarm said quietly.

"By God, there can't be two queens of spades in a deck!" Snore shouted. "I don't give a shit what rules you play by!" He looked around the table at his friends. "Ain't I right, Lefty? Morris?"

Perez said, "*Qué lastima*, Snore! Custees, he ees right. *La bromista*, eet ees what the man who hold eet say eet ees."

"Goddamn you, Perez! Whose side you taking, mine or that fucking stranger's?"

Perez shrugged without replying.

Lefty said quickly, "Listen, Snore, don't go—"

Snore was past listening. He fixed his eyes on Longarm and said, "Custis, you dealt yourself that hand on purpose! You're a dirty cardsharking son of a bitch!"

Snore knew quite well what his accusation and the words he'd used would call for. As he finished talking, he leaped to his feet and kicked his chair out of the way. His hand started for his gun.

Longarm did not stand up. By the time Snore was on his feet and reaching, Longarm's gun was already in his hand and coming out of his cross-draw holster. Longarm's bullet went home, and Snore started sagging to the floor just as his groping hand was closing on the butt of his revolver.

Chapter 11

Taking a step back from the table, Longarm made a quarter-turn and swung the Colt's muzzle to cover not only Snore's three companions, but the barkeep, who was hurrying up. Lefty, Morris, and Perez were still sitting in their chairs, with dazed expressions on their unshaven faces. The argument between Snore and Longarm had been so short and its explosion into gunplay so unreasonable that they still seemed to be trying to figure out what had happened and why.

"Godamighty!" Lefty finally exclaimed. "I never seen Snore act like that before!"

"Me neither," Morris gasped.

"Era un poco loco," Perez said, staring at the corpse.

Lefty's stunned expression slowly became a frown. He looked at Longarm and asked, "Who in hell are you, mister?"

"I gave you my name before I sat in on your game," Longarm replied, his voice flat.

"Oh sure. You said your name's Custis, but in these parts a name don't signify much sometimes."

"Custis is all you'll get," Longarm replied. He kept his Colt moving in a slow arc, though none of the poker players had

116

moved a hand toward a gun and the barkeep had stopped short when he saw Longarm's revolver.

"Snore enganarse," Perez said suddenly in the silence that fell after Longarm's reply to Lefty. *"Mira!"* He brought his arms up slowly, gazing at Longarm, keeping his hands well away from his sides. Reaching onto the table, he turned over his hole card. It was the fourth six. His voice puzzled, Perez went on, *"Mis cartas son mejor de el."*

"By God, you're right!" Morris agreed. "If Custis hadn't had that joker in the hole, you'd've took the pot!"

"That still don't prove he wasn't dealing crooked," Lefty pointed out.

"There ain't more'n fifty dollars in that pot," Longarm said. "If I was a cold-deck artist good enough to deal the hands that's turned up on that table, I sure wouldn't be wasting my time in a little town like Tascosa. I'd be in some fancy club in a big city, where I could hit for bigger games."

"Now that makes sense, Lefty," Morris nodded. "It does to me, anyhow."

"Yeah, I guess that's right," Lefty said slowly.

"Well, I'll say this," Longarm told them, his voice crisp with authority now. "I'm sorry I had to shoot your friend, but all of you seen it was him or me. And I'll ask you what you'd've done if you'd been in my boots."

A moment of silence followed Longarm's words. Then, like a pin-pricked balloon, the tense atmosphere suddenly dissolved.

Lefty said slowly, "All right, Custis. Looks like none of us figures this was your fault. We don't hold no grudge against you. Ain't that right, Morris? Perez?"

Unhesitatingly the others nodded agreement. Longarm lowered his Colt, then holstered it. The barkeep broke the silence that followed.

"What about him?" he asked, pointing to Snore's body.

"That ain't your worry," Lefty told him. "He was traveling with us. We'll see he gets buried proper."

"Take that money in the pot to pay for a decent funeral," Longarm told them. "It was me that done the shooting, so I ought to stand the expense."

"No, by God!" Lefty said firmly. "You won that pot with the high hand, and you won it square. Me and Morris and Perez will split the bill amongst us."

"I'll stand the drinks, then," Longarm said. "Just to show

there's no hard feelings between us." He jerked his head at the barkeep. "Bring a fresh bottle of whatever these men fancy. And pour me a drink out of that bottle of rye, and pour yourself one, while you're handing 'em out."

No one in the saloon seemed to be in a talkative mood while the drinks were downed. Snore had collapsed with his face to the floor when Longarm's slug took him, and Perez left his drink to get up and straighten out the limp body, turning it faceup, and cover the dead man's face with his hat. As soon as Longarm had picked up the pot from the table and paid for the drinks, the barkeep suddenly found that the bar was in need of polishing and worked himself away from the group with vigorous swirls of his moist towel.

Lefty broke the silence at last. He asked Longarm, "Mind saying where you're from, Custis?"

"Rode in from the north," Longarm replied tersely. Lefty nodded and did not pursue the subject.

When Longarm decided he'd stayed as long as courtesy and common sense dictated, he picked up his two bottles of Daugherty's and said, "I'll bid you men good night. I been a long time in the saddle today, and got another long ride ahead of me tomorrow. If we run into one another again, I hope you'll all remember what we agreed was the way this happened." He did not wait for an answer, but walked to the door and pushed through the batwings.

Walking slantwise across the street to the hotel, Longarm noticed the dim night light burning in Mickey McCormick's livery stable, and changed course to see if Lem Edwards had finished the saddle modification. Edwards was just getting up from his saddlemaker's bench when Longarm entered the shop.

"I ain't aiming to rush you," Longarm said. "I just happened to be going past and thought maybe you'd finished up a mite sooner than you figured."

"Just finishing," Edwards told him. "'Twon't take a minute to put a little stain on the job."

While Longarm watched, the saddlemaker brushed leather stain over the surface of the pokehole, and buffed it off until it was precisely the same hue as the rest of the saddle's leather. He took an awl and made a few random scratches on the newly buffed surface, then rubbed wax over the inserted piece until it took on the appearance of wear that matched the rest of the well-worn saddle. Then he stepped back and looked at his work approvingly.

"Looks just like that new piece has been there since the saddle come out of the factory," Longarm commented, inspecting the finished job over Edwards' shoulder.

"A-yeh. No use going to a lot of work if somebody can see it's new leather," Edwards said. "It satisfies you, then, Marshal Long?"

"It's a fine job. How much do I owe you?"

"For as much time and trouble as went into it, I'll have to charge you three dollars."

Longarm dug out three cartwheels and handed them to the saddlemaker. "I call it dirt cheap, for a rush job. You're a right good workman, Mr. Edwards."

"A-yeh. I was brought up to be."

Leaving the saddle with the night man at the livery stable, Longarm walked up the quiet, deserted street to the Exchange Hotel. In his room, he took even greater care than usual in his pre-bedtime preparations. He cleaned the Colt meticulously, even though it had been fired only once, and gave the ugly little snub-nosed derringer the same kind of attention before going over his Winchester.

Finally, after placing the cleaned and reholstered Colt in its accustomed position on the bed's headboard, and his vest with the derringer in its pocket over a convenient chair, Longarm decided to wake up a bit earlier than usual, and with that decision made, he went into his usual sound and dreamless sleep.

Sunrise found Longarm well on his way to the Red River. The piebald was frisky after his short ride of the day before and a full night of rest in a stall with a well-filled corncrib, and Longarm let the horse follow the southeastward slope of the ground. In less than an hour after he'd forded the Canadian just below Tascosa, he had left the river's shallow valley and was again riding across the same type of gently rolling prairie, complete even to the buffalo wallows which appeared now and then, that he'd seen on his way east from the Indian Nation.

Not until the sun had climbed almost to noon in a sky as broad and vacant as the prairie itself did the character of the land begin to change. This change was not abrupt, but gradual.

The rolling humps that had been so easy to ride over in a straight line gave way to an area of uneven, elongated hills. Because of the gentle downward slope of the land ahead of him, Longarm could see their ridges stretching to the horizon. It was a serrated landscape, but not a harsh one, for the slopes were grassed and there were clumps of sagebrush, and occasionally thin stands of stunted cedar or pinoak trees in the valley bottoms.

As fresh as the piebald had been at the beginning of the morning, it soon began to plod as rise followed rise, mile after mile. Longarm let the horse keep to its slower pace; he had a long ride ahead, and to force the animal to move faster on a trip that did not require him to hurry would have been both needless and foolish. At noon, when he came to one of the rare valleys that had a tiny brook trickling along its bottom, he stopped and let the horse rest and drink and graze while he ate a traveler's lunch of cheese and crackers and squatted at the edge of the little rill to scoop up a few swallows of water.

Soon after he'd resumed his journey, the land underwent its most abrupt change. Ahead, he saw the plateau across which he was riding drop away suddenly, and in the distance he could see high, steep cliffs of red and yellow, purple and orange, a palette of deep, varying colors in a generally monochromatic country. Riding to the edge of the dropoff, Longarm pulled up and looked down into the wide canyon that gaped below him.

For the first few minutes after he'd stopped, Longarm's eyes were so firmly fixed on the shimmer of colors displayed on the far wall of the canyon that he could see nothing else. After his first quick glimpse of them as he came upon the canyon's eastern rim, he'd been so engrossed in guiding the piebald safely to the very edge of the dropoff that he'd paid little attention to the western wall.

Accustomed as he was to the dun-hued monochrome of the prairie and the dull green of the vegetation that grew on the ridged section he'd just crossed, Longarm could not quite believe that the display he was looking at was real. The colors rose up the wall in layers, no two of them exactly the same tint, a mixture of red and blue and reddish brown and yellow and orange and purple and lavender. As he looked along the steep, almost vertical wall, he could see that it was broken by the mouths of smaller canyons, and that there were formations—pinnacles and small, jagged, irregular mesas—rising from the wall's base, extending at times for short distances onto the canyon floor.

Scanning the canyon wall led Longarm's eyes to the floor of the wide gash, and the river that flowed through its broad expanse of sandy soil. From his high vantage point, he saw that the river was at times a thin sheet of water that spread almost from wall to wall and at times narrowed to swift rushes and dark, still pools. There were trees along the edges of the canyon floor, pinoaks and cedars, and mesquite bushes growing as tall as trees, and here and there a few ocotillos.

This has got to be the canyon that shows on them Army maps, the one called Palo Duro, Longarm told himself. Except them maps don't show what a hell of a fine sight it is. But you ain't paid to sit on your butt and look at the scenery, old son. You better do your gawking while you make tracks on south. 'Course, there ain't any law that says you can't ride down that canyon, and when you come down to it, it's likely the easiest way to go.

Turning the piebald, Longarm started riding slowly along the canyon's rim, keeping a safe distance away from the jagged edge itself, while he looked for a slope gentle enough to descend to the floor. After a half hour he found a cut that bore the marks of much use by riders, and let the piebald find its way down. On the level, sandy soil of the canyon floor, the piebald moved more easily and at a faster gait.

Longarm pushed on steadily through the afternoon, stopping occasionally to let the horse drink and rest. Shortly before sundown he saw a buffalo-hide shanty on the riverbank. Except for a lot of hoofprints and dried blobs of steer manure on the sandy soil, it was the first man-sign he'd seen. He reached the shanty; the brand "JA" was burned into the stiff, inch-thick hide walls in several places, identifying it as a line shack of the Goodnight spread. Longarm looked inside, got a whiff of the odor of unwashed humanity, and decided he'd be better off camping on the riverbank.

Two or three times during the hours of darkness, Longarm woke up to the mournful song of a coyote echoing off one of the canyon walls, and toward daybreak he was aroused once by the distant blatting of a herd of steers.

He woke as the gray promise of false dawn showed over the rim of the canyon, and by sunrise was moving along the floor once more. The colors that had marked the walls so

121

vividly the day before faded as he rode through the morning, and the walls grew lower, more sloping. In midmorning, Longarm began to run into bunches of cattle grazing along the bank of the stream, and though he kept a sharp lookout for riders, he saw none. The floor of the canyon had grown broader as the walls sloped down, and the course of the river changed, curving more to the east.

Longarm halted to consult his map, and realized that this was about as far as the canyon extended to the south. It was time now to cut westward; if the map was right, he'd be riding across the Llano Estacado by sundown.

With the declining sun in his eyes to guide him, Longarm rode steadily over a flat plain. There were no humps in the ground here, no serrated ridges rising and falling. No trees broke the monotony of the bare, level landscape. There were no streams, nor was there any brush other than an occasional sparse clump of thin prairie grass.

At sunset Longarm made a dry camp, a dark camp, as there was no fuel to use for a fire. He ate jerky and cheese and crackers and rolled up in his blankets. The only sound that broke the night's silence was the soft sighing of a thin, chilly breeze that began its low whine at moonrise and continued until the sun rose and warmed the air enough to quiet the vagrant drafts.

Breakfast was a repetition of last night's supper, and before starting out again, Longarm decided it was time to take the precaution for which he'd prepared in Tascosa. He opened the pokehole and into it put his wallet and badge, most of his money, and his travel vouchers and maps. When he closed the hidden cache, there was nothing in his saddlebags or pockets to identify him as anything but a rider coming from nowhere in particular and going on his way until he found a place where it would be profitable for him to stop.

Keeping the sun at his back, Longarm rode on. He passed two or three water holes, shallow and scummed, their edges ridged with the alkali deposits that warned the informed traveler to avoid them. At the edge of one water hole that bore no alkali traces, a stake had been driven into the ground and to it had been nailed a piece of sun-bleached board into which a skull and crossbones had been burned as a warning sign.

In midafternoon the flatland was broken for the first time by a canyon in which flowed a little stream. Longarm followed the canyon south until it widened and twisted east. He urged the piebald up its low wall and continued to the west.

There were more water holes here; a few held clean water, but most of them carried the alkali taint. For the first time Longarm noticed signs that the land was used. The soil was ground into tufts of loose dirt by the small, sharp feet of sheep, and only low, ragged sprigs remained to show where grass had once grown in clumps. Late in the day, Longarm saw the herd ahead of him, dun-colored backs bobbing along under the low dust cloud that hung in the air along its path and obscured the dark silhouette of the shepherd and his dog, herding the sheep to the west.

Almost as soon as Longarm saw the herd of sheep, the dog sensed his approach and yelped to alert the herder, running back toward Longarm to draw the man's attention. The herder stopped, leaving the dog to attend to the herd, and waited for Longarm to reach him. He was squatting on the ground Indian-fashion, his legs folded in front of him, puffing at a cornhusk cigarette, when Longarm reined in the piebald a few feet away.

"Bue's días, señor," the man said, bobbing his head and smiling.

Even before the sheepherder's greeting, Longarm had tagged him as being of Spanish blood, probably originally from New Mexico. He nodded. "Howdy. Maybe you can tell me how far I am from anyplace right now."

"Where you go?" the herder asked.

"I ain't particular." Longarm could tell by the sheepherder's frown that his remark hadn't quite registered with the man. He lighted a cheroot, debating whether to ask the question he really wanted answered, then said, "What I'm looking for's a place called the Valley of Tears. You ever hear of it?"

Slowly the sheepherder nodded. *"Ay, sí. El Valle de Lágrimas."* He pointed in the general direction from which Longarm had just come, though more to the south than eastward. *"'Sta ahí, señor. Es puesto muy malo."*

"How'd I know it if I was to want to go there?"

For a moment the sheepherder frowned, the frown of a simple, unschooled man who has lived in a place all his life and knows it intimately from experience, but lacks the imagination and words to tell a stranger how to find a familiar landmark.

"You must only ride *al occidente, señor*, the way from

123

which you have come," the man finally replied. "It is a ride of half a day. *El Valle de Lágrimas*, eet ees canyon weeth river that flow *al sureste*. Ees not possible to go by and not see eet."

"There ain't any other valleys around I'd get it mixed up with?"

"No, *señor*," the sheepherder said, shaking his head. *"No hay valles lo mismo como El Valle de Lágrimas."* Again he remembered belatedly to speak English. "Ees only that way one beeg valley, *señor*. You cannot meestake eet." Then the man hesitated and said slowly, "Ees better you don't go there, *señor*. Don Feliciano, he don' like for nobody they go to thees place."

"Who's Don Feliciano?"

"Es mi patrón, Don Feliciano de Aguirre. Thees sheep, thees land, all belong to heem."

"Looks like I ought to go have a talk with him, then," Longarm said thoughtfully. "Whereabouts is he?"

"A su hacienda, señor. Su plaza." The man pointed west. "You go on thees way, you find it, two, three hour ahead."

"Thanks for the information. I'll tell your boss I seen you taking good care of his sheep, when I get there."

With a fixed destination ahead, Longarm pushed the piebald to a faster walk. Something more than an hour after he'd stopped to talk with the sheepherder, he began to come across trails: the narrow, shallow ruts worn by horsemen; the deeply incised tracks made by wheels of loaded wagons; the broad, almost invisible paths of herds of sheep being driven. The trails converged as he followed them, and another hour or so brought Longarm to the rim of a wide, deep saucer, where he could look down on the hacienda of Don Feliciano de Aguirre.

It was not the single mansion he'd expected to see, but a number of houses, small adobe dwellings, clustered around the sides and back of a big central structure. There were perhaps twenty of the small houses, and beyond them, on the bank of a good-sized stream that rose somewhere out of his line of vision and flowed out through a cleft in the side of the saucerlike hollow, there were stables and storage barns and a large corral.

Through the clear bright air, Longarm could make out most of the details of what lay below the rim of the saucer where he'd reined in the piebald to study the place before he rode closer, but he spent little time looking at the small houses or work buildings; his attention was drawn to the big main house.

It was a huge building, two stories tall, with a roof of red tiles. A massive wall enclosed the mansion, its wide gates open. Like the main building, the wall was made from adobe bricks. Both wall and building were whitewashed and gleamed dazzlingly, and even at a distance their details were so sharply etched that Longarm could see them plainly.

Turrets rose above the two front corners of the facade, their openings covered with cast-iron grills. The windows were set high and were longer than they were tall, which indicated to Longarm that the hacienda must be very old indeed, dating back to the time when such an isolated place had to be both home and fortress. The impression was heightened when he saw the *acequia* that ran between banks so uniformly even that they must have been dug by hand. The ditch curved through the compound enclosed by the wall, and the sun reflected in a bright silver ribbon from the surface of the water that flowed through it.

Longarm whistled under his breath as he looked at the estate.

This Aguierre fellow's really got him a castle way out here on the other side of nowhere, old son. No wonder they called their places plazas back in the old days, they're just like them big squares in the middle of towns, down in Old Mexico. That place looks like it's been there a hundred years, give or take a few months. And maybe it has; them old Spanish families begun coming up here from Old Mexico longer ago than that. If him and his family's been here all that long, he ought to be able to tell me a lot of things I'd sure like to know.

Kneeing the piebald ahead, Longarm rode down the slanting side of the saucer, up to the wall, and through its open gates. Just as he reined in at the massive double doors of the hacienda, they swung open and a man in the thin white cotton clothing of a house servant appeared.

"*Bienvenido a Plaza Aguierre,*" he said. "*Don Feliciano encontrarse y saludarse en su sala. Viena usted conmigo, señor.*"

Chapter 12

Longarm hid his surprise and dismounted. He hesitated, the piebald's reins still in his hand, looking around for a hitch rail and finding none.

"*No desasosiego, señor,*" the servant said. "*Viene momentito un posadero attende a su caballo.*"

As before, when he had spoken with Ramon Gallegos, it was not in Longarm's plans to show that he understood more than a few simple words of that language. He did not release the reins, but looked questioningly at the man. The servant pointed to the horse and to the back of the walled enclosure, to indicate that the horse would be led to the stables. Then he gestured for Longarm to follow him.

Longarm nodded, let the reins fall, and followed the man into the house. The servant led him down a wide hall floored with red-brown terracotta tiles, stopped in front of an open door, and bowed, motioning for Longarm to enter. Inside the large rectangular room to which the door led, Longarm turned to ask the servant a question, but the man had already disappeared.

Standing just inside the door, Longarm put his time to good use by studying his surroundings, seeking a hint of the kind

126

of people who lived in such a huge establishment.

He was standing in what was obviously a formal salon, and though the room was sparsely furnished, it gave him the impression of luxurious living. Wide, low divans upholstered in well-tanned steerhide faced each other in the center of the room, separated by an intricately woven woolen rug of Indian design on which stood a low table. Chairs that matched the rug were drawn up in groups in front of the small, domed, adobe fireplaces with arched hearths that occupied all four corners of the big room.

On the long wall opposite the high windows, the portrait of a Spanish grandee was hanging, the face of its subject obscured by the dark patina of generations. A pair of crossed sabers with jeweled hilts hung on one of the end walls, and a striped, Indian-woven blanket of fine wool decorated the other. Sconces holding fat white candles were spaced along all four walls. Large carved wooden cabinets stood against the inner wall on either side of the portrait, and on top of one of them was a steel helmet, its polished dome bearing the dents of long-ago combat. Longarm stepped over to the cabinet to examine the helmet more closely.

A man's voice spoke from behind him. "That helmet, *señor*, belonged to my great-grandfather. He wore it when he came from Mexico with Onate to recapture New Spain from the savages, more than one hundred years ago. Those swords were his also."

Longarm whirled to face the speaker, and saw a short, chunky man, who showed a small paunch under the lapels of his creamy, gold-embroidered *charro* jacket. His nose was thin and hooked, his eyes opaque brown under thin gray brows. His hair, once coal-black, was heavily streaked with gray, as was his short, neatly trimmed beard. The beard effectively disguised the contours of his jaw, but Longarm detected the bulge of a double chin.

"I am Feliciano de Aguierre," the newcomer continued. His English was softly modulated, not accented, and he spoke in the overly precise manner that is common to those using a language acquired by study rather than having been spoken since birth. He added, "You are welcome in my plaza. *A tu servicio, señor. Mi casa es tuyo.*"

"Well, those are mighty neighborly words, Mr. Aguierre," Longarm replied. "I don't speak your language, but I don't need to for me to savvy what you said. My name's Custis. I—well, I guess you'd say I'm just traveling through, and stopped in to pass the time of day."

"You will stay the night, of course," Aguierre said. "Or longer, if it pleases you to break your journey by honoring my house with your company." He looked at Longarm's three-day beard and dusty clothing. "Dinner will be served soon. One of my people will show you to a room. It will be my pleasure to talk with you later." With a quick, bobbing bow, Aguierre left the room hurriedly.

Before Longarm could recover from his surprise at Aguierre's abrupt departure, a manservant came in; he was dressed as had been the one who had greeted him at the door, in thin white cotton trousers and jacket. "Please to come with me," he said, bowing. "I am Esteban. So long as you are guest here, eet ees for me to serve you, because the good Engleesh I have. Your room ees ready now, *señor*, eef you like."

Still feeling strange in his new surroundings, Longarm followed Esteban into the hall and to a stairway at one end. On the upper floor, the man led him to a bedroom, where he got another surprise: His saddlebags were draped over a chair waiting for him, his Winchester stood in one corner. Beyond the open door in one of the inner walls of the bedroom, he heard water splashing; when he got far enough inside the room to peer through the second door, he saw a woman servant pouring water from buckets into a slipper-shaped, tin bathtub.

"Now hold on here, Esteban," Longarm protested. "I didn't stop in here to get free board and room for the night. All I want to do is talk to your boss for a little while."

"But eet ees late!" Esteban said, his face drawing into a worried frown. "Don Feliciano is say for me to feex bath, and when you feenish, bring you then to supper. He weel be very offend eef I do not do what he say."

"I don't want to step on anybody's toes," Longarm began, but before he could go on, a second man came into the bedroom.

"I apologize for intruding," he said to Longarm. "I am Hernan Maldonado, the *mayordomo*—what you would call the manager—of the Plaza Aguierre. I was coming from another room when I happened to hear what you were saying to Esteban, and took the liberty of coming in to explain to you about the Plaza Aguierrre."

128

"I guess that'd help me figure things out a little better," Longarm told him. "I wasn't aiming to stay here. I just stopped off to pass the time of day, and maybe find out the lay of the country hereabouts." While he spoke, Longarm studied the *mayordomo* without appearing to do so.

Maldonado was tall, almost as tall as Longarm, but of much slighter build. His face might have been handsome except for the scars that pitted it; to Longarm they looked like the marks of a very severe burn. He wore a dark brown *charro* suit—waist-length jacket, and thigh-hugging trousers that flared at the ankles—but his jacket did not have the elaborate gold braid that had ornamented Don Feliciano's.

"To be sure," Maldonado nodded. "It is this way. Don Feliciano expects all travelers who stop here to be the guest of the plaza as long as they wish to stay. It is an old custom of his family, you see. He will be greatly offended if you refuse his hospitality."

"I sure don't want to do nothing that'd put your boss out of sorts, Mr. Maldonado," Longarm replied. "I just ain't used to stopping in at fancy places like this one. Most quality folks don't even pass the time of day with—well, a saddle tramp."

A thin smile, no more than a flicker, twitched Maldonado's lips. "The Aguierre hospitality extends to everyone, *señor*. Of course, the local *peones* are made welcome in the houses of our people, as fits their station."

"I guess I see what you mean, Mr. Maldonado. Well, if you put it to me that way, I'll stay for supper. And it'll feel real good to have a bed, too."

"Of course." The *mayordomo* nodded and went on, "Now I have duties to perform. Esteban will help you with your bath and show you to the *sala* when you are ready."

Maldonado left, followed by the woman who'd been filling the bathtub. Longarm let Esteban help him off with his coat, and while the manservant was busy folding the coat over the back of a chair, Longarm managed to transfer his watch to the vest pocket above the derringer without Esteben noticing his movements. He put the vest aside, hung his pistol belt on the headpost of the bed, and managed to convey to Esteban that it was not to be disturbed. Then, though he found the manservant's attentions more of an annoyance than a help, he stripped off the rest of his clothing and stepped into the tub.

Esteban came into the bathroom just as Longarm was settling down in the tub. "*Señor*," he began, "You weel weesh me to—"

"Now you don't need to worry about me," Longarm told him. "I'm old enough to bathe myself. You go find something else to do while I finish and get into my duds again."

"Ees not to help weeth bath I am theenk," Esteban said. He straightened his forefinger and second finger and drew them down his cheek and across his chin. "I am make for you *afeitada*, no?"

Longarm rubbed the heavy stubble on his face thoughtfully. "I reckon I better have a shave, at that. And I purely don't like to shave myself. All right, Esteban. There's a razor in my saddlebags. I'll dig it out for you soon as I get out of the tub."

"Ees not necessary, *señor*. I have fine *navaja*." He took a straight-edge razor from the capacious pocket of his loose jacket. "Ees better I make *afeitada* while you een tub, yes?"

"I guess it's as good a time as any," Longarm agreed. "All right. Only that razor of yours better be good and sharp." He leaned back in the tub and tilted his chin. "Go ahead, Esteban. If you can stand it, I guess I can, too."

While Esteban's touch was not as quick and sure as that of an expert barber, he finished the shave without nicking Longarm's face or damaging the clean line of his longhorn-curved mustache. He stepped back when his job was finished and bobbed a small bow.

"*Acabado, señor*. Here ees towel. I am wait in other room while you make to dry."

How and when and where it had been done, Longarm could not figure out, but when he'd rubbed himself dry and went back into the bedroom, his clothes had been brushed, his coat and trousers sponged, his boots polished to a high sheen, though some of the scars of hard use still showed on them. He glanced quickly at his vest, which he'd folded and placed on a chair beside the bed, but it did not seem to have been disturbed.

Esteban stood by while Longarm dressed, handing him each garment as it was needed; the attention was one that Longarm could have done without, but that he could not manage to avoid. The manservant opened his mouth as though he were about to protest when Longarm reached for his pistol belt, but a look from Longarm's steel-blue eyes stopped him. Then, when Longarm donned his long coat, and the holstered Colt showed as a barely visible bulge, he smiled and nodded.

"Ees good," the manservant said. "Now I take you to Don Feliciano."

Aguierre was waiting alone in the room where he'd first greeted Longarm. The master of Plaza Aguierre had changed for dinner, and now wore a hip-length coat over gray trousers and an embroidered vest. He was smoking a cigar that might have been a twin to the cheroot Longarm had lighted as he'd left the bedroom, though the one Don Feliciano puffed was a bit larger in diameter.

"We will have a *copita* while we finish our cigars, Mr. Custis," the *hidalgo* said by way of greeting. "What do you prefer? Whiskey? Brandy? Wine?"

"I'd relish a tot of whiskey, Mr. Aguierre."

"Good. I have some from my *rancho* near Taos. That is where my wife is now, or she would be here to greet you. Each year at this season she takes the children there to visit her mother for a month."

While he talked, Aguierre was pouring their drinks from a small earthenware jug. He handed Longarm one glass and lifted the other. Longarm sipped at the liquor and could not keep from blinking. It was thinner in body than his favorite rye, but had a bite that in its own way was as distinctive, though it lacked the smooth edge of the well-aged rye. It also had a potent after-jolt that took Longarm unawares. Aguierre saw Longarm blinking, and smiled.

"You have not had what the people of the mountains call Taos Lightning, Mr. Custis?"

"Well, I had some once before, but it's been a while, and I forgot what a kick it packs."

"It has authority, yes." Don Feliciano drained his glass and nodded appreciatively. "My whiskey ranch is small, I get only sixteen barrels a year from it, but the liquor is of a good grade. Now we will go to dinner."

Maldonado, the scarfaced *mayordomo*, served the two in the dining room across the hall. Longarm and Don Feliciano sat at opposite ends of a long table, which made conversation somewhat difficult. The meal consisted of a chicken cooked in a sauce of sherry, sweet red peppers, onions, finely slivered garlic, and minced pinyon nuts. There were paper-thin tortillas to go with the chicken, as well as a dish of herbed rice. It was not a dinner such as Longarm would have ordered for himself,

131

but after all the cold catch-as-catch-can meals he'd eaten since leaving Tascosa, he found the change welcome.

Don Feliciano, after a few desultory remarks soon after they began eating, devoted his attention to the food. Longarm did the same thing, for it was impossible for either of them to talk in a normal conversational tone because of the length of the table that separated them. Maldonado stood behind Don Feliciano's chair throughout the meal, moving only to carry more food up to Longarm's end of the table. At last the *hidalgo* sighed and pushed his chair back.

"If your appetite has been satisfied, Mr. Custis, let us go back to the *sala*. We can speak together with greater ease while we enjoy a cigar. Maldonado will serve us coffee and our after-dinner *copitas* there."

Longarm followed his host across the hall into the salon. Don Feliciano indicated an easy chair in front of one of the corner fireplaces, where a small fire had been kindled. Longarm lowered himself into the chair, and the *hacendado* took the chair on the opposite side of the narrow little hearth.

Maldonado was at their sides almost as soon as they'd sat down, carrying a tray on which fresh glasses and a bottle of Taos Lightning stood beside coffee cups and a steaming porcelain pot. He served Longarm, then poured coffee and a drink for Don Feliciano, before retreating to the center of the room. Both Longarm and Aguierre lighted cigars.

"You sure dished me up a fine meal, Mr. Aguierre," Longarm said, looking at his host through a cloud of blue tobacco smoke. "I don't recall when I enjoyed chicken as much."

"Chicken cooked in the style of Jerez has been a specialty of the cooks in my family's kitchen for many years," Don Feliciano replied. "I am pleased that you enjoyed it."

"It tasted mighty good after having to live on jerky and parched corn and bacon and spuds on the way down here. There's a lot of miles between the Llano Estacado and where I started from, up north. But I guess I ain't the first one to mention that."

"Travelers who do not know the region are deceived by the distance they must go, Mr. Custis. The Plaza Aguierre is far removed from any settlement, but I do not think I would have it otherwise. So far we have escaped the problems that have caused such trouble to my friends who live in more settled places."

"You're talking about the land-grabbers, I guess?"

Aguierre nodded. "I bear your people no ill will, but your cattle ranchers have forced many of my friends in the north away from the estates they have created since the Spanish conquest of this territory. I would not want to see the Plaza Aguierre suffer the same fate."

"It don't look to me like you got much to worry about," Longarm said. "Just about all the country I rode over on the way down south ain't good for anything but sheep. There ain't enough graze or water for cattle ranching."

"There are land-grabbers who are interested in sheep as well as cattle, Mr. Custis," Aguierre reminded him.

Longarm nodded, but said nothing. Maldonado appeared at his shoulder so silently that even Longarm's sharp ears had not heard him approach, and refilled their glasses and coffee cups, then left as quietly.

"Tell me, Mr. Custis," Don Feliciano asked, after they had begun sipping their drinks again, "are you traveling on some errand to do with your business?"

"Why, I don't have what you'd rightly call a business, Mr. Aguierre. I just take what jobs I find that need to be done."

Don Feliciano frowned. "It is not my affair, of course, but I find myself curious. What sort of jobs do you seek?"

Longarm gambled. He hardened his voice. "I take on whatever jobs need to be done. I heard up north that the Comancheros are stirring around again down here on the Llano Estacado."

"Comancheros?" Don Feliciano shook his head. "There have been no Comancheros here since the Comanches were defeated in the Palo Duro some years ago. There have been no Comancheros come to the Valley of Tears since then."

"Maybe so. But even if there ain't any Comanches around nearby, looking to trade for guns and ammunition and whiskey, there's a lot of Apaches right close that ain't on a reservation. From what I hear, they're still raiding and robbing and stealing women, and they'd need guns and suchlike."

Don Feliciano shook his head. "I am afraid you have been deceived by a rumor, Mr. Custis."

Longarm shrugged. "Well, that's the chance a man in my line knows he's got to take. All I'm doing is betting a little bit of my time that there's enough Comancheros left over from the old days that's interested in starting up the trade again."

"You have had a long ride for nothing," the *hacendado* said curtly. "There are no Comancheros on the Llano Estacado today, Mr. Custis."

Longarm replied blandly, "I'll look around, all the same. Comancheros spells trouble, and wherever there's trouble, I most generally find there's somebody needing help."

"That is your choice, of course," the *hacendado* said with a blandness that matched Longarm's. "But I assure you that if the Comancheros had indeed returned, I would know of it."

"Oh, I don't guess they'd've bothered a place like the one you got, Mr. Aguierre. Why, you wouldn't be interested in trading with 'em, anyhow."

"No, most certainly I would not!" Aguierre exclaimed. "But I would not want such evil men close by, attracting the Apaches, who would slaughter my sheep flocks, perhaps even raid my plaza! I remember from my early childhood how my father was forced to lead our people in defending our lands against both the Apaches and the wild Comanches. I wish only for peace, Mr. Custis."

"Sure," Longarm said. "I guess when you come down to it, that's all anybody wants." He tried to stifle a yawn, failed to, and while yawning, stretched hugely. He said, "It ain't that I don't enjoy talking with you, Mr. Aguierre, but that good supper and your Taos Lightning has got me a little bit sleepy. If you don't object, I think I'll just take myself to bed."

"Of course," Don Feliciano replied. He stood up, as did Longarm. "You will be my guest for another few days, I hope, Mr. Custis, while you rest from your long trip."

"No, sir, I think I better be moving on tomorrow. I thank you for the invite, but if I stick around here, I'm likely to get to liking it so much I'd want to stay."

"As you choose, then. Esteban will wake you in time for breakfast, unless you choose to sleep late."

When Longarm got back to the bedroom, he found that the bed had been turned down and a fire kindled in the corner fireplace, and the manservant was waiting sleepily.

He said, "Now look here, Esteban, I can get into bed by myself. You go on to wherever you belong. I'll take care of putting myself to bed."

"Eef you are sure, *señor*—"

"I'm sure. Now go on."

Longarm dug the opened bottle of Daugherty's out of his

saddlebags when Esteban left. He lighted a final cheroot and had a nightcap while he undressed and observed his regular bedtime routine.

While he was hanging his gunbelt in its usual place on the bedpost, he went over in his mind his talk with the *hacendado*.

That Aguierre fellow was just a little bit too smooth when you begun talking about Comancheros. There was something about him that wasn't just right. I'd say your first job's going to be to stick close by this place a few days after he thinks you've moved on, and see if you can't dig up what all you can do is smell right now, and have a look at it.

He blew out the lamp, and by the soft glow of the tiny blaze in the little domed fireplace, he finished undressing while he smoked the cheroot to a stub and had a final sip of rye. Then he yawned, stretched, and yawned again before crawling into the waiting bed. No squeaking or rasping of metal springs followed when he lowered his weight on the bed. He dropped a hand to its frame and felt the roughness of the rope that supported the mattress.

He'd slept before on this kind of bed, in which crisscrossed, taut ropes supported the mattress, and the thought flashed through his mind that he faced an uncomfortable night. He was past being merely ready for sleep, though. Stretching out as he lay down, he felt the soft resiliency of a wool-filled mattress gently cradle his relaxing muscles, and even before they had relaxed completely, he was asleep.

Longarm's first move when the infinitesimal sound from the doorway aroused him was one of pure reflex action of the muscles he'd trained, rather than any conscious awareness of an intruder coming into the room. Simultaneously with waking, he swept his Colt from its ready holster into his hand and sat upright. He was fully awake, sitting up in bed, the Colt in his hand, before he noticed the total darkness of the bedroom, became aware that the fire had burned itself out, and realized that he must have been asleep for quite a long while.

He kept his eyes fixed on the door across the room, but all he could see was the rectangular outline of its frame; he could not tell whether the door itself was swinging inward. He flicked a quick glance at the high-set window. It was barely visible as a light rectangle in the wall; the moonless night was itself so dark that there was little difference between the darkness inside and that outside the room.

A faint, shuffling whisper came from the direction of the door. Longarm's reasoning told him the intrusion was not likely to be an effort to kill him; if that had been the object of whoever was visiting him, the door would have burst open and a blaze of gunfire would have followed immediately. However, he had no intention of taking useless chances. Long ago he'd trained himself to move noiselessly. Not even a whisper came from the bedclothes, and the springless bed gave no squeaks of protest as he slid off on the side away from the door. He crouched there, his body shielded now by the thick mattress that he knew would stop the slug from any weapon, and waited.

A soft whisper of disturbed air broke the silence, and a second whisper, only a shade louder, followed as a man's voice said, "Señor Custis?"

Longarm recognized the voice, despite the changed timbre given it by the whisper; it was that of Hernan Maldonado. Keeping his own voice low, he replied, "I right here. What's your business with me at this time of the night, Maldonado?"

"It is night no longer, the morning is already late."

"What time it is don't make no difference. I asked you what you want in here. Suppose you tell me."

"To talk, only to talk, *señor*. Will you permit me to strike a light?"

"If you're set on talking, I guess you better. I don't much like having a palaver with somebody I can't see."

"Your caution does you credit, *señor*," Maldonado said.

A match rasped and flared into flame. Longarm slitted his eyes until they adjusted to the brightness, but kept the Colt's muzzle fixed on the scarfaced man as Maldonado stepped over to the bureau and touched the match to the lamp wick. He turned to face Longarm, and smiled. The upward twist of his lips gave his face an even more sinister expression than did the scars that pitted it.

"I could not keep from overhearing the conversation you had with Don Feliciano about the Comancheros returning to the Llano Estacado," Maldonado said.

"That'd follow, seeing you was with us in the room. Now tell me what it's got to do with you being here?"

"Only one thing, Señor Custis. If you are looking for a way to earn a great deal of money quickly and easily, and if you are the sort of man I think you must be, perhaps we can help one another."

Chapter 13

Longarm stared at Maldonado for a long minute before he asked, "What give you the idea I'm looking for help?"

"Perhaps I should express my thoughts a bit more clearly," the *mayordomo* replied smoothly. "I meant only that we might both find an advantage in working together."

"How do you figure on us doing that, Maldonado? Seems to me you got pretty much of a full-time job working for Mr. Aguierre. What kind of deal have you got in mind that'll help us both? About the best I can see you offering me is a job herding sheep, and I sure as hell ain't interested in that kind of work."

"I would not insult a man of your skill by offering him such employment, Señor Custis."

"Then what've you got in mind? Have you got the idea I'm in some special line of work that your boss needs done?"

"Don Feliciano has no connection with the work I speak of," Maldonado said. "I am thinking of something more in your regular line of employment."

"You sure you know what that is?"

"I am no fool," Maldonado said curtly. "Do not make the mistake of thinking that I am."

"As far as I know, you got as much brains as the next man, Maldonado. Only you ain't showing 'em right now."

"Señor Custis. I heard you remark that you are looking for employment. I examined your saddlebags and rifle when you first arrived. There is nothing in the bags to identify you, and your rifle is better kept than any of the men you called 'saddle tramps' would keep a weapon. Only a man who thinks of his weapons as tools of a trade would give them the kind of care yours show."

"Meaning you figure I got a gun for hire?"

Maldonado exhaled a patient sigh. "Let us speak openly. We are reaching no conclusions with this kind of talk."

"I'm ready to open up anytime you are," Longarm told the *mayordomo*. "All I been hearing from you so far don't say much of anything, though."

"Then I will ask you the question direct, Señor. Would you be interested in a dangerous job, one that would perhaps require you to use the guns you attend to so carefully?"

"I wouldn't carry them guns if I wasn't ready and able to use 'em," Longarm replied truthfully.

"Ah. That is what I have been waiting to hear you say." The *mayordomo*'s pitted face broke into the wolfish smile he'd shown before. "Now we can talk frankly, no?"

"You said you come here to talk. Talk, then. I'll listen to whatever you got on your mind, soon as I step into my pants." Longarm stood up, the Colt still in his hand, and pulled on his trousers. As he donned them he said, "It makes me sort of feel like whoever I'm talking to's got an edge on me, if he's all dressed up and I'm buck-ass naked."

Maldonado moved a chair from the wall closer to the bed. He said, "If we are to discuss our mutual concerns frankly, I would expect more trust than you are displaying now, *señor*."

Longarm moved to the bureau. Laying down his Colt, he picked up a cheroot and lighted it. He left the big revolver lying where he'd put it, walked back to the side of the bed, and sat down in the chair over which he'd hung his vest.

"Start talking," he told Maldonado.

"You were very foolish when speaking with Don Feliciano," he began. "Men have been killed for talking with unguarded lips."

"I don't recall saying anything out of line."

"Even innocent questions about Comancheros on the Llano Estacado can be dangerous. Not everything that is happening near the Plaza Aguierre reaches the ears of *el patrón*."

"Meaning there's Comancheros working someplace close by, and your boss don't know about 'em?" Longarm shook his head. "It don't seem to me like you'd be doing your job if you didn't tell him, Maldonado."

"Perhaps you will think me cowardly, but I value my own skin much more than I value my job."

"And maybe the Comancheros are greasing your palm to keep your mouth shut," Longarm suggested.

Maldonado shrugged. "Think what you wish. The Comancheros gather at a place in Yellow Horse Canyon. It is not on the land of the Plaza Aguierre. I understand it is easy to find; the canyon is a large one, with a stream flowing through it. There are only a few canyons hereabouts which carry water, as I am sure you saw while you were traveling across the *llano*."

"Look here, Maldonado," Longarm said, his voice hard. "You just as good as told me you got some kind of tie-in with them Comancheros. You was wanting us to put our cards face-up a minute ago, now you're backing away. I don't trust a man who'll do that."

Maldonado sat thoughtfully silent for a moment, then said, "I will make no confession to you, Custis." Longarm noted that the *mayordomo* no longer thought it necessary to address him in the more polite form, but said nothing. Maldonado went on, "Let us just suppose the Comancheros reward those who help them. Let us suppose that I have learned they are looking for men who know how to use their weapons with skill, a man such as you are."

"So they'll pay you off for sending me to where they meet?"

"I did not say this," Maldonado said quickly. He stood up.

"Wait a minute!" Longarm protested. "I want to know a lot more'n you've told me before I go looking anyplace for anybody!"

"I have told you nothing," Maldonado replied.

While they were talking, the blackness beyond the room's windows had grown gray. Now the faint sound of voices could be heard outside. Maldonado started toward the door.

"Hold on!" Longarm said.

"I must go quickly, I have duties that will not wait," the *mayordomo* said over his shoulder. "Think well on what I have told you, Custis. What you do is your own decision."

Longarm reined in the piebald, and sat listening. He had left the Plaza Aguierre shortly after breakfast, and it was now late in the morning. He had ridden steadily, but not hard. He took the military map from the pokehole in his saddle; when he had put the map into the hiding place, he'd found it necessary to fold and refold it to fit it into the pokehole. He unfolded it, smoothing the creases carefully. Since leaving the hacienda, he'd ridden with only the sun as his guide, but now it was time to set a more certain course.

Lighting a cheroot, he studied the map. Yellow Horse Canyon cut through the flat plain for a distance of fifty miles, somewhere ahead of him. The canyon ran generally southeastward, and was the only geographical feature of any size that had been noted by the army cartographer, other than a few water holes and ponds. Longarm suspected that most of these were nothing more than buffalo wallows like those he'd seen elsewhere on the Staked Plains. He had an idea they held water only during the days after the thaw of winter's snow and during the short, uncertain rainy season late in the year.

All you got to do, old son, is to ride on east until you run across that canyon. Then it'll be a job of going up and down it till you see signs where there's been some camps made lately. That ought not to be too big of a job.

He was rolling the map, trying to smooth out some of the more stubborn creases, when a slight smudge in the lettering that denoted the canyon caught his eye. He quit rolling the sheet of flexible, tough paper and held it up to the sunlight.

Like most mapmakers, the army cartographer had used pencil to sketch topographical outlines and rough in the words that identified them, and had later gone over the penciled lines with india ink. The smudge occurred at a spot where penciled markings had been erased, and holding the paper against the sun, Longarm could see the faint outline of the word that had first been written in pencil. He frowned for a moment, trying to make out each of the shadowy letters, then nodded with satisfaction.

"*Rescate,*" he said aloud, trying the pronunciation of the

140

erased Spanish word he'd been able to read. "*Rescate*. Sure has got a familiar sound. I heard somebody say it not too long ago. *Rescate*, now." He frowned, summoning memory, and suddenly his face brightened. "Sure! It was the old Comanchero up at Tascosa, Ramon Gallegos. 'Ransom,' that's what *rescate* means. Must be the place where the Comancheros used to meet the folks that'd come to pay 'em to get back their relations the Comanches had sold."

Looking at the sun, Longarm calculated the direction he'd have to ride to reach the place marked on the map. He fixed the sun's angle firmly in his mind, twitched the piebald's reins, and toed the horse into its slow, steady walk.

Noon had passed and the sun was westering before Longarm got to the rim of Yellow Horse Canyon. The wide trough that split the prairie was shallower than the Palo Duro, and was neither as large nor as colorful. The stream that curled along its bottom—Yellow Horse Creek, according to his map—was not as wide nor as deep as the fork of the Red River that coursed through the much larger canyon.

Longarm gauged the canyon's width with his eyes; it was, he judged, between two and three miles wide at the point where he'd stopped. From the rim where he overlooked it, he could see that there were smaller canyons breaking its walls, and there were also places where one of its sloping sides arced inward to give it greater than usual width for as much as a mile or more. Looking along it to the south, Longarm saw that the canyon grew wider as it curved toward the mouth. Going by his map, he'd reached the canyon almost at its midpoint.

Like the horse from which its name derived, the canyon was predominantly yellow. Yellow sandy soil covered the bottom on each side of the stream, and the baked earth and rocks of its walls were in shades ranging from yellow to light tan. There were a few trees, mostly cottonwoods and a few small cedars, along the course of the stream and huddled close to the protection of the walls. There were patches of thin grass on the canyon floor, and a few reeds grew in the sandy bottom of the little creek.

Tossing the stub of his cheroot to the bare, rocky ground, he turned the horse's head south and started it moving along the rim at a slow walk, looking for a place where the wall slanted gently enough for him to descend. He found such a spot after he'd covered less than a mile. The piebald stiff-legged it down to the canyon floor.

Longarm's stomach reminded him that a number of hours had passed since breakfast; he backtracked along the south wall of the canyon until he reached a place where the rise was steep enough to provide a strip of shade, and dismounted. After he'd let the horse drink, he tethered it beside a patch of grass where it could graze, and squatted in the shade to eat a cold lunch of jerky and cheese and parched corn from his dry rations.

As he ate, Longarm's eyes were busy scanning the new terrain he'd just entered. What he saw was much the same, whether he looked north or south. He finished eating and smoked, then remounted and began a slow ride toward the place his map hinted might be the spot of the old rendezvous point he sought.

There were signs of the canyon's use that Longarm's trail-wise eyes noted as he rode. None of them looked new. In that land of scant and infrequent rain, the traces left by men stayed visible for many years, and all the signs Longarm saw were old. There were Comanche firepits, readily identified by their size and shape and by the bleached buffalo ribs that lay scattered around them. There were the crumbling coals left by fires of sheepherders, coals in heaps that a man's outspread hands could easily span.

A scattering of brass shell cases marked a place where a brush between some exploring cavalry troop and a band of roving Comanches or Apaches had taken place; a trail of the outsized cases of the big dragoon revolvers carried by the cavalry told their own story of a small, short skirmish, the Indian retreat, and the troop's pursuit. Longarm did not bother to follow the trail to its end.

In midafternoon, when the canyon narrowed, he splashed the piebald across Yellow Horse Creek and turned south again, still riding close to the wall of the canyon. An hour or two before sunset he found what he'd been looking for, the old Comanchero camp indicated on the map.

Shards of pottery demijohns and jugs were strewn over the ground; old bones picked clean by passing coyotes lay here and there around a mound of black coals and ashes that spoke of fires kindled in the same place year after year. At a distance from the fire there were the low, weather-eroded, rectangular humps of two old graves. He looked for footprints, but the dry ground was stone-hard and no layer of dust covered it.

Longarm pulled up the piebald and dismounted. The camp-site was located in the center of one of the deep arcs that cut back the canyon wall, and ended in a narrow vee where the skeleton of a mule and scattered piles of dessicated and long-dry manure showed that the vee had been used as a corral. As he walked farther back to the point of the vee, Longarm encountered lumps of fresh manure, scarcely affected by the weather. Here he found hoofprints of horses and mules, both shod and unshod, deeply incised in soil that must have been wet from a rain when the prints were made. A closer, more careful look disclosed signs of a few bootprints and one or two smeared tracks made when heelless, moccasin-shod feet slipped in mud.

At one side of the vee's apex he found the ashes and coals of new fires, and a few sticks of recently cut wood. His sharp eyes also spotted the glint of broken glass; he squatted and examined the shining, fresh shards of a broken bottle.

Looks like you've found what you're looking for, old son. This place is where the old Comancheros made camp, all right. Them pieces of busted jugs go back to the days before whiskey come in bottles, and them dry horse turds in that deep cut are as old as the hunks of jugs. It's been a lot of years since them graves were dug, too.

Now that new sign can't mean but one thing. It's for damn sure there's somebody that knowed about the old ransom-place connected up with the new bunch that's using it now. So it looks like the best thing you can do is stop right here and wait till they come back. It's sure going to be a hell of a lot easier to settle down and wait for them to come find you instead of chasing ass-over-appetite, trying to find them.

In the waning light, Longarm made camp in the mouth of the vee at the back of the canyon wall's deep curve. He tethered the piebald in the back of the vee-cut after letting it drink from the creek. At the mouth of the vee, close to the canyon wall, where the night's shadows would be deepest, he smoothed a place for his bedroll and spread his blankets. Then he gathered up the scattered sticks of wood and found he had enough to cook bacon and potatoes for supper and breakfast. He built the smallest fire he could kindle in the center of the vee-cut's mouth, and while it was burning down to cooking size, he placed his saddle and saddlebags midway between the fire and the spot he'd chosen for his bed.

By this time the fire had dwindled to a few small tongues

143

of flame running along the charred surfaces of the four sticks of wood he'd lighted. Squatting by the fire, he grilled pieces of bacon while a pair of potatoes roasted in the heart of the tiny bed of coals.

Longarm ate slowly, watching the flames as the fire flickered away. He had a sip of water to wash down his spartan supper, and after lighting a cheroot he took the opened bottle of Daugherty's rye out of his saddlebag and sipped from it while he smoked. The night was moonless, and though the sky was studded with stars, they gave no light by which he could see more than a few yards beyond the embers of the dying fire.

Working by the faint glow that was all that remained of his supper fire, Longarm pulled the saddle and saddlebags into line and draped his coat over them. He spread his slicker over the coat. The result was a long, almost shapeless bundle that, in dim light or no light at all, could have been taken for the figure of a sleeping man.

Returning to his blankets, Longarm took off his pistol belt and crawled between the covers, fully clothed from vest to boots. He placed his Winchester on his left side and stretched his pistol belt along his right side. He slid the Colt from the holster and placed it ready to his right hand. For a short while he lay looking up at the stars. Then, with a final glance at the few tiny embers left from his supper fire, Longarm slept.

Slowly increasing dawn light was beginning to pale the stars over his head when Longarm snapped awake, his senses fully alert. He did not know what had roused him, but lay motionless while he listened and watched. Darkness had not yet been broken, and he could not penetrate the gloom no matter how hard he stared. The fire had died away; no coals glowed at the center of the vee, but a faint aroma of woodsmoke still hung in the breezeless air.

A faint noise broke the predawn hush—the scraping of a foot or perhaps the shod hoof of a slowly moving horse. Longarm was unable to locate the source or direction of the sound in the gloom. He looked back at the end of the vee, but it was in deep shadow and he could not see the piebald. The small noise sounded again, and this time Longarm could tell that it came from the mouth of the wide arc that broke the canyon's sheer wall.

Moving silently, he slid the Winchester from beneath the

top blanket and laid it across his thighs, where he could grasp it and bring it up immediately. He picked up the Colt and freed it from the bedclothing too, resting his right arm across his chest so that simply by raising his wrist he could level the revolver at whatever might now present itself.

A faint squeak, the creaking of saddle leather, audible only because the predawn silence was complete, reached Longarm's ears. He did not move, but lay quietly waiting, while a whispering of boot soles on the baked earth sounded briefly, then stopped.

Minutes dragged by and the morning slowly brightened, though the ground close to the wall of the canyon where Longarm lay was still shrouded in deep gloom. Above his head Longarm could see the canyon's irregular rim becoming defined as the dawn light increased. He glanced toward the floor of the canyon and could now make out a large dark shadow that he knew must be the horse ridden by the new arrival. There was no sign of the rider yet, for the sky light had not become bright enough to lift the darkness from the canyon's floor.

Imperceptibly the dimness brightened. Longarm kept his eyes moving, but even though the outline of the standing horse was now visible, he still could not see its rider. With startling suddenness the stillness was broken. The low voice of a man broke the hush.

"Put your hands up, you under the blanket! But lie where you are. If you move, you are a dead man!"

Longarm had located the speaker by the time he'd said three or four words, and had snapped up his Colt to cover the vague form that he could see now through the lifting darkness. Night was lifting swiftly, the transition from darkness to daylight speeding up as the sun began to brighten the sky from below the horizon. What had a few seconds earlier been only a vague manlike shape was now clearly defined as a man kneeling beyond the dead ashes of Longarm's supper fire. He was leveling a rifle at the dummy that Longarm had placed between the fire and his real bed.

Longarm said nothing until the newcomer spoke again, this time with a sharp snap of command in his tone.

"Get up your hands, I tell you! Move, now!"

From the intonation, though not from any accent, Longarm judged the speaker to be Spanish or Mexican. Longarm lay quiet, his finger firm on the Colt's trigger. He waited until he saw the man move to raise the rifle he was holding.

"Drop the rifle!" he called. "I'll cut you down before you can swing it!"

When the newcomer did not obey, Longarm snapshot and sent a slug from the Colt plowing into the dirt a foot from the kneeling rifleman. The dust raised by the bullet proved to be a convincing argument. The man opened his hands and let the rifle fall to the ground in front of him.

Chapter 14

"That's fine," Longarm called. "Now just hold real still while I get up close enough to take a look at you!"

Keeping his Colt aimed at the kneeling man, Longarm walked over and stopped in front of him. With a boot toe he snaked the rifle out of the newcomer's reach. There was enough light now for him to see the man clearly, and he found something familiar about his face, although specifically what it was hovered just beyond recall.

Aside from the haunting feeling that the kneeling man's face was one he should know, Longarm found nothing unusual in his appearance. The stranger's face was thin, his cheekbones high. His nose was narrow, with nostrils that flared suddenly, and the eyebrows that framed it were black, heavy, and straight. His eyes were dark, and they watched Longarm with an intensity that was almost fierce. The man wore a short-trimmed black beard, thickly shot with gray, that hid the line of his jaw, but judging by his other facial features, Longarm imagined that his jaw was thin and protruding.

There was as little unusual about the newcomer's clothing as there was about his face. He had on nondescript clothes: a tan shirt open at the neck, a woolen suit jacket that did not

147

match his closely woven convert-cloth trousers, a leather vest. His boots were high-heeled, with a pointed toes. Longarm recognized the butt of the revolver protruding from his holster as an ancient lever-action Volcanic repeating pistol, the lineal ancestor of his own Winchester. The gun, he thought, must be at least twenty years old.

He told the stranger, "You ought to take a closer look at what you got in your sights before you open your mouth. There wasn't a time I couldn't've put you down while you was aiming at that dummy bed I fixed up."

"What makes you think I didn't know it was a dummy?" the stranger asked. "I might have been just testing you to see what you'd do if someone sneaked up on you." Then, in spite of his upraised arms, he somehow managed to shrug as he added, "Or it may just be that I've gotten old and careless, Custis."

Longarm's jaw dropped in surprise. He asked, "Now how in hell did you get hold of that name?"

"Surely you didn't think I came to this place by accident?" the man said, his voice casual.

"You mean you was looking for me to be here?"

"I was looking for you to be in Yellow Horse Canyon, but I didn't realize you'd managed to locate this place until I picked up the scent of your fire and followed it. If you're going to join us, you'll have to learn to be a lot more careful."

"Us, meaning who?"

"We can talk about that at breakfast."

"I ain't sure yet that I'll want to eat breakfast with you. Not till I know more about you, anyhow. Like your name and where you found out mine."

"Call me Zarzalo. You and I both know there's only one place I could've gotten your name and found out where you'd be. Now if you'll holster your gun and let me put my arms down, we'll both be a lot more comfortable."

"Just one more thing. I'd be inclined to listen to you if you'd tell me the name of the man that said I'd be here."

With a smile, Zarzalo nodded. "At least you're careful. I feel better about you already, after seeing how you set up your camp, and the way you took me."

"We can talk about that later on," Longarm told him. "I want that name before I listen to anything else from you."

"Does Maldonado satisfy you? Or do you want his first

name too? It's Hernan, if you insist."

Zarzalo's reply did not surprise Longarm; he'd half expected it to be either Maldonado or Don Feliciano Aguierre whom the man would name. After his talk with Maldonado, Longarm had been sure that the plaza's *mayordomo*, and perhaps its owner as well, were somehow involved in the new Comanchero activity. He kept his face expressionless, then nodded and slowly holstered his Colt.

"All right, 'Zarzalo," he said. "Get up and I'll see what I can stir up for breakfast. It ain't going to be much. I'm traveling on sort of short rations."

"I've got enough food to tide us both over for a few days," Zarzalo said, rising and stamping his feet to shake the dirt off his trouser legs. "And if you haven't already found it, there's a cache of pots and pans back in the cut where your horse is."

"It didn't occur to me to look," Longarm said as they walked over to the ashes of his dead fire. "I could see there'd been somebody using this place lately, but I didn't figure they'd get here often enough to cache anything."

"Caching things like pots and dry grub that won't go bad saves a lot of trouble," Zarzalo pointed out. He stepped to one side long enough to pick up the reins of his horse, and led the animal back as he rejoined Longarm. "If one bunch gets here early, they don't have to worry about the rest being late."

"By which I take it there's more'n you coming, and the rest are on the way here?" Longarm asked.

Zarzalo was busy pulling small cloth sacks out of his bulging saddlebags. He nodded a "yes."

"You got this thing pretty well planned out, I see."

"Any man who doesn't plan is a fool," Zarzalo said curtly. "Come along, I'll show you where the cache is."

Leading his horse again, Zarzalo motioned for Longarm to accompany him. They started toward the apex of the cleft. Zarzalo halted to tether the animal. He pointed to a large flat rock that was leaning against the canyon wall near the point of the little cut.

"It's behind that rock," he told Longarm. "Just grab it by the top and pull it over. You'll find some pots and a spider and a bag of cornmeal and flour. I'll gather up a little bit more wood down by the stream and start a fire while you get the pans and grub out of the cache."

Before he touched the big thin stone slab, Longarm examined both the stone and the area around it. Even his sharp eyes saw nothing to indicate that the slab had not simply slid down the canyon wall and come to rest in its present leaning position.

Whoever put that piece of rock where it is sure knew how to make it look like nobody'd ever touched it or even come close to it. If this bunch of Comancheros is as smart as it looks like they might be, you're going to have to step light and easy while you're with 'em.

Grasping the top edge of the slab, he pulled. For such a sizable stone, the slab was surprisingly light. It gave way readily to his tugging. He held it balanced on edge for a second or two, then lowered it to the ground.

Moving the stone revealed a miniature cavern, its floor paved roughly with thin pieces of the same kind of stone that had been used to seal the mouth. The opening extended some four feet into the canyon wall, and its jagged top was a full yard above the level of the ground. In the tiny cave were two cotton sacks and three large wooden boxes. Two iron pots, one inside the other, and a tripod-legged cooking spider stood on the boxes.

Longarm took out the sacks and placed them to one side. He moved the cooking utensils and put them beside the sacks, then lifted the hinged wooden lid of one of the boxes; it contained a quantity of mixed ammunition and two pistols, one a Colt, the other a Remington. He lifted a handful of the cartridges and found them to be of unsorted calibers for both rifles and pistols.

He opened the other two boxes, but they were both empty. Levering up the cover slab, he leaned it back in place, but did not try to disguise the fact that it was not the face of a huge boulder that was embedded in the canyon wall. Carrying the bags and cooking utensils, Longarm walked back to the mouth of the cleft.

Zarzalo was hunkered down beside a four-stick fire, coaxing it to life. Several small bags were piled a short distance from him. He jerked his head toward them.

"Grub," he told Longarm. "We won't be needing too much, this time out. All I brought was some tortillas and a chunk of beef and a little garden truck, onions and turnips and such, for a stew."

"That's a lot more'n I got," Longarm said. "Bacon and

some jerky and parched corn and a few spuds. I guess some of it'll go good in a stew, though."

Zarzalo nodded, intent on blowing life into the young blaze. Longarm squatted beside him and lighted a cheroot. He said, "A while ago you said there's somebody else on the way. When do you figure they'll be here?"

"It's hard to say. At a guess, they ought to be showing up a while before dark."

"Anybody I'd be likely to know?"

"You might. It's hard to tell. Men rub up against each other in funny places all over this part of the country. If I called names, the chances are they wouldn't mean much to you, though. We'll wait and see who shows."

Longarm watched the fire in silence for a moment before asking his next question. "What kind of job will we be riding on? It can't be a train we'll be after, there ain't no railroads inside of a couple of hundred miles. No bank, neither, and I never heard of nobody rustling sheep. I'd like to know, because I got to admit I'm a mite curious."

Zarzalo shook his head. "You'll just have to be curious until the others get here. Everybody will learn at the same time where we're going and what we're going to do. There's no chance of anybody spilling information that way."

"Are you the head man of the outfit, then?"

"As far as you're concerned, I am." Zarzalo had gotten to his feet, satisfied that the fire would burn properly, and was rummaging in the sacks he'd brought. He answered Longarm's question in an offhand fashion, without taking his eyes off what he was doing.

Longarm had been debating ever since he'd heard Maldonado's name just how far he ought to push to get useful information from Zarzalo. He said, "I ain't so certain I want to go out on a job if I don't know whether it's going to be worth my time."

"You wouldn't be here if you weren't broke and needing cash to tide you over," Zarzalo pointed out.

"Maybe so and maybe not. I know I can get my price if I go on a ways. It ain't like I got to stay here."

A knife suddenly appeared in Zarzalo's hand. Almost of its own volition, Longarm's hand started for his Colt, but he realized in time that the move was not hostile, and stopped before Zarzalo noticed his movement. Longarm saw that the knife had no hilt; it was a sleeve-sheathed blade, drawn with a quick wrist-flip. He marked the knife down in his mind as a weapon to remember if he should ever have to face the other man in a showdown.

Zarzalo took a big chunk of boneless meat from one of the sacks he'd brought. He knelt, placed the meat on the sack he'd taken it from, and began cutting paper-thin slices. To Longarm, the piece looked like it had come from a sheep's hindquarters. Mutton wasn't a meat for which he had a great deal of liking, but as he waited for the Comanchero to answer, he resigned himself to eating it on this one occasion.

For a moment Zarzalo devoted his full attention to his careful slicing. Then he said, "You're new with us, Custis."

Longarm smiled inwardly; until now he'd avoided addressing Zarzalo by name, just as the Comanchero leader had carefully refrained from calling Longarm "Custis." Longarm took the other man's words as an indication that he'd passed his first test; men on the wrong side of the law in the West were careful not to use names among themselves unless they were very sure they were with their own kind.

"I don't usually make a new man an offer like this," Zarzalo went on. "You seem to be brighter than most, so I'll make an exception. When everybody's here, and I explain what our job's going to be, if you don't like what you hear, you can ride out and no hard feelings. Is that fair enough to suit you?"

Longarm waited to answer long enough to make his attitude convincing, then replied, "Fair enough to do me, I expect."

"Good."

Zarzalo put the spider on the fire. He picked up a sack and took a stack of thin tortillas from it; to Longarm they looked exactly like those he'd been served at the Plaza Aguierre, but he realized that one tortilla looked pretty much like the next one. Zarzalo put the tortillas in the spider and watched it carefully. When the edges of the bottom tortilla began to curl, he slipped the knife under it, yanked it from the bottom with an expert jerk that did not disturb the others resting on it, and placed the tortilla he'd removed on top of the pile.

"Hand me that little pot," he said over his shoulder to Longarm. "I need it to keep the tortillas warm in."

By the time Longarm had put the pot down at the edge of the small hot fire, Zarzalo was moving a second tortilla to the top of the stack. When the entire pile of a half-dozen had been

152

heated, he lifted them and transferred them to the pot. Reaching into a second sack, he took out a large crimson-red pepper and dropped it on the spider. He let it stay there for only a short time, turning it every few moments with the point of his knife. He lifted the pepper off the hot spider with his knifepoint and held it out to Longarm.

"Here," he said. "Gut this out and cut it into strips while I cook the meat."

Longarm held the pepper, looking at it blankly. Surprisingly, it was not hot enough to make his hand uncomfortable. He said, "Hell, I never gutted one of these things in my life."

Zarzalo was putting the thin slices of meat on the smoking surface of the spider. Without looking at Longarm, he said, "Do it like you'd gut anything. Slit the skin and peel it off, cut it open and get rid of the stem and core and seeds."

Opening his pocketknife, Longarm followed instructions. The paper-thin skin slid off almost of its own accord. He opened the pod, cut around the stem, and flicked stem and seeds into the fire. Zarzalo had turned the pieces of meat by now. He speared them with his knife and shook them off into the pot with the tortillas. He saw that Longarm was still holding the pepper and grinned.

"Cut it in strips," he said. "Six tortillas, six pieces of meat, six strips of pepper. That should hold us until noon."

Longarm held red pepper in about as much esteem as he did mutton, but he watched his companion and followed his example. Zarzalo took a tortilla, topped it with a slice of meat, put a strip of pepper in the center, and folded the tortilla around both. Zarzalo was already eating, and Longarm bit into his own roll. To his surprise, the pepper was sweet instead of hot, and the meat tasted nothing at all like the greasy mutton he remembered.

"This ain't bad at all," he told Zarzalo. "I looked for that pepper to burn my mouth."

"This is sweet red pepper. If you want to burn your mouth, there's some ground-up hot pepper in one of those bags."

"No thanks. This'll do just the way it is."

"I expect you'd rather have ham and eggs," Zarzalo said, his mouth half full, "but this is better than nothing."

"I've got a lot worse in some cafes," Longarm admitted. "Sure tastes better'n I figured it would."

"Don't look for me to do any cooking for you from here

on," Zarzalo warned. "You'll be expected to do your share of it."

Longarm nodded. "I'll try not to poison nobody."

They finished their breakfast in companionable silence. Longarm strolled over to his saddlebag, removed the disguise he'd draped over the bags and his saddle, and took out the opened bottle of Daugherty's Private Stock. He carried the bottle back to where Zarzalo was standing gazing at the dying fire, and held it out to the Comanchero leader.

"This'll have to do instead of coffee," he said.

Zarzalo took the bottle and looked slit-eyed at Longarm. "You feel like you got to have liquor?"

"No. I drink it because I like the way it tastes. If you mean am I drinking to get drunk, the answer's no again."

Zarzalo nodded. He tipped the bottle, took a conservative swallow, and wiped the neck before handing it back to Longarm. "I wasn't insulting you, Custis," he said. "Just asking as a matter of information."

Longarm nodded. "No offense taken, Zarzalo. I got no use either for a man that's got to have a crutch to help him."

"Then we understand one another, no?" Zarzalo's smile was a thin one, but Longarm decided it was the widest smile of which the other man was capable. Zarzalo went on, "I've been riding most of the night. You keep an eye on things while I get some sleep."

Longarm could not decide whether this was another of the Comanchero's tests, or a mark of acceptance. He chose to take it as acceptance, and nodded. He went back to his bed and stretched out, lighting a fresh cheroot. Zarzalo unsaddled his horse, put his blanket roll down a few feet away from Longarm's, and went to sleep as soon as he'd lain down.

Slowly the morning wore on to noon, and past noon. Longarm grew tired of lounging. He got up silently and took the horses to the creek to drink, then tethered them in the biggest patch of grass he could find close by. He went back to his bedroll and took his time cleaning the Colt before he slid a fresh cartridge into the chamber to replace the one he'd fired to warn Zarzalo.

By the time midafternoon had arrived and Zarzalo still slept, Longarm began to get restless. He was thinking of waking his companion when he heard hoofbeats. Reaching for his rifle, he stood up, but before could call a warning, Zarzalo snapped awake and rolled to his feet, picking up his own rifle as he stood. He saw Longarm standing ready and nodded.

"We'll take cover," he said. "It's sure to be the men we're waiting for, but there's no use taking chances."

Together they walked across the mouth of the cleft and stood at a corner of the opening, where a quick backward step would put them in the cover of the canyon wall. The hoofbeats grew louder. Longarm tried to separate their rhythms, but echoes from the walls made it impossible. From the volume of the muffled drumming, though, he guessed there were at least three or four men approaching.

Longarm and Zarzalo waited in silence while the riders came closer. The new arrivals rounded the curve in the canyon walls that had hidden them, and Longarm counted four. He looked questioningly at Zarzalo, who nodded.

"They're our men," he said. "No need to worry."

Standing at the corner of the cleft, they waited. The sun had dropped low in the west by now, and was in their eyes. Longarm did not recognize the approaching riders until they were within a few dozen yards. Then he saw that three of them wore familiar faces: Lefty, Perez, and Morris. Longarm did not recognize the fourth rider. He clamped his jaws shut in exasperation and turned to Zarzalo.

"I ain't one to borrow trouble," he said quietly. "But those fellows might be bringing it. I had a little run-in with three of 'em up in Tascosa a few days ago, over a poker game. There was four of them there, then. I had to cool one of 'em. Beats me who the new man is they've picked up."

Without taking his eyes off the four, who were now almost at the mouth of the cleft, Zarzalo said, "Glad you mentioned it. Now I'll expect you to keep quiet while I settle things between you, if any trouble starts."

"I don't say there'll be trouble, but I don't say there won't either," Longarm replied. "I'll go along as far as I can with you. Just don't look for me to go too far."

Zarzalo nodded. The four riders pulled up a few yards from where he and Longarm stood, Zarzalo slightly in front of Longarm. Lefty was the first one to recognize Longarm.

"What the hell you doing here, Custis?" he asked belligerently. "We seen all we wanted of you in Tascosa!"

"Just hold your mouth, Lefty," Zarzalo said before Longarm could reply. "Custis is going to be with us for a while."

155

"Hell you say!" Morris chimed in. "Did he tell you how he cut Snore down?"

"Not until a minute ago," Zarzalo replied. "What difference does it make if he did?"

Longarm thought it was time for him to say something. He faced Lefty and his companions. "You know why I had to shoot your friend. I had a drink afterwards with you, and all of us agreed there wasn't going to be any hard feelings."

"Is that right, Lefty?" Zarzalo asked. "Morris? Perez? Any of you object to riding in the same bunch with Custis?"

For a moment the trio sat their horses in silent consultation, eye to eye. Finally, Lefty shook his head.

"I guess we can stand it," he said. "I'll say this much for Custis, he can hold his own with anybody when it comes to handling a gun."

"Then you ought to be glad to have him with us," Zarzalo pointed out. He waited, looking from Lefty to Morris to Perez, and when none of them spoke, he added, "We'll call it settled, then. I don't want to hear any more about Snore, understand?"

"Sure," Lefty said.

Morris and Perez nodded. Longarm relaxed. He'd been too intent on the trio from Tascosa to do more than glance at the fourth rider, but now he looked at him. The man was Spanish, with perhaps some Indian blood, he decided. His face was incredibly wrinkled, his hands gnarled with age and work. His eyes were black and clear, though. When he swung off his horse as the newcomers dismounted, Longarm realized for the first time how small he was; the man's head came barely past Longarm's waist.

Zarzalo noticed Longarm examining the old man. He said, "This is Magro, Custis. Don't let him fool you. He'll carry a lot more than his own weight when we get moving."

Magro acknowledged the introduction with a quick nod, but did not speak.

Lefty asked Zarzalo, "You got any grub? We didn't stop to eat at noon, just chewed some jerky while we rode. My belly thinks my throat's been cut."

"There's meat for a stew," Zarzalo told him. "And the rest of the fixings. You men can get it started while I talk to Magro a minute. There's a few things we need to work out before we start for where we'll be going."

Of the four who drew the stew-making job, Longarm was

156

the only one who did not wear a sheath knife. In the surprisingly short and good-natured discussion that settled the division of labor, he drew the potato-peeling assignment. Perez chopped the meat with a huge bowie knife that fell just short of passing for a saber, Lefty dealt with the turnips, and Morris uncomplainingly took on the onions. They worked for the first few minutes in silence, squatting or kneeling a short distance from the fire that Perez had rekindled, tossing the cut-up pieces of meat into the big stewpot.

Finally Lefty said, "It ain't none of my business, Custis, but how'd you come to get connected up with Zarzalo?"

"You know how things like that happen, Lefty," Longarm told him. "You ride awhile and keep your ears open and look around. Pretty soon you've found what you're after."

"I guess," Lefty agreed. "None of us wasn't looking to see you again, after we pulled outa Tascosa. Not that it makes no difference."

"Is like we say een Tascosa," Perez put in. "We do not put on you blame because you keel Snore."

"No reason why you should," Longarm reminded them.

"Sure. Grudges don't help nobody," Morris agreed.

They worked on until the stewpot was full and simmering over the fire. Zarzalo and Magro came up.

Looking at the bubbling pot, Zarzalo nodded approval. "Good," he said. "Let it simmer while we're talking. Then, as soon as we've eaten, we'll ride. Tonight we're going to do the job you three"—indicating Lefty, Morris, and Perez—"have been wanting to get to."

"You mean the Guthrie place?" Lefty asked.

"That's right," Zarzalo said. "The Guthrie place. It'll take all of us to handle that. Then, when it's finished, we'll leave the house to burn and Magro and Perez can move Guthrie's sheep while the rest of us go to that new homestead and take care of it. And all of you remember, don't set fires until I've got all the homestead papers from both places. Now let's eat and get moving. We can finish talking on the way."

Chapter 15

Grimly silent, Longarm stood aside and watched while the others dug into their saddlebags for tin plates or frying pans and ladled stew into them. Thinking hard, he walked slowly over to his own bedroll and dug into his saddlebags for his big all-purpose cup. On his way back to get his portion of the stew, he was still mulling over the problems he faced.

You've sure drawed a hand in a wild game this time, old son. From what Zarzalo said, this bunch ain't Comancheros at all. They don't do no trading with the Comanches, they just go out and raid like the Comanches used to, which makes 'em plain out-and-out bandits! And there sure ain't no U.S. marshal in his right mind's going to ride with a bandit gang, not even to get the evidence he could use in court to send 'em up.

What you got to do now is play your hand like it was a good one. You got to figure out how to handle this whole bunch by yourself. You can't just stand still and watch these bastards burn out two places tonight, steal a flock of sheep, loot the houses before they set fire to 'em, and kill God knows how many innocent people.

You sure can't join 'em, neither, like they're expecting you will. Now, five to one ain't good odds, but you've won out on worse deals than this is. So start thinking, old son. It'll take some doing, and you'll need to know just what moves to make and when, and every move you make has got to be just right, regardless of whether the odds is five to one or ten to one against you.

Still silent and preoccupied, Longarm spooned himself up a sizable helping of the stew and went over to where Lefty and Morris and Perez were sitting. Their mouths were full, but they nodded in friendly enough fashion, as though making him welcome, when he hunkered down close to them and began eating. Zarzalo and Magro were sitting a little apart from the rest, talking in low tones. They were too far to hear anything that he might say to Lefty or Morris or Perez, Longarm noticed.

He began eating, waiting for one of the others to begin talking, relying on his skill at guiding a conversation to give him some of the answers he was looking for. Morris gave him the first opportunity.

"How'd you get hooked up with Zarzalo, anyways, Custis?" he asked. "You wasn't on your way down here when we seen you in Tascosa, was you?"

"I wasn't on my way to much of anyplace. You men know what you do in our line of work when you're looking for a job."

"Sure," Lefty nodded. "Just prod till you land one."

"Except I didn't figure this job for what it's turning out to be. Damn it, I was told this outfit was Comancheros. Now I took that to signify I'd be swapping with the Comanches, which is what the Comancheros always done."

Lefty guffawed loudly. "Well, maybe you ain't as smart as I reckoned you to be, Custis! Hell, man, there's not any Comanches to trade with no more! That's just a yarn Zarzalo begun spreading around so's folks would blame the raids on the Indians!"

"Well, that sort of puzzled me for a while," Longarm frowned. "But I heard a while back, when I was over in the Indian Nation, that there was a lot of young bucks jumping the reservations to come down here and trade for guns and whiskey with Comancheros. In my book, that's a nice easy way to make money. What this looks like to me now is a damned hard way to make anything."

"It ain't all that bad," Morris told him. "Sure, we do a lot of hard riding, mostly at night. And there's some shooting too.

We don't get shot at as much as we shoot, though."

"You've all rode with Zarzalo before," Longarm said. "I ain't. What I don't see is how you get enough out of these little bitty ranches to make the job worth a man's time."

"It sure wouldn't, if all we got was the little bits of jewelry and whatever cash we find," Lefty said. "Or what the sheep bring in, either."

"Where does the money come from, then?" Longarm asked.

"Homestead rights. You heard Zarzalo talking about being sure to save the papers a minute ago, I guess?"

"Sure. I didn't rightly understand what he meant, though."

"Property papers. Like deeds and homestead grants and such. Zarzalo's got somebody on the string that buys 'em. Later on, I guess whoever buys 'em claims the land they cover."

"Hell, I didn't know land was worth all that much in Texas," Longarm said. "Especially in these parts."

"It ain't, unless it's got water on it," Morris put in. "We don't bother the dry-landers. But from the way I understand it, even a little old ma-and-pa homestead's worth considerable if there's a live pond or a stream or a spring on it."

"Well, now. That's right interesting," Longarm said. "I don't guess it makes any difference who finds these papers, as long as Zarzalo gets 'em? What I mean is, we share and share alike, don't we?"

"Everybody gets paid the same, if that's what you mean," Lefty replied. "And money's money, Custis. Even if we take a chance or two, and dodge bullets for a little while, it sure as hell beats punching cattle."

"Just the same, I'd rather all we'd be doing is swapping with the Comanches, like the real Comancheros used to," Longarm said. "I guess there ain't no Comancheros left now, though."

"Magro, he ess old Comanchero," Perez volunteered. "He ees like to talk weeth me because we talk in the Espanish. *Ay, caramba!* What kind of life ees the real Comancheros they have! New woman every night, wheesky all they want, money!"

"That Magro, he might not look like much," Lefty said to Longarm. "Don't think he ain't plenty of man, though. He's one of the real old-time Comancheros, like Perez said. Tougher'n a boot sole and mean as a tarantula. Keep on his good side, if you can find out which one it is. Me, I ain't found much good about the old bastard yet."

160

Thanks," Longarm told Lefty when he'd swallowed. I'll keep my eye on him." He spooned up another bite of stew, but before putting it in his mouth he asked, "How much do you figure a job like this one tonight's going to be worth to us?"

"We oughta get—" Lefty began, but before he could finish, the thudding of many hooves on the ground reached their ears and all of them dropped their plates and scrambled for their rifles. As one man, they started toward the mouth of the cleft. Perez, small and wiry and the closest man to their objective, was the first to reach a point where he could get a clear look up the canyon.

"*Madre de la Virgen!*" he called, skidding to a halt and bringing up his rifle. "*Vienen los Comanches!*"

Longarm had been watching the approaching riders. There was no mistaking them for anything but what they were. There were at least a dozen, riding on the flat leather pads they preferred to white man's saddles, bare but for breechclouts, bronze skins shining in the glare of the low-hanging sun. Out of the corner of his eye, Longarm saw Perez bringing up his rifle to fire. He turned toward him to warn him not to shoot, but before he could speak, a shout sounded behind them.

"Perez!" a hoarse voice commanded. "*Quedarse! No tira si 'stan verdaderos Comanches!*"

"*Son absolutamente verdaderos!*" Perez replied, but he lowered his rifle.

Longarm looked around to identify the source of the command; it had come from Magro, who was hustling toward them as fast as his aged legs could carry him. Zarzalo was close behind him. Magro reached the four men and pushed between them to step in front of where they stood. Zarzalo went to stand beside Magro.

Longarm was close enough to the two men to hear what they were saying. They spoke in Spanish, and while he wasn't certain that he was catching every nuance of their words, he did get the general gist of what was being said.

"*Veramos en apuros?*" Zarzalo asked Magro.

"*Aun no conozco,*" the old man replied impatiently, his eyes fixed on the approaching Indians. "*Son jovenes. Asechamos a vemos que quieren.*"

"*Es claro que quieren!*" Zarzalo snapped impatiently. "*Mira! Tienen una mujer. Vienen a trato, quieren whiskey y fusiles!*"

Looks to me like Zarzalo's got it right, Longarm told him-

161

self. *They come looking to swap that woman for whiskey and guns.*

Urgency in his voice, Zarzalo said to Magro, *"'Pues, habla con ellos, viejo! Dice que no tenemos whiskey o fusiles ahorita, pero tienen a poco tiempo, tal vez mañana. Retrasen cuando pensamos!"*

"Sí, sí, Zarzalo," the old man answered. *"No desasosiego, hombre. Conozco hacer!"*

Zarzalo gestured for the men to stay where they were, and he and Magro began walking forward to meet the oncoming Indians. Longarm could no longer hear what they were saying, but he'd lost interest in their conversation when he heard Zarzalo mention that the Comanches had a woman with them. Shading his eyes from the sun's glare with his hand, he stared hard at the Comanche band. The riders were closer now, and he saw the blur of a white-shirted figure in the middle of the band, almost hidden by the bronzed bodies of the leaders.

As the Indians drew closer, their ponies shifting from side to side to avoid the rough spots on the canyon's floor, Longarm could see the white-clad figure more clearly. Even at a distance he could make out the swell of female breasts under the shirt. Then, when the Comanches began reining in their mounts, he saw that a flour sack had been pulled over the woman's head, perhaps, he thought, to keep her from seeing where she was being taken. Her hands were tied to the horn of her saddle, and her booted feet were held in the stirrups by looped rawhide thongs. A rope lariat around the neck of her horse was held by the Indian riding in front of her.

Longarm turned his attention to the Comanches. Of the dozen men in the party, only one was elderly, and he wore an antelope-hide jacket and leggings. The others were young, their faces unwrinkled, and they had on only breechclouts and moccasins. Five of them carried rifles across their thighs; Longarm noted that of the five rifles only two were modern repeaters; the three remaining were single-shot breech-loaders. Two of the others had on broad belts above the strings of their breechclouts, and holstered pistols dangled from the belts.

When the Comanches were within fifty or sixty feet of the spot where Zarzalo and Magro stood, they pulled their horses up. The Indians did not dismount, but sat looking down at the white men, waiting for them to speak first. It was a typical display of Comanche arrogance, an attitude acquired during the century that had ended a mere ten or fifteen years ago, when the Comanches were lords of the broad prairie, and lesser tribes—including whites—were expected to greet them humbly.

Magro knew the tradition. He raised his right hand, spread wide to show he held no weapon. *"Amigos,"* he said. *"Encontrarse en paz."*

"Talk English, old man," the Comanche on the lead horse told him. He could have been any age from twenty to forty; his broad face showed no lines. His black hair was braided with strips of red cloth and the two braids hung down on each side of his short, chunky torso. He went on, "We have been to school. We speak English now better than we do your tongue."

"I good," Magro said. He tapped his chest with a forefinger. "I am Magro. Come sit with us, we are talk."

"Pat-Cha-No," the Comanche leader replied, making the same sign.

Magro pointed to the woman. "You wan' to trade with us?"

"If you are the ones we heard are traders, like the men who traded with our fathers in the Shining Times."

"We are the ones you hear of," Magro nodded. "What for do you wish to trade?"

"We want guns," Pat-Cha-No replied. "New ones. Rifles."

"Where have you get the woman?" Magro asked.

"In the north, near the river Piedroso, the one the white men call Canadian. She will be worth much to you, there are those who will pay to have her given back to them."

Magro shook his head, then began the preliminary ritual of trading. *"Rio Piedroso* is too close to the soldiers' fort. Is bad to go there for us the same as for you. Go! Take back where you are get her the woman. Trade for her with the ones you say will pay for her."

Now it was Pat-Cha-No's turn to object. "No. If we try to trade her, the soldiers will know who took her. Then we must fight them, and for that we do not now have the guns we need."

"Is too much danger for us too," Magro said.

"If you take her back, the soldiers will not know of us," the Comanche leader pointed out. "That is why we brought her here. Why do we not talk more of this thing, and see if we can trade?"

Magro shook his head slowly. "Today is not good day that we talk of trading."

"Why not?" Pat-Cha-No demanded. "We are here, we have

the woman. We have no time to waste waiting."

"Our wagons do not get here until later," Zarzalo said. "Until they come, we have no food, no whiskey, no guns to trade."

Pat-Cha-No frowned. "When will the wagons be here?"

"Tomorrow." Zarzalo shrugged to show that time was of no importance. "Or perhaps the next day."

"Then we will wait."

"And if they do not get here tomorrow?" Zarzalo asked.

"If you have enough whiskey, we might wait another day. But we cannot be away from the Nation too many days. If the agent counts heads and we are not there, it will be bad."

Magro went back to the trading preliminaries. "Maybe it is no good if you wait. Not yet do we see the woman good. She maybe is not worth trading for "

"She is young, a strong young one! A woman worth many good rifles!"

Pat-Cha-No wheeled his horse and toed it to the woman's side, then wheeled again to face Zarzalo and Magro. He leaned across to the captive and pulled the sack off her head.

Longarm's jaw dropped, but he quickly composed his face to a studied neutrality The Comanches' prisoner was Ellen Briscoe.

She sat blinking for a moment in the strong unfiltered sunlight, her eyes darting from one to another of the Comancheros. She saw Longarm and her throat worked convulsively as she tried to call to him. Her struggle brought out only a choked bubbling sound through the strip of cloth that had been pulled across her mouth. Her eyes were wide open, and Longarm read in them the plea she was trying to make as she stared at him.

Longarm could see that Ellen did not grasp the danger that would threaten both of them if either the Indians or Zarzalo and his men realized that they knew one another. Quickly he took a cheroot from his pocket to mask the real reason for moving his hands. He brought the cheroot to his mouth and fumbled it clumsily as he put a finger across his lips and shook his head almost imperceptibly.

Ellen's brow wrinkled for a moment, then the frown vanished. She flicked both eyes closed, at the same time dropping her head in a quick nod to show that she understood. She moved her eyes away from Longarm at once and gazed fixedly ahead, her chin tilted upward defiantly.

Magro and Zarzalo had been inspecting Ellen. They put their heads together and whispered for a moment, then Magro told Pat-Cha-No, "*El jefe* say the woman is not much good, but he will talk to you about trading for her."

"It is good," Pat-Cha-No nodded. He drew the attention of his men with a gesture and signaled for them to move over to the side of the arc farthest from the area where Zarzalo's group was camped. "We will wait and drink whiskey until your wagons get here. Then we will talk of trading."

"Thought you said your men didn't trade with the Comanches," Longarm remarked to Lefty as they walked back toward the fire.

"We don't. Or we ain't, not before now," Lefty replied.

Morris put in, "These is the first bunch of Comanches that's ever come looking to trade."

"Then why'd Zarzalo spin that redskin them lies about having wagons coming with guns and whiskey?" Longarm asked.

"You'd have to ask him that. Why, shit, Custis! We never have had no wagons hauling stuff in here!"

"Them Comanches is apt to be riled when they find out Zarzalo's lying to 'em." Longarm frowned thoughtfully. "But maybe he's got some kind of trick in mind."

Exactly what kind of trick their leader had in mind was explained to them very soon. Zarzalo and Magro were the last to return; they'd remained standing where the parley had taken place, talking to one another—arguing, to judge from the angry gestures that Magro made from time to time. The Comanches had moved to the spot designated by Pat-Cha-No, and tethered their mounts. Longarm had watched them as closely as he could without giving any indication of his special interest in the Indians or their captive. Zarzalo motioned for the others to gather around him.

"I have changed our plans," he told them abruptly. "I did not expect these Indians."

"Wait a minute now!" Lefty broke in. "We rode a hell of a long ways to get here, Zarzalo. We ain't going to hightail outa here without the pay that you promised us!"

"Be silent, Lefty!" Zarzalo snapped. "I did not say we will not do as we intended. And you will be paid, I promise you." He waited, looking from one to another of the men, and when none of them objected further, he went on, "We will leave earlier than I had planned. As soon as it is dark, we will muffle

165

the hooves of our horses. One man at a time, we will lead the horses down the canyon far enough so the Indians will not hear us ride away—"

"Yeah," Lefty interrupted, a sneer in his voice. "I figured you'd come up with some scheme like that! Then we just fade away and forget the job we was going out on!"

"No!" Zarzalo shot back angrily. "When we are out of hearing of the Comanches, we will ride as I have told you before. But there is one change in the plan. Because we will be one man short, we will first go west to the new homestead, and when we are through there, we will attack the Guthrie ranch."

Morris frowned. "How'll we be a man short?"

"Someone must stay here to keep a fire burning and make some noise now and then," Zarzalo explained. Before any of them could ask further questions, he looked at Longarm. "You have not ridden with us before, Custis. You will stay behind and make the Comanches think we are all here."

Longarm had been trying to think of some means by which he could rescue Ellen Briscoe, and now he realized that Zarzalo's new plan was giving him what he wanted. He was too wise to accept the risky job of decoy without protesting, though.

"Now hold on there, Zarzalo!" he exclaimed. "I joined up to ride with you! I ain't figuring to play setting duck for a bunch of wild Comanches! No, sir!"

"If you are the man you pretend to be, you will have no trouble deceiving them," Zarzalo replied, a mixture of anger and persuasion in his tone. "We will ride slowly, and when you see it is safe for you to go, you will follow us."

"Not a chance!" Longarm said curtly, shaking his head. "I don't know the country here like you do. How in hell you expect me to find you in the dark?"

"It will be easy," Zarzalo shrugged. "The house at the new homestead will be burning before you catch up with us. A fire can be seen many miles here on the Llano Estacado. You will have a big one to guide you."

"I don't like that one damned bit! Seems like you're giving me the shitty end of the stick! Why don't we draw cards for it?" Longarm suggested.

"Sounds like a good enough scheme to me," Lefty announced. He looked at Morris and Perez. "How do you take it?"

Perez nodded agreement at once, and Morris joined him a few seconds later. Longarm kept his face fixed in an angry scowl to hide the pleasure that he felt at having Zarzalo solve the problem that had been puzzling him.

Drawing out his words reluctantly, Longarm said, "I guess I ain't got much choice but to go along, then. But if I'm going to be stuck with that kind of job, I ought to get paid extra for it!"

Zarzalo thought this over for a moment. "If Lefty and his friends do not object—" he began.

"We won't mind, if we don't get shorted too bad," Lefty said quickly. "I sorta think Custis is right."

"All right." Longarm nodded. "I'll take it on." Then, as though it were an afterthought, he said, "Wait a minute! What about that white woman them Comanches has got? What's going to happen to her?"

Without hesitation, Zarzalo replied, "Whatever the Comanches decide to do with her is no concern of ours. We did not ask them to bring her here."

Longarm lighted a cheroot while he made a show of thinking about Zarzalo's statement. Then he nodded slowly. "Well, I'll have to agree with you there. Anyhow, I sure as hell ain't going to worry about her. I got enough to do here the way it is."

"It is settled, then," Zarzalo announced. "Begin to get ready as soon as it is dark. Magro will go first, then Lefty and Perez and Morris, and I will be the last to leave. We will meet at Agua Toro Creek."

"You better tell me how to go to get to that homestead too," Longarm said. "I don't aim to go messing around in the dark in country I don't know."

"Before I go, I will tell you," Zarzalo promised. "There is much time for that."

During the next hour, while dusk settled in and the others moved with seeming casualness in making their preparations for a quick departure, Longarm studied the Comanche camp without seeming to do so. There was very little to see. The Indians had set up a picket line for their horses and kindled a fire at the deepest belly of the arc that swept in from the main canyon, and for the most part they simply squatted around it, talking.

Straining his eyes through the gathering dusk, he saw at last where they had put Ellen. She was lashed to a high, thin splinter of stone that stuck at an angle out of the wall of the arc, a snag that was high enough to prevent her from working the loop of the rope over its peak, yet low enough to allow her to sit on the ground at its base. So far as he could tell from a distance, her gag had not been removed.

Time seemed to drag more slowly than usual while he waited. The first stars appeared, bright pinpoints in a deep blue velvet sky, and the night-hush settled down. The small fire Zarzalo had kindled cast a glow only a few yards around it. Following the instructions Zarzalo had given him after describing the route he must take to reach the homestead, Longarm walked slowly between the blaze and the Comanche camp. The dark, humped figures of the squatting Indians showed as black silhouettes against their own bigger fire.

One by one the Comancheros slipped away, until only Zarzalo and Longarm were left. The Indians gave no indication that they had noticed anything amiss. Zarzalo intercepted Longarm as he walked in front of the fire, and stopped him.

"We will talk for a moment. Let the Comanches see that more than one man is here, before I go," he said. "You have no more anger that I have given you this job to do, Custis?"

"Hell, I didn't get mad but for a minute. Anyhow, it looks like this scheme of yours is working out."

"It will be safe for you to leave in another hour. With the directions I have given you, the homestead should be easy to find."

"You're pulling out now?"

"Yes. Do your job, Custis. You will be well paid for it!"

Longarm nodded. Zarzalo turned and walked away. Longarm stood where he was for a moment, listening, but he heard no noise that would carry as far as the Comanche camp to betray Zarzalo's departure.

Well, old son, he told himself as he walked behind the small fire, *you got your real job to do now. And you damned well better get at it, before some of them Comanches gets up a thirst and strays down here looking for whiskey!*

Chapter 16

Since the moment when Pat-Cha-No yanked the flour sack away from Ellen Briscoe's face, Longarm had been trying to think of a scheme to get her free. After Zarzalo had outlined his new plan for the night's activity, Longarm's concentration had doubled. He realized that the plan he now began to put into effect was chancy at best, but it was the only one he'd been able to work out.

He went to the fire and added two sticks of wood from the diminishing supply to the waning coals. Both of the iron pots were empty; he made a fast, silent trip to the stream to fill them with water, and put them on the fire. From his pocket he took the small sack of ground-up hot red pepper he'd slipped out of Zarzalo's saddlebags when the man was having a last private talk with Magro. He emptied the sacks into the water, trying to divide the pepper in ratio to the different sizes of the two vessels.

From his own saddlebags Longarm took the quart of pure grain alcohol the stableman at Fort Elliott had given him to use in place of horse liniment, and poured it into the pots, dividing it as he had the pepper.

He tested the water with a fingertip. Its temperature seemed to him about right, just warm enough to insure a good blending of the alcohol and red pepper. He smiled.

It sure ought to be strong enough to get a dozen Comanches so drunk they'll be a mite careless, but not so drunk they can't get around.

Carrying the pots by their bails, he stepped back to his saddlebags and took out the opened bottle of Daugherty's Private Stock. The bottle was not quite half full. He uncorked it and took a healthy swallow before dividing what remained of the liquor between the two pots.

"Sure is a sad waste of good drinking whiskey," he said regretfully as he stirred the Daugherty's into the mixture. "But this popskull's got to smell enough like real liquor to fool them Comanches into thinking it's at least as good as the stuff them whiskey ranches in the Nation puts out."

More than one of Longarm's cases had taken him into the No Man's Land that bordered the Indian Nation, and he'd encountered some of the products of a few of the scores of illicit stills that were in operation there, as well as in the Nation itself.

Bending down, Longarm smelled the brew he'd concocted. Its fumes hit his nose like the breath of a sick skunk. He dipped a finger into the liquid and touched it to his tongue, gasped and spat, then hurriedly lighted a cheroot.

"It'll do," he muttered. "It'll *have* to do, seeing as I ain't got anything more to put into it. Well, hell, after they swill down a swallow or so, it won't matter all that much, of course."

Picking up the pots, he started toward the Comanches' campfire, a hundred yards away.

Hearing his boot soles scraping on the ground, the Indians who had been hunkered down around their fire got up, and when Longarm came into the circle of light cast by the flickering flames, and they saw the pots he carried, they crowded around him, chattering to one another in the harsh, guttural Comanche tongue.

Longarm did not say anything to them, but quickly counted and found that all twelve of them were there, which meant that no one was guarding Ellen or keeping watch over the picket line. He was careful to show no special interest in that area as he looked around, trying to single out Pat-Cha-No's face in the gloom. He saw the leader at last, pushing his way through his men.

"You bring us food?" he asked, peering at the pots, which

were half hidden in the shifting shadows cast by the group.

"No. I got you some whiskey," Longarm replied. "We ain't got much, but our chief said we ought to share it with our Comanche brothers."

"That is good," Pat-Cha-No said. "We have been dry today. But why did your chief not come with you?"

"He said you'll have to excuse him tonight, he don't feel so good. Got a bellyache or something. He was going to bed when I left, but he said to tell you he'll drink with you tomorrow, when the wagons gets here."

Pat-Cha-No did not question Longarm's quickly improvised reply; the Comanche leader was too interested in sampling what he could smell in the pots. Leaning forward, he sniffed the surface of the brew Longarm had concocted, then bent down and tilted the pot while he took two big gulps.

"*Ai-ee!*" Pat-Cha-No exclaimed, gasping. "This is good whiskey! It is very strong!"

"Well, you and your friends enjoy it," Longarm said, holding the pots out to the Comanches on either side of him. To Pat-Cha-No he added, "There'll be a lot more whiskey tomorrow. Now I done what my chief said to do, so I'll bid you good night."

Longarm waited until he was outside the circle of firelight before he stopped and looked back. He shielded his eyes and tried to see if Ellen was still tied to the stone shaft, but the night was too dark for him to make out anything beyond the range of the firelight.

He turned his attention to the Comanches. They were passing the pots from hand to hand, gulping the potent alcoholic mixture. Longarm decided that by the time he was ready to return for Ellen, the Indians' usually sharp senses would be dulled sufficiently to allow him to move around close to their fire with reasonable assurance that they would not detect him. He went on back to the deserted Comanchero camp and gathered up his gear, then saddled the piebald. Leaving the horse tethered, Longarm went to the cache and opened the box in which he'd seen the two pistols and the loose ammunition.

Working in the dark, depending only on his sense of touch, it took Longarm what seemed to be a long while to fumble through the mixed-up ammunition until he'd found enough cartridges of the right caliber to fill the five-round chambers in each of the two revolvers.

It'd be a sight easier if you could just toss a handful of these

171

shells on that fire, old son, he told himself as he worked matching cartridges to cylinders in the blackness. *But that wouldn't fool them damn Comanches for a minute. A cartridge that's set off from getting hot don't make the same bang as it does when it goes off in a gun's cylinder. So take your time and do the job right, because you sure as hell ain't going to get but one chance to pull off this stunt. If it don't work the first time around, it ain't going to work at all.*

When he'd finally filled the cylinders, Longarm carried the guns back to the fire and, using a stick of wood as his shovel, scraped away at the live coals until he'd formed a flat bed of red embers. Longarm laid the pistols on the glowing coals and covered them hastily with more hot coals, tossed the piece of wood on top of the mound, and hurried to his horse. Hugging the base of the canyon wall, he led the piebald as quietly as posible toward the Comanche camp.

Looking at the Indians silhouetted against the waning flames of their fire, he could tell that his popskull brew was lasting longer than he'd thought it would, and that the alcohol-heavy mixture was already having its effect. The Comanches were still passing the pots of liquor from hand to hand, but some of them were beginning to stagger.

As Longarm watched, one man fell on his face, then got to his knees and stayed there, swaying from side to side. Occasionally one of them would let out a garbled, shaky whoop when a swallow of the liquor hit bottom, but most of them were simply drinking as much as they could manage to put away, as often as they got their hands on one of the pots.

Longarm had covered almost half the distance to the Comanche picket line when the first cartridge got hot enough to explode. There was a burst of sparks from the coals in which he'd buried the guns, followed at once by the bang of another cartridge going off. Then the night was torn by a barrage of gunfire as the shells that were still left in the cylinders of the two revolvers exploded in quick succession.

Among the Comanches, an explosion of a different kind had started when the first gunshot cut the night. The liquor was forgotten. The Indians who were holding the pots dropped them to join their companions in scrabbling for their guns. Within the space of two or three minutes the Comanche camp was deserted. Hurrying to cover the remaining distance to where the Indians' horses were tethered, Longarm could see silhouettes of the running Comanches beginning to show up against the dim glow of the few coals that were left from the fire the exploding shells had scattered.

Reaching the picket line, Longarm discovered that fate had dealt him a mixed hand. Feeling his way among the horses tied along the stretched, staked-out lariat, Longarm felt a surge of relief when he discovered that Ellen's mount had not been unsaddled. He was not as pleased to find that the Indians had not taken the saddle-pads off the backs of their horses, either. He slashed the picket line with his knife and, while holding tight to the reins of Ellen's horse, started the Comanche ponies bolting.

At the stone needle to which Ellen Briscoe was still tied, Longarm cut the ropes holding her and then freed her mouth of the cruelly tight gag. She flung her arms around Longarm's neck and sagged down as her stiff muscles refused to support her. She was trying to speak to him, but her tongue was cramped and sore, her lips numb. All that she could manage was an incoherent mumble.

"Don't try to talk," Longarm told her. He took Ellen's arm and half led, half carried her to her horse. While he was helping her into the saddle he said, "It'll only take them Comanches a few minutes to find out they been fooled. When they do, they're going to be buzzing around us like a nest of burnt-out wasps."

Ellen replied with a few strangled, unrecognizable sounds, but Longarm could see the white blur of her face bobbing up and down as she nodded to show him she'd understood.

Slipping her booted feet into the stirrups, Longarm went on, "Now you just keep even with me when we start out of here. We'll go a little ways, far enough to shake off the Comanches, then we'll hole up and rest a spell."

Again, Ellen nodded. Longarm swung onto the piebald and jabbed its flank sharply with his toe. The horse took off, and Ellen got her mount into motion. Riding abreast, they gained speed as they moved across the level ground that lay inside the sweeping curve of the canyon walls. They heard the angry yelling of the Comanches when the thudding hoofbeats drew the Indians' attention, but by that time they were out of the sweep of the arc, and onto the floor of the canyon itself.

Staying close to the banks of the stream, on the level ground swept clear when Yellow Horse Creek was in flood, Longarm kept their horses at a gallop as long as he dared. He judged that they had a start of perhaps ten minutes on the frustrated, angry Comanches, and strained his eyes in searching the steep walls of the canyon, trying to pierce the darkness and find a cut that was wide enough and deep enough to conceal them. The horses were breathing hard before he spotted a gap, a black streak that cut the lighter walls. He yanked the reins and turned the piebald toward the opening. They splashed across the shallow creek, and moments later were hidden in the dark mouth of a broad gully.

Ellen's voice was still unsteady and rasping, and she was sobbing as much as speaking when she said, "Oh God, Longarm! I don't know how I can thank you for getting me away from those Indians! I've never been so scared in my life!"

"You know you don't need to thank me, Ellen," he said, then asked her, "They didn't hurt you, did they?"

"No." Ellen's voice was calming down now. In a matter-of-fact tone she went on, "They didn't rape me or anything like that. Maybe they had to keep moving, and didn't have time. We only made two stops all the way down here from the Canadian."

"You're tired out, but don't let up yet. We still ain't off free and clear, you know."

"I'll be all right, Longarm. Oh, my mouth's still sore, and my arms and legs are stinging me, but I think I'm more scared than hurt."

"You can forget about being scared," he assured her. "They ain't apt to see us in here. Likely they'll just go on past."

Ellen sat silent for a moment, then said, "When I saw you with those men, I knew you'd come for me, but it seemed like I waited forever."

"I couldn't get there no sooner. It took a lot of luck for me to get there at all."

"No. I know better. You're the kind of man who makes his own luck, Longarm."

Taking advantage of the limited time he knew they had before the Comanches would catch up with them, Longarm lighted a cheroot before asking Ellen, "How'd them Comanches get hold of you, anyhow?"

"I—I don't really know. I was riding, but I'd only gone three or four miles from the LX. There wasn't any sign of them, and nowhere for them to be hiding, just flat prairie.

Then, all of a sudden, there they were."

"Comanches have got a way of doing things like that, from what I've heard about 'em. They—" Longarm stopped short as the noise of hoofbeats reached his ears. He cautioned Ellen, "Sit quiet now, and keep your horse on a tight rein. Sounds to me like the Comanches is getting close."

They sat in silence, listening to the approaching hoofbeats. Longarm drew his Winchester from its saddle scabbard, though he didn't think he'd need it. He was sure the Comanches were still drunk enough to gallop past them, thinking only of the chase. If they'd been sober, the Indians would have advanced more slowly, investigating every possible hiding place, and their keen eyes would have missed nothing.

Beside him, Longarm heard Ellen give an involuntary gasp as the hoofbeats grew louder. He said, "Now don't start worrying, Ellen. Chances are they'll ride right on by us."

"I know I'm being foolish, but I can't help it."

"It'll likely take you a little while to get over it, I guess. Now hush and stay still. They're almost here."

Ellen reached across the narrow space that separated them, and clasped Longarm's wrist. He took her hand in his and held it, feeling her tremble as the thudding hoofbeats came closer, until the Comanches were opposite the mouth of the gully.

Longarm released her hand from Ellen's grasp and held the Winchester ready. They watched the dark figures of the Indians streaking past on the other side of the creek, intent on their chase. If the Comanches saw the gully that sheltered Longarm and Ellen, they did not break pace to investigate it. Over the fading hoofbeats of the Indian ponies, Longarm heard Ellen exhale the breath she'd been holding, a deep sigh of relief.

"It wasn't as bad as I was afraid it'd be," she said. "We can ride on anytime you're ready, Longarm."

"We'll sit here a minute. Let the Comanches get a good lead on us. But we'll have to move on pretty soon. That bunch of men I was with is up ahead, and I'd like to catch up with 'em in time to maybe save some innocent people a lot of grief."

"Whatever you say," Ellen told him.

"If you want to stretch your legs, we can dismount and walk around a minute or two," he suggested.

"I need to, if you don't mind."

Longarm suddenly understood. He dismounted and helped Ellen out of her saddle. She said, "I'll be right back." He heard her footsteps fading away, then in a few minutes she returned.

"I can walk by myself now," she said. Her voice was more normal, she sounded almost cheerful. She came to Longarm and put her arms around him, turning up her face. He bent to kiss her, a kiss without passion. In the dimness he could see Ellen's smile as their lips parted.

She said, "I guess I needed that too, to prove to myself I'm still alive. Whenever you want to, we can ride on."

They left the cleft and rode back out into the main canyon. Longarm set a steady pace, a deceptively slow, easy canter that the horses could keep up without strain and that rapidly ate up the miles. They'd been riding for an hour or more when he saw that the canyon walls no longer towered quite as high above them. As they forged ahead, the walls on both sides opened wider and the land seemed to rise upward. Then they were out of the canyon and on the level prairie again. They moved on steadily, keeping Yellow Horse Creek on their left. A strange glow began growing in the sky on their right.

"If that's dawn, I'm all turned around," Ellen said. "And it's been the shortest night I've ever lived through."

"You ain't turned around, Ellen," Longarm told her. "That ain't sunup you're looking at."

"But it looks to me as though it's getting brighter."

"Only because we're getting closer to it."

"If it's not sunrise, then it's a fire."

"That's what I figure it is."

Longarm's curt reply discouraged Ellen from asking any more questions. She followed him without a word when he turned the piebald in the direction of the narrow line of light. The glow took on color as they rode on. It became a bright orange glare that appeared to be pulsing in the sky.

After they'd been riding for several minutes, she asked in a low, quiet voice, "It's a ranch house, isn't it, Longarm?"

"More'n likely it's a little homestead on a new claim. I was hoping I'd get there in time, but it looks like I'm too late."

"You know all about it, then? You knew it was going to happen and you stopped to save me from the Comanches?"

"Getting you away from them didn't hold me back none, Ellen. Don't go blaming yourself for a thing. I had to move the Comanches out before I could leave that place, and getting you away from 'em was the quickest way to do it."

"Will we get there in time to help?"

"Not much chance. When you're riding over this kind of prairie, you can see about seven miles. That fire's a good ten miles away. That'd be more'n an hour's ride, unless we risk riding down our horses. Wind-broke nags won't help us, so we'll just go on like we are now."

They rode on in silence, watching the glow as it began to fade until it was little more than a bright spot on the horizon's rim. As the miles faded steadily behind them, the night began to lighten. Dawn's thin white line appeared on the eastern rim of the prairie as the stars faded almost imperceptibly. They'd covered about half the distance that Longarm had estimated lay between them and the burning house when they heard the shooting. Ellen flinched when she heard the first reports, distant in the stillness of the wide plains.

"That—those are guns I hear, aren't they, Longarm?" she asked hesitantly.

"They're guns, right enough. Sounds to me like the Comanches caught up with that bunch I been riding with."

"Aren't you going to do something about it? You're a U.S. marshal!"

"That's dogs killing dogs, Ellen," Longarm said quietly.

By now the sky was light enough for him to see Ellen's face wrinkling into a puzzled frown. She shook her head. "I guess I don't understand."

"My bet is that the Comanches have run into the men that set that homestead on fire, and they're killing each other off. I wouldn't lift a finger to help either outfit, even if I could."

"What a strange thing to say! I thought your job was to keep the peace."

"You ain't been out here but a little while, Ellen," Longarm told her soberly. "If you had, you'd have learned that the only way to keep the peace in country like this is to get rid of the ones that break it."

They rode on silently while the gunshots diminished in volume and the short volleys that had sounded at first dwindled to widely spaced, individual shots. Longarm could almost chart the progress of the fracas when the high, sharp barking of rifles was replaced by the deeper-toned booming of heavy-caliber revolvers. After a short while the shots no longer sounded, and quiet reclaimed the night.

"Is—is it over?" Ellen asked hesitantly.

"Sounds like it is. We'll find out soon enough."

They followed the almost invisible glow of the dying fire until they could see what was left of the homestead, a few lines of flickering flames along what had been the rafters and joists of a small dwelling. Longarm reined in before they got close to the ruins.

"Maybe you better stay here while I go take a look. There ain't a thing we can do about what's over and done with, and there might be some sights in them coals that ain't right pretty."

"No. I want to see what it's like for myself," she replied, her firm determination showing in her voice.

"All right. We'll both look, then."

They rode as close to the smoldering debris as the heat would allow them. All that had survived of the house was the stove. It stood erect, its pipes bent and crumbled around it. Dark red coals glowed along the heavier timbers that had not yet been completely consumed. Lying along one outside wall was a long, coal-covered lump. Even without the rifle barrel that protruded from it, Longarm would have recognized the form hidden by the coals as having once been human.

He did not point out the form to Ellen. His eyes searched the rectangle of smoldering coals until he found a second long hump, near the center of what had been the house. He said nothing about this one, either.

Ellen turned away. "What kind of animals would do a thing like this?" she asked, riding beside Longarm as he guided the piebald away from the ruins, heading west.

"About all you could call 'em is human animals, I guess."

"I'm glad there's somebody like you trying to lock them up," Ellen said. Then she added soberly, "And I'm glad it's not my job. I don't see how you stand it."

"Somebody's got to do it," he pointed out. He waited for Ellen to reply, but she said nothing.

Longarm zigzagged along until he found the hoofmarks he was looking for. They were faint on the baked soil, but he followed them well enough, and they gave him the direction the raiders had taken when they left the homestead.

After Ellen had followed his zigzag course for several minutes, her curiosity could no longer be held back. She turned to Longarm and said, "I don't suppose it matters, because I'm going right along with you, but where are we going now?"

"I got to find where that shooting we heard took place and

178

see what it was was all about, even if I've already got a pretty good idea. If you're getting tired, we can stop and rest awhile before we do any more riding, though."

"After seeing what was left of that house, I don't have much appetite. And my nerves are so tight I couldn't rest if we did stop, so let's go on."

They did not have far to ride. In the distance they saw riderless horses, some standing, some moving aimlessly around. Drawing closer, they could see sprawled bodies scattered among the clumps of thin, high grass that dotted the prairie. Before any details of the scene became visible, Longarm reined in.

He said, "What's up ahead of us is going to be even uglier to look at than what you seen back at the homestead, Ellen. You sure you want to look at it?"

Ellen pressed her lips together for a moment as she gazed at the bodies strewn on the ground. After a moment she said stubbornly, "Yes. It might make me sick, but I do. People from where I was brought up don't know that things like this still happen here in the West. Yes, I want to go with you."

Longarm nodded. "As long as you're sure."

He twitched the piebald's reins and led the way to the scene of the fight.

Chapter 17

As Longarm and Ellen rode closer to the still forms that lay
in clumsy sprawls, the horses that the dead men had ridden
began to shift around. Longarm counted them; there were three
with saddles on and nine bearing the doubled pads of hide that
marked them as Comanche ponies.

*That means two of the bunch I was after got away, and
three Comanches must've made it off free*, Longarm thought.

He did not pass his conclusion on to Ellen. She was sitting
rigidly on her horse, her back ramrod-straight, her eyes fixed
on the ground, her lips compressed so tightly that the skin
around her mouth showed white.

Longarm was studying the terrain, visualizing the way the
fight must have gone from the pattern in which the bodies lay.
It was not hard for him to deduce what had happened. Zarzalo
and his men had been riding east, on the way to the Guthrie
ranch, when they encountered the Comanches. The Indians,
galloping south from the mouth of Yellow Horse Canyon, had
cut across their path at an angle from the north.

There were three Comanche bodies lying to the north in an
almost straight line, an indication that Zarzalo's force had
brought them down with rifle fire while the Indians were still

closing in. Apparently, Zarzalo's riders had never been able to get into a group. The Comanches had kept them separated, and the encounter had turned into several individual combats, two or three of the Indians against each of the men with Zarzalo, for the bodies were clumped in separate groups of two or three or four, the groups spaced widely apart.

Longarm and Ellen reached the first body; while they were still several yards away it was obvious that the corpse was that of a Comanche. Getting closer, Longarm saw that a bullet had taken him in the chest. He lay on his back, arms sprawled, a pistol beside his right hand. Longarm did not stop, but merely glanced at the contorted face to be sure that dead man was not Pat-Cha-No.

A dozen yards from the dead Comanche lay Morris, his body twisted at the waist, his face turned up, the dead man's glazed eyes staring sightlessly at the brightening sky. Morris's hand still grasped his revolver. He had not been scalped. Longarm rode on, past the body of another Comanche that lay some distance from the other corpses, to the huddled heap that had been Perez.

He was lying facedown, the back of his shirt one massive bloodstain, his rifle beside him. His hat was still on his head, his revolver had never been drawn from its holster. There were no Comanche bodies close by; Perez had fallen early, Longarm thought, before the Indians closed in, but he must have been able to keep firing, to judge from the position of the Comanche corpse that lay just beyond him. This dead Comanche was not Pat-Cha-No, either.

Though there were other Comanche dead lying ahead, Longarm had concluded by now that he would not fine Pat-Cha-No's body among them. As their leader, he was the only one who could have stopped the fight and ordered the three surviving Comanches to retreat. And only Pat-Cha-No could have commanded that no scalps be taken, that the weapons of both the Indians and whites who had fallen be left behind.

Fifty yards to the north lay the body of a dead horse, with several human bodies around it. The corpse of an Indian was draped over the fallen horse and hid the face of whoever its rider had been. He reined the piebald closer, and recognized the horse as Lefty's. Though he was certain the dead white man must be Lefty, Longarm felt compelled to confirm his conclusion. With Ellen following, he rode up to the scene.

Lefty had died hard. His body lay twisted under the corpse of a Comanche, and a second dead Comanche lay beyond the tangle that marked the end of what must have been a last-ditch battle, Lefty against the two Indians. Longarm rode only near enough to be sure of the dead man's identity, then pulled the piebald's head around and started for the last of the huddled dead.

Four more corpses lay ahead, three of them Comanches. The bodies were some distance from where Perez lay, and as they rode toward the dead, Longarm glanced at Ellen. She had not spoken since she'd insisted on accompanying Longarm. He saw that her expression had not changed. Her body was still rigidly erect and her face frozen and immobile.

They reached the last cluster of corpses and pulled up. The three dead Comanches lay in a semicircle, and one of the Indians had dropped only an arm's length from Zarzalo's inert form. Zarzalo's eyes were closed, and bullet wounds showed in his chest and abdomen. His rifle lay a few feet distant, and his old Volcanic lever-action repeater was still in his hand.

Longarm turned in his saddle to tell Ellen that they'd seen enough, and to ask her to ride away from the scene of the fight while he rounded up the horses of the Comancheros and put the bodies on them. What he was about to say froze on his lips when he saw Ellen's face. Her eyes were fixed on the ground, and her face was a ghastly white.

"He moved!" she gasped breathlessly. "He's not dead! I saw him move!"

Longarm swiveled, his eyes following Ellen's gaze. He found himself staring into Zarzalo's open eyes, and knew that when he'd first looked, those eyes had been closed. While he was still staring, Zarzalo opened his right hand, letting the pistol fall from it, and began to raise his arm.

Leaping from his horse, Longarm stepped up to the recumbent Zarzalo and bent over him. Zarzalo's effort to raise his arm had failed, but Longarm saw his chest heave and heard him gasp as the Comanchero leader drew air into his lungs.

Without looking around, Longarm called, "Quick, Ellen! Hand me my canteen! He's still breathing!"

Zarzalo's eyelids fluttered shut, then opened slowly, and he looked up at Longarm. He tried to speak, but only a few weak coughs came from his lips, followed by a trickle of bright blood. His face twisted in a sudden contortion and his eyes closed once more. Ellen handed Longarm the canteen; he poured water into his cupped palm and wiped it over Zarzalo's face. A few seconds passed while Zarzalo lay motionless, his eyes still shut. Then they opened slowly and he looked at Longarm.

"Don't try to talk," Longarm said. He uncapped the canteen and held it to Zarzalo's lips. "Here. I'll pour a little bit of water in your mouth, and you try to swallow it."

As Longarm let the water trickle slowly into Zarzalo's mouth, the wounded man's throat jerked convulsively, but he managed to swallow most of the water.

"I'm going to lay you back down and see how bad you're hurt," Longarm said. He started to lower Zarzalo to the ground, but the Comanchero shook his head weakly.

"Don't...bother," he managed to say. "You can't...help me...Custis. Seen enough men...shot...to know...I'm dying..."

Longarm had also seen men shot. He knew that Zarzalo was right, even though he would not say so. Instead he said, "You ain't dead yet. And as long as you ain't—"

Again, Zarzalo moved his head from side to side. "Can't waste...time..." he gasped. "Want whiskey..." his words trailed off into unintelligible gibberish as his breath trailed out in a sigh, and his eyes drooped shut once more.

"There's a bottle of whiskey in my saddlebag," Longarm told Ellen. "Hand it to me, fast as you can!"

Letting Zarzalo down to lie on the ground, Longarm took the unopened bottle of Daugherty's that Ellen gave him, hit the bottom of the bottle firmly on the butt of his palm to start the cork, then yanked it out with his strong teeth. He pulled Zarzalo's chin down and dribbled a small stream of the rye into his mouth.

Zarzalo's body shook and his throat spasmed, but he swallowed the whiskey. His eyes fluttered open and he lay for a few moments staring up at the bright morning sky, then struggled to get up. Longarm helped him by slipping an arm under his shoulders and raising him until he was half sitting, half reclining. Zarzalo's eyes focused on the whiskey bottle and Longarm held it to his mouth again while he took another sip.

"Don't ask...questions..." he whispered, his voice so weak that Longarm had to bend forward to catch his words.

183

"Just let me . . . talk." Longarm nodded and the dying man went on, "Aguierre started this . . . my half-brother . . . legitimate son . . . I'm the . . . bastard." His head sagged as he fought for breath. Longarm put the bottle to his lips again, but Zarzalo moved his head to one side. "Don't waste . . . good whiskey . . . on a . . . dead man."

"Never mind the whiskey. Go on and talk," Longarm told him.

"Father treated us . . . alike," Zarzalo whispered. "Feliciano and . . . me. Clothes, money, college . . . until he died. Then old . . . family custom . . . no bastards in . . . wills."

Zarzalo stopped and closed his eyes again, his chest heaving. Longarm forced another swallow of whiskey down his throat, and his irregular breathing became smoother. He opened his eyes and began talking again.

"Feliciano . . . paid my way . . . took care of me until he got tired . . . quit supporting bastard. No place in world for . . . man like me . . . never learned how to work." Zarzalo stopped to gasp for breath, then continued, "Mistake . . . was coming back. Got me started . . . doing dirty work. Lately . . . water underground . . . make Llano Estacado . . . green. Make Feliciano . . . richer."

Zarzalo's breathing faltered once again, but when Longarm tried to pour more whiskey into his mouth, he turned his head away as he had before. He lay quietly for a moment, his eyes closed, his breathing labored and shallow. He recovered his strength more slowly this time, and did not show as much vitality when he began talking.

"You don't owe me . . . Custis," he said. "But humor . . . my vanity. See me buried . . . at Plaza Aguierre . . . collect pay from . . . Feliciano. Find Magro. If he's still alive . . . he'll be at plaza . . . he can tell . . . whole story . . . help you get pay . . . from Feliciano." He paused again, his chest heaving as he tried to breathe. A bit more strength flowed back into his frame and he went on, "Tell Magro . . . I wanted you . . ."

Zarzalo's body arched. He began to cough. Gouts of blood gushed from his mouth. He twitched, stiffened, and then went limp under Longarm's supporting hand, his sightless eyes staring up into the sunrise.

Longarm lowered Zarzalo's body to the earth and stood up. Ellen had been standing just behind him. He took a cheroot from his pocket and lighted it before he turned to face her.

"There wasn't anything anybody could have done for him,"

he said, wondering why he felt any explanation was needed. "Not all shot up the way he was." He lifted the bottle of Daugherty's and looked at it. "When I was a little tad down in West Virginia, my mother always said 'ladies first.' Now I'm going to have me a drink. Before I do, you feel like one too?"

"Yes. Too much has happened too fast for me to understand, Longarm. I suppose a drink will help, even if I already feel a little bit giddy."

Longarm handed her the bottle and picked up his canteen. He held the canteen out to her after she'd choked down a swallow of the rye. Ellen shook her head.

"My father drank whiskey straight, like you do, Longarm, and he had a sort of saying like your mother did. But his was, 'Why start a fire if you're going to put it out right away.'"

Longarm took his drink and puffed meditatively on his cheroot for a moment. He said, "You've done a lot of riding, Ellen. I know you're tired, but do you feel like you can stand a little bit more?"

"Since that's the only way we can get away from here," she replied, "I guess I'll have to stand it. This isn't the most pleasant place in the world right now."

"I'd take you straight back to the LX, if I could, but I've got to stay here and close out my case. It won't take much longer, though, after what Zarzalo told me."

Ellen frowned thoughtfully. "I heard most of what he said, Longarm. It didn't make much sense to me. Did you understand what he was trying to tell you?"

"Some of it didn't make much sense to me, either. He done me a real favor, though. I got the lead now I've been looking for all along. But I guess that won't make much sense to you, either. I'll tell you the whole story, or as much of it as I can, while we're riding."

Her eyes swept over the seemingly endless prairie that surrounded them. "Riding to where?"

"That Plaza Aguierre that Zarzalo was talking about. It ain't too far from here. I'll hurry up what I got to do, and I guess it'd be a good idea to hustle around and get it done quick. Comanches generally pick up their dead after a fight, and what's left of Pat-Cha-No's bunch might be heading back here right now."

"You're going to—" Ellen stopped and indicated the bodies.

Longarm nodded. "They wasn't much account, them fellows, but a man's got a right to be buried decent. If the Comanches come back, they'd likely scalp 'em and cut 'em up."

"Then I'll help you."

"It ain't your job. I'll tell you what. You get on your horse right now and start riding west. Before you're out of sight, I'll have everything done I need to do. Then I'll catch up with you."

"I'd rather stay and help you than ride away alone."

Longarm shook his head. "I misdoubt you can, Ellen. It ain't a nice job, rolling dead men up in their blankets and loading 'em across a horse's back. It ain't something a young woman like you are would have much stomach for."

"My stomach's stronger than you think, but I do need something to help settle it after looking at this. If I can have one more drink of that whiskey, and one of your skinny cigars, I'll be able to help. Just tell me what has to be done."

"I'll make you a deal, Ellen. There's three horses with saddles on 'em in the bunch that's scattered around. You mount up and lead them three horses to where I'll need 'em, and I'll do the rest."

Starting with Lefty, whose saddle gear was at the spot where he'd died, Longarm rolled the four bodies in their own blankets and slung them across the backs of the horses as Ellen led them up. Perez's and Zarzalo's mounts had lariats draped on the saddle pommels; he cut one into lengths to lash the bodies in place, and used the other for a lead rope. The sun mounted higher as they worked; it was morning before he and Ellen started west, the three horses trailing them, carrying their grisly burdens.

They pushed steadily along through the day, making only two stops. One was to let the horses drink at the Lagunas Coronadas waterhole, the only watering place shown on Longarm's military map. The other was a brief halt at noon to rest the animals and to eat dry rations from Longarm's saddlebags.

As they rode, Longarm gave Ellen an abbreviated account of the case he was now close to bringing to an end. When he'd finished, she took a sweeping look at the parched country on all sides of them and shook her head.

"I can understand why water's so important here, Longarm," she said. "But is it important enough to kill people for? And burn out little homesteads like the one we saw?"

"It wouldn't be to me," he replied. "Maybe to somebody

like that Aguierre fellow. I don't rightly see what he's up to yet. But Magro's an old man, he's been here a long time, I'd judge. If I find him, maybe he can tell me something I don't know."

Leading the three laden horses made their progress slow, and it was late afternoon before Longarm and Ellen mounted the long upward slant that led to the Plaza Aguierre. They'd ridden for the last few miles in silence. Ellen was sagging in her saddle, her head falling forward occasionally as she dropped off to sleep. Longarm, too, was feeling the drain of twenty-four hours of almost uninterrupted activity. He pulled up the piebald as they reached the top of the rise, and they sat for several moments looking down on the big, white, turreted hacienda that towered above its encircling wall.

"Why, that's a palace!" Ellen gasped, surprise overcoming her sleepiness. "How could they build such a huge place out here in the middle of nowhere?"

"Slaves don't draw wages, Ellen," Longarm pointed out. "And all they needed to make 'dobe bricks was dirt and water and straw. I guess they took their time too. A place that big wasn't built all of a piece."

"It still took a lot of work and a lot of time," Ellen said. "I thought the LX main house was pretty nice, to be so far away from everything, but this is—well, I can't quite believe it."

"Oh, it's real enough." Longarm lighted a cheroot and took a few puffs before he went on. "Now, when we go down there, I'll ask you to remember what I told you about this case I'm on. When I stopped here before, I let on that my name's Custis, which it is, my first name, anyhow. I didn't say I was a U.S. marshal, and I don't want to talk about my job, at least not yet."

Ellen nodded. "I understand what you're saying, and most of what you're not saying. At least I think I do. Don't worry, Longarm. All women are devious, and I can keep quiet if that's what you want me to do."

"I won't ask you to lie for me," Longarm told her seriously. "But if you just don't say too much, I'll be right obliged." He toed the piebald and they started down the slope to the Plaza Aguierre.

Maldonado must have been informed of their approach, for

187

he was waiting for them at the gate. He looked silently for a moment at the blanket-shrouded bodies and stared hard at Ellen, his scarred face as expressionless as a statue carved from stone.

He said, "I did not expect to see you here again, Custis."

"There wasn't much of anyplace else for me to go, Maldonado," Longarm replied levelly. "You see what happened out there on the prairie. Those men hanging over the horses was jumped by a bunch of Comanches. I guess I'm the only one left, and we got some business to settle between us."

"Yes. We will get to that later." Maldonado looked again at the bodies, then fixed his eyes on Ellen. "I can understand what you say about the Comanches. The woman, though—I do not know where you found her or why you have brought her here, but that can wait until later, as well."

"I can tell you now, just as easy. The Comanches took her prisoner up by the Canadian. I got her away from 'em before . . ." He jerked his head back to indicate the bodies. "You sure wouldn't expect me to come away and leave her by herself on the prairie, would you?"

Maldonado said quickly, "This is not the time or place for your explanations, Custis!"

Longarm went on as though the *mayordomo* had not spoken. "Now if you don't want us here, we'll ride off and I'll come back by myself later on. It'd put me out some to do that, so I'd just as soon get my business settled and move along. If you—"

"Enough, Custis!" Maldonado interrupted angrily. "The hospitality of Plaza Aguierre will not be lacking. I will see that she is shown to a room while you lead the horses back to the stables. Men are waiting there to unload them. You will occupy the same room you used before. Esteban will be there to attend you. Now go!"

With a reassuring nod, Longarm told Ellen, "You go along with Mr. Maldonado. I won't be too far off, if you need me."

Ellen dismounted, and Longarm led her horse with the others around the big house and back to the stables. There were a half-dozen men waiting, and Maldonado had apparently told them exactly what to do, after he'd seen Longarm approaching. The men unloaded the horses, placing the bundled corpses inside a shed next to the stables. Longarm waited until his saddlebags had been taken off the piebald, slung the bags over his shoulder, took his Winchester from the saddle scabbard, and walked back to the hacienda. As Maldonado had promised, Esteban was waiting for him at the door.

"Bienvenido, Señor Custis!" the manservant exclaimed, taking Longarm's saddlebags and rifle. "Come, I take you upstairs."

As they reached the head of the stairway, Longarm saw a maidservant carrying buckets of water into the room across the hall from the open door of the bedroom he'd occupied during his first stop at the plaza. He stepped past Esteban and reached the door before it closed. Ellen was standing on a chair, looking out the high window. She looked around and saw Longarm.

"Oh, Longarm!" She sighed in relief. "I—well, this big house, and being by myself, and everything happening so fast—"

"Now stop worrying, Ellen. I'll be in the room across the hall if you need me for anything," he said quickly. "But right now, you rest up. I'll see you at supper."

Longarm looked for a moment at the bed when Esteban closed the door of his room. He knew that he should follow the advice he'd just given Ellen, and rest for a few minutes before doing anything more. He told Esteban, "I need a bath and a shave, but let's put 'em off for about an hour. Right now I need shut-eye a lot more'n I need anything else."

Esteban frowned. "What is thees 'shoot-eye' *señor?*"

"Sleep," Longarm replied. "I'm going to take off my boots and have a nap. You rouse me in about an hour."

It was not Esteban who roused Longarm, but Maldonado. As exhausted as he was, the slight scraping of the metal door latch was enough to wake Longarm from the deep sleep into which he'd fallen the instant he stretched out on the bed. Longarm had taken his usual precautions before lying down; his gunbelt hung on the headboard of the bed, and once again the *mayordomo* found himself staring into the revolver's muzzle when he turned around after closing the bedroom door.

"You do not need the gun, Custis," Maldonado said. "I have no reason to harm you."

"A man in my job never is sure who his friends are when he's in a strange place," Longarm replied. He lowered the Colt, but did not return it to the holster. "What've you got on your mind, Maldonado?"

"A great deal has happened," Maldonado replied. "Things

of which I know too little. I must have your explanation of how the job you were supposed to do was finished, and if it was not done, then I must know that too."

"I ain't inclined to do a lot of talking right now," Longarm said. He knew he had very little with which to bargain, but he intended to make the best use of what he had. "I'm in about the same situation as you are. There's a whole lot behind this job you hired me for that I don't know about."

"You knew all that you needed before you left here," Maldonado said harshly. "Instead of bringing back news of a success, you have brought back four bodies. Why should I tell you anything now?"

Longarm did not reply at once. He knew of only one key that would unlock the door leading to Aguierre, and that was Magro, the old Comanchero. Finding Magro on his own might be impossible, but Longarm was reasonably sure that Maldonado knew where the old man was, if indeed Magro had returned from the fight on the prairie. If Magro had not returned, then he would be forced to look for another key to Aguierre's door. He decided to gamble.

"Before I tell you anything, Maldonado," he said firmly, "there's a man I got to talk to. I guess you'd know him. His name's Magro."

"Why must you talk to this man? I am the one who employed you. I am the one to whom you should tell your story."

"I aim to talk to Magro for one reason. Zarzalo was still alive when I got to where him and the others fought the Comanches. He told me to talk to Magro before I said a word to anybody else about what happened."

Maldonado's slitted eyes widened and an entirely new expression took shape on his scarred and pitted face. "Zarzalo told you to do this? Why?"

"I don't know exactly why. He said some things I didn't understand, just before he died. I was trying to keep him alive, but he was too far gone."

"If Zarzalo told you to talk with Magro, then you must do so," Maldonado said. He spoke as though he were talking to himself; his voice lacked its usual harshness. The abrupt change puzzled Longarm. Maldonado stood up. "Very well, Custis. You will wait for me here in this room after dinner. Then I myself will take you to see Magro."

"How come you changed your mind so fast when I brought out Magro's name?" Longarm asked.

"Because I know him. And because I know that Zarzalo would not tell you to speak with him unless it was important." Maldonado hesitated, then said abruptly, "You see, Custis, Magro is my grandfather. And Zarzalo was my father."

Chapter 18

Longarm stared at Maldonado, his mouth open in surprise. He realized now the reason why Zarzalo had reminded him of someone, why he'd felt he should have recognized him. Maldonado had his father's profile and thin face, but the scars that marred the son had disguised the resemblance between him and his father.

"I didn't know that," he told Maldonado. "And I'm sorry if I said anything about him that hurt your feelings. Zarzalo struck me as being a right good man, even if he was in a bad business. If things had been a mite different, him and me could maybe have got along pretty good together."

"He did what was forced on him," Maldonado said stiffly. "He might have had a different life if it had not been—" He stopped and pressed his lips together tightly. "In my language there is a saying, '*No hay rosas sin espinas.*' 'There are no roses without thorns.' It was my father's way to pick the roses and pay no attention to the wounds he got from the thorns."

"He told me about him being Mr. Aguierre's half-brother," Longarm went on slowly. "Asked me to make sure he was buried here, instead of out on the prairie. That's one reason I come back, to bring his body."

His eyes fixed across the room on nothing, Maldonado said, "The burial service will be held at sunrise tomorrow. There is no longer a priest living at the plaza, so Don Feliciano will read the service. It will be a family affair only."

"Maybe I'm stepping on a sore toe, but I got the idea your daddy and your uncle didn't get on too good."

Maldonado did not have to answer Longarm's question with words. His outthrust jaw locked and he shook his head angrily. Sitting up, Longarm reached for the cheroots and matches that lay on the chair beside the bed and lighted up. Then he said, "But if you're Zarzalo's son, that makes Aguierre your uncle. How come he's got you working for him like a servant?"

"To tell you everything would take far too long. There will be time to do this later."

"Why in hell didn't you say something about all this family business before?" Longarm asked.

"It had nothing to do with our arrangements before."

"Well, it sure does now. When we was setting up the deal we made, you didn't say a word about your uncle being mixed up in it. As I recall, you acted like you was doing all that make-like-Comancheros business on your own."

"I was doing what Don Feliciano had ordered me to do. He did not want it known that the scheme was his."

"Maldonado, you better sit down right now and spill the whole story, so I'll know where everybody around here fits in."

Maldonado shook his head and started for the door. "Not now, Custis. What you call the whole story must wait. I will come for you after dinner tonight, we will go together and talk with Magro."

"Magro's here?" Longarm asked. "He got away from that fight without getting hurt?"

"He got away, but not without harm. He was badly wounded. I have not been able to talk with him yet. He was almost senseless with pain when he arrived, and the *curandera* gave him some laudanum. He should be waking soon. By nightfall he will be able to talk with us."

Longarm frowned. "Does Aguierre know he's back?"

"No. I cautioned the *peones* who knew to say nothing. Now I must go back to my work before Don Feliciano misses me."

When Maldonado had gone, Longarm stretched out again,

but the new information he'd gotten from the *mayordomo* kept buzzing through his mind, and sleep would not come.

You're into a real big tangle of mighty slippery fish, old son. There ain't any kind of a fight worse'n a family fight, and that's what this thing's turned into somehow. Blood being thicker'n water, and you being a son of a bitch from outside, the whole damn Aguierre family's apt to gang up against you when the cards is all on the table. So step light and keep one eye behind you, and maybe you'll get this untangled and find out whether Aguierre or Maldonado or Magro ought to go to jail, or whether you'll want to nab all three of 'em.

He got up, swallowed a good-sized drink of Daugherty's, and lighted a fresh cheroot before he laid down to do some further thinking.

At dinner, refreshed as much by a bath and shave as by the short rest he'd had, Longarm faced Don Feliciano de Aguierre across the length of the long table. Ellen Briscoe sat at one side of the long, narrow table between the two men. Her presence put an atmosphere of mutual cordiality on what might otherwise have been a taut and uncomfortable meal.

Don Feliciano was almost curt in his treatment of Longarm. He concentrated his attention on Ellen, whose imagination had been caught up in the hacienda from the first moment she'd seen it. The idea of such an establishment in so deserted an area fascinated her, and she kept the conversation going with a series of questions about its history and the manner in which it had been built.

Don Feliciano's conversation with Ellen revealed that he was not a widely traveled man. His orientation was not toward the United States, which to him and his contemporary *hacendados* was an alien power that had invaded and conquered the homeland that had been settled by their ancestors nearly three centuries before. Until he discovered that Ellen was not a Texan, but came from faraway Boston, he had been as cool to her as he was throughout the meal to Longarm. Don Feliciano did not consider himself a Texan, though the Plaza Aguierre had become a part of Texas long before his birth.

After receiving several near-snubs from his host, Longarm made no effort to take part in the stream of talk that flowed between Ellen and Don Feliciano. He did not want to draw too much of his host's attention; being virtually ignored suited him perfectly. He sat back and enjoyed the meal and listened.

When dinner ended, Don Feliciano rose and said, "We will go into the *sala* for coffee and brandy, and continue our talk there, Señorita Briscoe. There is a great deal I have not yet told you of the plaza, and of how my family has enlarged it over the years."

"I know your family's story is interesting, Mr. Aguierre," Ellen said. "I do want to hear more of it, but I'm terribly tired. Would you mind if I excused myself from joining you men for coffee? I need to go to bed and catch up on my sleep."

"Of course," Augierre said apologetically. "It was thoughtless of me not to remember what a great strain your experiences must have been. But you will remain as my guest until you have recovered fully and can travel easily again, so there will be other times for us to talk together."

"Thank you," Ellen smiled. "I'll say good night, then."

Longarm took the opportunity to escape an after-dinner session with Don Feliciano. As soon as Ellen had gone, he said at once, "I guess I'll beg off too, Mr. Aguierre. I'm just about as worn out as Ellen is."

"To be sure." Aguierre shrugged. "As you wish, Señor Custis. We too will talk later."

Longarm did not have to wait long in his room. He'd had a quick swallow of Daugherty's and was lighting a cheroot when Maldonado slipped in the door.

"I have been watching to see how long Don Feliciano was going to keep you and the woman in the *sala* with his stories," he said. "If you are ready, we will go now to talk with Magro."

"Ain't your boss apt to spot us if we go downstairs now?" Longarm asked.

"We will not go down the main stairway. There is a small one the house servants use. If you are ready, let us start."

Maldonado led Longarm down the hall to an inconspicuous door near its end. Maldonado opened the door to reveal a small landing and a narrow spiral stairway.

"This stair was used in the old dangerous days," he said, motioning for Longarm to follow. "It goes down to the serving-pantry off the kitchen and to one of the turrets on the roof. When Plaza Aguierre was first built, there were sentries posted in the turrets day and night to watch for Apache and Comanche raiders."

Longarm heard women's voices laughing and chattering in

195

the kitchen as he followed Maldonado across the deserted serving-pantry and out a door. He found himself at the side of the big main building. Maldonado led the way past the stables and the small one- and two-room huts of the hostlers and household servants to a narrow gate in the wall that encircled the hacienda. A footbridge spanned the *acequia* just outside the gate. Along the course of the ditch that carried water to the walled enclosure, the lights of a number of small houses twinkled in the darkness.

Maldonado did not tell Longarm where they were going, but started walking briskly along the well-beaten footpath that ran beside the *acequia*. The night was dark, lighted only by the stars, but Longarm's eyes quickly adjusted to the gloom as he walked beside Maldonado, skirting the area dotted with the small houses—enough of them to make up a sizable village—that were occupied by the people of the plaza. There were only two of the houses beyond them when the *mayordomo* stopped and tapped on the door of one of the little adobe huts. A stooped and ancient woman, her face seamed with deep wrinkles, her head wrapped in a *rebozo*, opened the door.

"*Como 'sta Magro?*" Maldonado asked.

"*Es convencido. He sido hablando,*" she replied.

Maldonado gestured for Longarm to follow him inside. The ceiling of the little one-room house was so low that Longarm had to stoop slightly to keep his hat from brushing it. The interior walls were whitewashed like the outside, but the plaster here was intact except for a few cracks.

A religious plaque depicting a haloed, winged figure with its arms raised in the gesture of a blessing hung on one wall by a wooden peg driven into the adobe. Candles on a low shelf behind a small woodburning stove and on the table that occupied the room's center provided a flickering light as their flames wavered in the draft from the closing door.

Magro lay on a narrow bed that stood along one wall. His head was bandaged, and a second bandage held one arm pressed to his chest; the bandage extended over the shoulder. Longarm had seen enough men suffering from bullet wounds and the shock that went with them to know that Magro was in very bad shape. His breathing was so shallow that the rise and fall of his chest was barely noticeable. He lay on his back, his obsidian eyes glistening in the candlelight as they darted from Longarm to Maldonado to the *curandera* in turn.

"*Meneste que hablamos con el,*" Maldonado said.

"*Solamente para poco tiempo,*" she replied. "*Es cansado!*"

"*Conozco, conozco!*" Maldonado told her impatiently. "*Pues, vete a su casa para la cena. Volve en dos horas, menos o mas.*"

"*Bueno. Pero cuidarse que no hace fatigoso Magro,*" she warned, shaking a gnarled finger under Maldonado's nose. "*Es muy debilidemento.*"

As soon as the woman had closed the door behind her, Maldonado pulled the room's two chairs up to the side of the bed. He motioned for Longarm to sit down and settled into the second. For a moment he sat studying Magro's drawn, wrinkled face.

"*Abuelo,*" Maldonado began, "*Es tiempo de dolor entrambos, pero se meneste continuan la vida.*"

"*No diga que no conozco,*" Magro replied hoarsely, his old voice a rasping whisper. "*Zarzalo no sera el primero de mis compañeros que se muerte, y no sera el ultimo.*" He stopped when a fit of coughing siezed him, then asked, "*Qué quieres ahora, Hernan, tu y el pistolero Americano?*"

"*Es que dijo mi padre al Americano, antes de muertando,*" Maldonado said. "*Y habla Inglés, abuelo, como entiende Custis.*"

Longarm welcomed Maldonado's request that the old man speak English. He'd barely managed to get the gist of the rapid-fire conversation between Maldonado and the woman, and even though at the slower pace of the men's speech he could pick up enough words here and there to follow them more easily, he didn't want to risk any misunderstanding in what was to follow.

Magro turned his head slowly and painfully until he could look into Longarm's eyes. "What is it *mi yerno* say to you, *hombre*?"

Longarm hid the new surprise that Magro's question had just given him. Nothing he'd seen during the time he'd observed Zarzalo and Magro together had given him a hint that any family ties connected them, nor had Maldonado mentioned that his mother was Magro's daughter. He'd thought when Maldonado had called the old man "grandfather" that he'd only been following the Spanish custom of addressing all old men by that title. The skein of relationships at Plaza Aguierre seemed to be getting more tangled the further he saw it unwinding.

Speaking slowly, he said to Magro, "Your son-in-law told

197

me to ask you how all this raiding out on the Llano Estacado come about. That's all. He didn't even say you was related."

Maldonado broke in before Magro could reply. "*El patrón* does not like to be reminded of his father's habits. It is not discussed on the plaza."

"*De verdad,*" Magro agreed. He shifted his gaze back to Longarm. "You are *Tejano*, no?"

"No. I come from back East. Place called West Virginia."

"Is good. I talk to you, then. I speet on *Tejanos*," Magro said. He frowned. "Is begin long ago, these raidings. When *los diablos Tejanos* is try to steal from *Nueva Mexico* these land where *Plaza Aguierre* is build so long ago, *la gente Aguierre* are always fight with *Tejanos*. Before *los Tejanos* come, we are fight for the land against *los indios*—Apache, Comanche, Kiowa. Now, when *Tejanos* take the land, we are stop to fight *los indios* because they fight *los Tejanos* for us. We are help these *indios* by trade them guns, powder, lead, all like so. From this we are call 'Comancheros' by *los Tejanos*."

His long explanation had exhausted Magro's strength. He sagged back on the pillow, his eyes closed. Longarm said in a low voice to Maldonado, "That's real interesting, but what I want to know is why them raids is going on now."

"Be patient, Custis. My grandfather will tell you that too, but we must let him do so in his own time."

Magro stirred, opened his eyes, and looked to make sure he was still holding Longarm's attention. Then he went on, "In the time of my father and his father, is always one of Aguierre men to lead *los Comancheros de Aguierre*. Is *pundonor*." He looked at Maldonado and asked, "*Conoce el pistolero acerca el linaje de su padre, hijo?*"

Maldonado said, "*Sí, abuelo.* He knows of my father's parents. Go on."

Magro nodded and resumed, "So you are know Raimundo is *bastardo*."

"Wait a minute!" Longarm interrupted. "We ain't talking about no Raimundo, we're talking about Zarzalo."

"*Es lo mismo,*" Magro said. "Is nobody from plaza keep true name when he go to be Comanchero."

Maldonado explained, "Men from the plaza went under assumed names in case the Texan ranging patrols caught them. My father called himself Zarzalo because he said it fitted his

198

life. In English, you see, it means thorny."

"*Lo mismo como Magro significa* 'skinny,'" the old man said. "Me, I am always so thin like *palillo de frijoles*. But is not my name, Magro, *de verdad se llama* Antonio Gonzales."

Longarm nodded. "I get it now. What we—" He caught himself in time and went on, "what the lawmen call an alias, so if you got in trouble, they couldn't trace you back to the Aguierres."

Maldonado nodded, and gestured for his grandfather to go on. Longarm felt sure he could guess most of the rest of the story, but there were still points he wanted to clear up. He looked at Magro attentively as the old man resumed.

"Is make good Comanchero, Zarzalo. I am teach him myself. He is not like idea to start, is make heem do this thing, Don Feliciano."

"*Abuelito*," Maldonado said, "I will tell him about Don Feliciano later, myself. Save your strength now. Tell him what you have done lately."

"*Bueno*." Magro nodded. "So, we are to be Comancheros no more when soldiers is beat Comanches and put them to *reservaciones al norte*. Then a little while since now, is say Don Feliciano we must be Comancheros again, only now we are not go to trade with *los indios*, we are to make raid on *ranchos*, on the little homesteads, kill those who live in them, steal the animals, put fire to the houses. But what is say *más importante*, Don Feliciano, is we are to find *los papeles de propriedad* of these places, and bring them to him."

"Why?" Longarm broke in to ask.

"Is not say why to me, Don Feliciano. But Zarzalo is know. If Don Feliciano have *los papeles*, these places belong to him, the law say."

"Did Zarzalo—" Longarm stopped and turned to Maldonado. "Excuse me. I just can't think about your daddy by his right name, I guess."

"It's not important," Maldonado shrugged. "It does not hurt my pride, Custis. Not as much as thinking of the reasons why my father had to become Zarzalo. But what were you going to ask my grandfather?"

Longarm turned back to Magro. "Your Don Feliciano's got more land then he's got use for, it looks to me. Why'd he want them little bitty homesteads and the ranches that ain't ever going to get no bigger till somebody figures a way to get enough

199

water to 'em so's they'll carry a good cattle herd?"

"Ah." Magro smiled. "Is know this thing, Don Feliciano."

"He's figured out how to get water where there ain't none?" Longarm frowned. "Hell, if he can do that, he don't need to go outside the law to get rich. He can do it by selling water."

Magro shook his head. "Is not enough he should sell *la agua*. Is want all the land, all the water himself. Is very greedy man, Don Feliciano."

"You know this secret way he can get water to flow where there ain't none there to start with?" Longarm asked.

This time Magro nodded. "*De verdad*, I am know. I am with Don Feliciano and Zarzalo when is find out how."

"You really got my curiosity humped up now," Longarm said. "Maybe you'd feel like telling me about it?"

His eyebrows raised questioningly, Magro looked at Maldonado, who nodded. The old Comanchero said, "Was happen two, three years ago. Is then no more Comanchero trade, so I am to be *ganadero*."

"Sheepherder," Maldonado translated in a half-whisper.

Longarm nodded without taking his attention away from Magro. The old man's eyes looking into the past, he went on with his story.

"Is *balnerio*, like you say, water hole, big *laguna*, where I am take sheep. Is dry, the little spring that keep *balnerio* full. So I tell Zarzalo, and Zarzalo tell Don Feliciano we must find new range for sheep. But Don Feliciano is make angry, he esay we make *bomba*, maybe it open up spring and make run again. So we do this thing, and when is go off, *la bomba*, is come big water, ten, twenty times so much as old spring. Is *agua artesiano, puro y claro*."

"You reckon all the little springs and ponds around here'd pour water that way, if somebody was to blast 'em?" Longarm asked thoughtfully.

"*Seguro*," Magro assured him. "Don Feliciano is do this at other places. Always is come big water, big *como un río*."

"Did you know about this blasting business?" Longarm asked Maldonado.

"I have heard of it. My father mentioned the matter once or twice."

"Hell, I don't wonder that Aguierre wants every bit of all the land he can grab!" Longarm exclaimed. "All the Llano Estacado needs to turn it into prime cattle country's a little bit more water, and if Magro's right, he didn't figure out how to get just a little bit. If it's artesian water, it'll be a big lot!"

A long, low sigh from the bed drew the instant attention of both men to Magro. The old Comanchero lay quite still, his eyes closed. Longarm leaned closer to the bed, and could see Magro's chest rising and falling regularly.

"He's all right," he told Maldonado. "Just got tired out from talking, and went to sleep. Well, there ain't any use in us tiring the poor old fellow out anymore. I can guess at what happened after that. Aguierre decided he'd just get the title to as much land as he could, fair or foul, and set about doing it."

"What he did not tell you, I can," Maldonado said. "Though I do not see why you wish to know. The job you were hired to do ended when the raids failed, when the Comanches attacked your companions and you were not there to fight beside them."

"You can't blame me for that, Maldonado. It was Zarzalo told me to stay behind. Just like he told me to come here and have a talk with Magro. I've found that when things go wrong, a man like me is apt to have a hard time collecting his pay."

"I have not discussed that matter with Don Feliciano," Maldonado said stiffly.

"Are you saying he might not feel like paying me?"

"I am saying nothing until I talk with *el patrón*."

For a split second Longarm debated revealing to Maldonado his real identity, but decided to wait. He sensed that Zarzalo's son was angry and bitter, but did not know whether the anger was directed against him or against Aguierre, or whether, if his anger was with Aguierre, it cut deeply enough to overcome what seemed to be a blind loyalty to Don Feliciano. Longarm decided to play what few cards he had very close to his chest indeed, and even to do a bit of bluffing to make them seem better than they were.

"That *patrón* of yours, he sure don't give you much room to make up your own mind, does he?" he asked. "Seeing as you're his nephew and doing all the work, it'd seem to me he'd trust you a little bit more. After all, if push comes to shove, you ought to have Zarzalo's rightful share of this place."

"My father was not left a share in my grandfather's will. The fault is not that of Don Feliciano," Maldonado said stiffly.

"Just the same, if he'd done the right thing by your father, you'd be Don Feliciano's partner instead of just working here.

But I guess you've thought about that before now."

Maldonado's face turned livid. He started to reply, but before he could speak, Magro's hoarse voice broke the silence.

"He is right, *nieto. El pistolero Yanqui dice que es verdad*," the old man said. "*Dijera a su padre muchos tiempos.*"

"*No es su asunto, abuelo!*" Maldonado snapped. He turned to Longarm. "We will go now. There is nothing more Magro can tell you, I am sure."

"No, I guess there ain't," Longarm agreed. He did not think it necessary to tell Maldonado that he'd learned far more than he expected.

Maldonado bent over Magro and kissed his forehead. "*Duerte, abuelo*," he said.

"*Bueno, Hernan. Y oye que dice este pistolero. Es hombre muy sabido.*"

"*Sí, sí. Descanso, ahorita. Hablamos más mañana.*"

Maldonado walked back to the hacienda in silence. When he and Longarm reached the door to the spiral staircase, he said, "Don't worry about getting paid, Custis. I will make it a point of honor to see that you receive what is owed you."

"Now I take that real kindly, Maldonado. I'll see you in the morning, then, and me and Ellen will be riding out early."

"Not too early. There will be the funeral. But it should be finished by eight or nine o'clock."

"I ain't expected to go, am I?"

"It will be for the family only. Not even the servants will attend. Now I will bid you goodnight. I still have a duty to perform."

Longarm lighted a cheroot and stood outside the door, watching Maldonado walking into the night's gloom. He saw a light appear in the stable, and realized what Maldonado's duty was: to keep vigil beside Zarzalo until time for the burial service. He shook his head thoughtfully and mounted the stairs.

He turned the knob of the door leading to his bedroom and started to push the door open, but stopped after it had opened no more than a crack. He remembered that he'd left the lamp burning in the room when he'd left. Drawing his Colt, he flung the door wide and slid inside with his back against the wooden panels, his Colt fanning out to cover the room.

"My goodness, Longarm!" Ellen Briscoe exclaimed. "I hope you aren't getting ready to shoot me!"

By the faint light that spilled into the room from the hall, Longarm could see Ellen now. She was sitting up in the bed, the nipples of her bare breasts dark dots in the dim light.

"All I knew was, somebody was in here," Longarm told her. "If I startled you, I'm sorry."

"When I saw the gun I was scared, but now that I see it's you, I'm not a bit frightened," Ellen said. "Why don't you close the door, put your gun away, and come to bed?"

Chapter 19

"I wasn't expecting you to be here," Longarm said. "After supper you said you was tired and wanted to go to bed, so I just figured you'd be asleep." While he was talking, he holstered his Colt and closed the door. He stood in the doorway for a moment, waiting for his eyes to adjust to the dim light of the room.

"I was tired then," Ellen told him. "And I slept until a little while ago. I don't know why I woke up, but I did. Then I couldn't get back to sleep because I started thinking about all the death and killing I've seen the past day or two."

"There's times when things like that's better forgotten."

"I know that," Ellen replied. "But it's too fresh to forget it. I needed to be with somebody to prove I'm still here, still alive. Oh, I guess all the time I was thinking about you being right across the hall, and remembering our night at the LX—a hundred years ago, it seems like—and, well, here I am."

"And I'm right glad too." Longarm could see well enough to move around the room now. He'd found the Daugherty's on the bureau and swallowed a nightcap, and was going through his bedtime routine of hanging his gunbelt on the headboard, his vest on a chair. He sat down to lever off his boots.

"You sound glad, Longarm, but you don't act like you are," Ellen said, a hint of disappointment in her voice. "I thought you'd be glad to see me."

"Now you know I am, Ellen. I'm hurrying as fast as I can to get rid of these clothes so I can show you how much."

Longarm stripped off his trousers and balbriggans and stood up. Ellen threw back the covers and slid to the side of the bed. She put her hand out and found him, and Longarm felt her warm, soft fingers close around his beginning erection.

"I can feel that you're really starting to be glad now," she said, holding him cradled in one hand while she gently stroked his swelling shaft with the other. She leaned forward to bring the pebbled rosettes of her breasts to touch his tip, and traced around them with gentle pressure.

For several moments Ellen continued to caress her breasts as Longarm's erection grew firmer. Then she pulled her body closer and pressed his shaft into the valley of flesh between the two firm globes. She held him while she slowly twisted her shoulders from side to side.

Ellen's skin was warm and soft, and the gentle friction that resulted from her body's movements quickly brought Longarm fully erect. He put his hands on her shoulders. Ellen turned her face up to him, and he bent to kiss her, opening his lips to take in the questing tongue that quickly sought his. He felt her hands on him again, closing around him, clasping and squeezing, then stroking him with velvety fingertips, lifting and fondling his heavy pouch.

She broke the kiss with a sigh and gasped, "I can't wait for you another minute! Now, please, Longarm!"

Ellen released him and fell back on the bed, lying across it. She brought her hips up and dropped her elbows to the bed to brace herself with a hand on either side of her hips. She lifted her legs high, her calves resting on Longarm's broad chest, her own body suspended, only her shoulders on the bed.

Longarm understood what Ellen wanted. He grasped her ankles and spread her legs wide. Taking a step forward, he freed one hand long enough to position himself, and when he felt the warm, moist softness that waited for him, he slid into her slowly, inch by inch, until he was fully inside her.

Except for an occasional quiver of pleasure as she felt him sinking ever deeper into her, Ellen had lain passive. Now, for the first few moments after she felt him filling her, she still did not move. Longarm remained motionless too, making no effort to thrust, simply pressing into her at full length.

Slowly at first, then more rapidly, Ellen began to rotate her hips. Longarm took this as her signal for him to begin stroking. He began in the same slow, deliberate fashion that she was moving, with a shallow withdrawal and a deliberate return to bury himself completely, then held his groin hard against her moist pubic hair for several moments before beginning his next slow stroke. Then, as Ellen suddenly stopped her twisting and began to rock her hips up and down, her buttocks suspended in midair, he withdrew farther and plunged in faster.

Ellen was panting now. Between her deep inhalations she gasped, "I know it takes you longer that it does me, so I'm going to let go. I can't hold on any longer!"

"Go on, take your pleasure," Longarm replied. "I still got a while to wait."

In the dim light he saw Ellen's eyes close tightly. Her lips parted as she rocked her hips faster and faster while he responded by driving deep and hard, and then when she began to quiver, Longarm grabbed her soft buttocks and pulled her upward to meet his long swift thrusts. Ellen's breathing grew erratic, the soft flesh of her buttocks grew firm in his hands as she squeezed to hold him with her inner muscles. Longarm drove hard during the final few seconds before she cried out in a little smothered scream and surrendered to her body's release with a last wild upthrust of her quivering hips.

Longarm pulled her buttocks to him, buried himself in her all the way, and held her there while she gasped and shivered and her stiffened muscles slowly grew soft again as she relaxed with a soft, fulfilled sigh.

After she'd lain limp for a short while, her hips supported in midair by Longarm's hands, she opened her eyes and looked up at him through the soft gloom and said, "You're a very satisfying man, Longarm. Big and long-winded, and willing to help a woman do what she enjoys the most. I wish I could do as much for you as you do for me."

"Why, you do, Ellen. A man won't do a woman much good unless he helps her take pleasure while he's having his."

"And it doesn't bother you if a woman likes for a man to give her pleasure in more ways than one, does it?"

"Not a bit. As long as she's enjoying it."

"Come lie down, Longarm," Ellen said. "Strong as you are,

you must be getting tired of standing there holding me. But don't break away from me. I like feeling you in me too much to want to let you go, even for a minute."

Ellen pulled herself farther onto the bed while Longarm stepped forward and lowered himself on top of her. They rolled across the bed together, turning in unison without breaking the connection that held them together, and lay side by side, one of Ellen's thighs under Longarm, the other draped over his hips.

"I want to please you for a while now," she told him.

"You are pleasuring me, like I just said."

"But I want to pleasure you still more, Longarm. Help me move now, so we can roll around a little bit without having to come apart. Because just feeling that big shaft of yours still hard in me is making me want more."

Guided by the pressure of Ellen's hands, Longarm moved as she silently directed while she turned her body until he was lying on his back and she was kneeling above him. She drew her knees up and lifted herself with a hand braced on the bed. Longarm raised his head to kiss her budded rosettes, drawing his tongue over their pebbled surfaces and pressing her protruding nipples between his lips.

Ellen shivered with pleasure as she felt the rasping of his tongue, but did not stop what she was doing herself. She was poised above him, rotating her hips, lifting her body and then letting it fall heavily, then slowly raising herself again to repeat her sudden fall.

Longarm lay back and let her ride him at her own pace. She lifted her hips high and brought them down with a quick, hard jerk, and raised and lowered herself until she'd found the tempo that suited her best. For what seemed to be a long while, Ellen bounced up and down on his hips, then when her bouncing grew more frenzied, she pushed herself erect and brought her feet under her thighs and hunkered down straddling his hips, trying to take him even more deeply.

Longarm was bracing himself to respond to her orgasm when she stopped the bouncing of her hips and lifted herself up until he was in her only shallowly. He felt her hand on him, rubbing around the point where he entered her, then her hand moved to the crease of her buttocks and returned to grasp him again. She raised her hips, freeing him.

Ellen arched her back, bending forward, then Longarm felt

his shaft slick with Ellen's juices, slide along in her buttock-crease until it reached the small puckered orifice above the nest he'd just left. Ellen rubbed the tip along her crease for a brief moment before she began to lower herself. She gasped as she took Longarm in, and stopped. He put his hands into her armpits and held her erect, feeling her body trembling as she poised rigidly above him.

"You can let go now, Longarm," she said, her voice trembling. "You're the biggest man I've ever had in me this way, but I'm going to take you in there no matter how much it hurts me!"

Longarm released her and Ellen let herself down slowly, now and then drawing a sharp, quick breath as he penetrated her, but she continued to lower her body until he felt the cheeks of her taut buttocks resting on his hips. She found one of his hands and pulled it to her crotch, and he slid his forefinger into her while she put his thumb on the small, firm button that nestled in her brush.

Slowly Ellen started rocking up and down, and with his fingertip, Longarm could feel his shaft moving inside her. Her buttocks grew firm as she tightened the inner muscles encircling him and began to rock her arched back gently.

Suddenly Longarm's fingers were wet as Ellen's juices began flowing while she shuddered and writhed, laughing in little gasps that were half sobs trickling from her throat as her entire body shuddered. She jerked into a rippling spasm that held her for what seemed a small eternity before her spasm ended and she let go with a wild cry and her body shook even more violently than it had before and she fell forward, only to cry out in pain and pull herself erect, away from him.

"I didn't mean to hurt you, Ellen," Longarm said as she lay shaking on him. He caressed her back with his hands, smoothing the muscles that he felt still twitching under her silken skin.

"You didn't hurt me," she said, kissing him gently. "It was just too much pleasure for me to stand. It always is, but I knew it'd be the best I'd ever had, because you're so big and can stay hard so long. I just had to have you that way, even if it was selfish of me."

"It wasn't if it pleasured you all that much."

"I wasn't thinking about you, though." Ellen closed her hand around Longarm's erection, still firm between her sprawled legs, and said, "I'll think of you, this time. You must be ready now, after staying hard so long."

"I am, if you're sure you are."

Ellen slid off Longarm and pulled him to her. She slid her thigh under him and guided him into her while they lay on their sides, face to face. She raised her lips to his, and he met her tongue as it slid out for him. Longarm brought his hips up in a quick thrust that sent him fully into her, and Ellen sighed and cuddled him into the soft embrace of her thighs, holding him to her while he stroked on and on, unhurriedly.

When Longarm felt Ellen's thigh muscles begin to tighten on his waist, he speeded up. He did not hold himself in check this time, knowing that she was building as he was. He rolled on top of her as he drew closer to the time when his body would take control, and speeded the tempo of his lunges when she began heaving up her hips to meet his thrusts.

Ellen reached her peak a few seconds before Longarm, her body heaved under his quick, hard plunges, and he felt her melting away in the instant before her smothered gasps began. Longarm was pounding by then, and as Ellen writhed and cried out, his hot spasm began and his body jerked as he drove into her for a few final plunges before he was totally drained, then he let his head down on the resilient cushions of her breasts and both of them sighed and lay quiet and spent.

They went to sleep still joined, and did not wake up until the sound of a rooster, heralding the false dawn, filtered through the high narrow window. Longarm stirred to look out; the stars had faded from the rectangle of sky visible through the window. His movement roused Ellen. She rolled away from him with a sigh, sat up and stretched and yawned.

"I haven't slept with a man in me all night since my honeymoon cooled off," she said. "I'd forgotten how good it is to wake up and feel someone filling me."

"And your husband died a while back, you told me," Longarm remarked. "How long were you married, Ellen?"

"Three years. And he died two years ago. But in case you're worried, I'm not looking for another husband. I like the idea of being free."

"I wasn't thinking about that, Ellen. Anyhow, you wouldn't want a husband like me, never at home much."

"Speaking of home, Longarm, how much longer will you have to stay here? I'm sure Bob and Annie must've given me up for lost, and I feel badly about that. If there were just some way to let them know—"

"I'm afraid there's not. But if everything goes smooth, I

ought to be able to close out my case today, and if you ain't too tuckered out, we can start on back sometime after noon."

"I still don't understand everything that's going on, but I can wait to hear about it until we're on the way back to the LX."

"Soon as I've got things wound up, I'll let you know."

"And I'd better get back to my own room before the maid comes to wake me up."

Ellen kissed Longarm quickly and slid off the bed. She picked up a robe from the floor and put it on. She opened the door a crack, listened to make sure the hall was deserted, and, with a smile and a quick goodbye wave, was gone.

True dawn was lighting the window now; the soft gray of the before-sunrise sky spilled enough light into the room to dispel most of its darkness. Longarm got up and padded to the bureau to pick up the bottle of Daugherty's and take an eye-opener. He carried the bottle back to the bed, put it on the chair, and lighted a cheroot.

He had a second sip of the rye, savoring its smooth bite, and began thinking of the day ahead. It occured to him that his badge was still in the pokehole of his saddle, and that he'd need it when he faced Don Feliciano de Aguierre. He remembered the funerals then, and realized that the little shed where the bodies lay was next to the stables. Within a quarter hour, a half hour at the most, the area around the stables would be buzzing with activity. He decided to retrieve his badge while he could still open the pokehole unobserved.

Clamping the cheroot in his strong teeth, Longarm dressed quickly: balbriggans, shirt, trousers, and boots. He strapped on his cross-draw rig, set his hat dead center on his crisp brown hair, and started down the hall.

He moved quietly, though the silence of the deserted hall told him that the hacienda was not yet astir. However, Longarm's plan was to avoid Don Feliciano until after the funerals had reminded the *hidalgo* of his own mortality. To be safe, he took the turret stairway. No sound of pots rattling or servants' chatter came from the kitchen when he passed through the pantry that separated it from the dining room. Longarm opened the narrow outer door and stepped outside into the phantom light of the pre-sunrise dawn.

Lights were just beginning to show in the small houses along the *acequia*, but no one moved around in the area enclosed by the wall. Longarm walked hurriedly to the stables. A peg-fastened hasp held their wide doors shut. He took out the peg and slipped inside; the shutters along the back wall had not been left open overnight, and the darkness was thick with the smells of manure and horse sweat and leather saddlery.

Some of the horses in the stalls stamped and whinneyed when they heard Longarm enter, but they quieted quickly when he pulled the door closed, leaving it cracked open for a few inches to let a breath of fresh air and a bit of light into the big shed. He stood quietly while his eyes grew accustomed to the almost total darkness. As his vision returned, he saw saddles and harness and other tack lined up on racks along the wall on both sides of the door, but in the gloom he could not make out his own gear.

Longarm began groping along the racks to his right, trying to locate his McClellan saddle by feel, but the job was a slow one. He had not encountered his saddle when he came to the end of the rack. He turned back, and halfway along the left-hand wall his fingers identified the familiar hornless pommel.

Fumbling with the catch of the pokehole in the darkness, Longarm opened it and took out the wallet that held his badge in its fold. He slid the wallet into his pocket and closed the pokehole, then started back toward the door. He pushed the door open and was stepping outside when he saw a lantern bobbing along the *acequia*, its light glinting off the surface of the water that ran in the ditch. Maldonado was carrying the lantern, Don Feliciano walking beside him. Longarm slid back into the darkness of the stable, but did not close the door, for the two men were close enough now to see its movement.

"*Mira, Maldonado,*" he heard Don Feliciano say petulantly as the two came abreast of the stable. "*Algún tonto no he asegure la aldaba!*"

"*Pues, arreglarte, patrón,*" Maldonado replied.

Longarm stepped back away from the door as he saw Maldonado's hand reaching for the hasp. The door closed and he heard the soft scrape of the peg being put in place. The footsteps of the two men outside faded away.

Knowing it was useless, Longarm pushed against the door, but it was securely closed. He put his eye to the narrow crack that showed a strip of light between the door's two halves, and saw men from the huts walking toward the stables; they must, Longarm thought, be the ones assigned to carry the corpses to the family cemetery that Maldonado had told him about.

Longarm took a match from his pocket and rasped his thumbnail across its head. By flaring flame he saw that the shutters on the opposite wall were secured by inside latches. He sidled through the nearest stall and unlatched the shutter. It took him only a few seconds to lever himself over the sill and drop to the ground behind the stable. Just as his feet touched the ground, a wild cry of anguish mixed with rage sounded from the shed where the bodies had been placed.

Longarm froze in his tracks. Looking around, his hand ready to sweep out his Colt, he saw no one. The wild cries he'd just heard had subsided quickly, replaced by a jumble of voices. A quick look around revealed the source of the voices. The shed was a lean-to attached to the stable, sharing a common wall. The shutters at the back of the shed had been left open, and it was through the window that the voices were coming.

Longarm moved quietly along the stable wall until he could peer into the shed. Don Feliciano de Aguierre knelt in the center of the shed, his arms upraised. Maldonado stood behind him, and men from the plaza were crowded in the doorway. None of them would have noticed Longarm even if he had not kept well back of the window through which he was looking. All eyes were fixed on the side wall of the low-ceilinged shed.

Along that wall, lashed to planks that leaned against the whitewashed adobe bricks, stood the bodies of Zarzalo, Lefty, Perez, and Morris. The corpses had been stripped to the waist to show their bloodstained torsos, pocked by the wounds of the bullets that had killed them. Narrow strips of wood had been affixed to the planks to support the right arm of each corpse, and the fingers of each extended hand pointed accusingly at the center of the small room. As a final grisly touch to the tableau, the eyelids of the dead men had been pulled open and their glazed eyes appeared to be staring with fixed intensity at the center of the shed.

Longarm needed no explanation of the scene inside the little building. He understood at once the impact the gruesome sight must have had on Don Feliciano when it was revealed by the light of the lantern as he preceded Maldonado into the shed. He looked at Aguierre. The *hacendado* was slowly lowering his arms, but his body was still trembling as he rose to his feet.

"Quién coloquia este infamia?" he demanded, his voice

shaking. He turned to the *mayordomo*. "*Maldonado, conoces algún de esta cosa espantosa?*"

Maldonado shook his head slowly, his eyes fixed on the body of his father. "*No, patrón. No se de algún.*"

"*Porqué no pode centinela anoche?*" Aguierre asked angrily.

"*No parece que sera necesario!*" Maldonado protested. "*Antes de medianoche, esta aquí yo mismo, orande para la alma de mi padre!*"

Don Feliciano had brought himself under control by now. He said, "*Pues, descubre que perpetrado esta espanto, y castigarle! Ahorita, dice algunas de este hombres cubiertan los cuerpos, y vemos al enterramiento!*"

Longarm stepped back from the window and took stock of his situation. The wall that encircled the hacienda rose only a few yards from the back of the stable where he was standing. The sun was rising, flooding the enclosure with light, and he could see no way of getting back to the main house until the bodies were being taken to the burial ground.

With a philosophical shrug, Longarm accepted the inevitable wait. He squatted down, his back to the stable wall, and waited. By the noises that came from the shed, he could tell when the little procession left for the burial grounds. After he'd given them enough time to get outside the wall, he walked along the back of the stable, crossed the *acequia* on one of the wide planks that spanned it at intervals, and went on to the hacienda.

By the time he got to the door leading to the turret stairs, the kitchen was buzzing with activity. None of the women noticed him as he passed through the pantry and climbed the stairs to the second floor. The corridor between the bedrooms was still deserted, and within a few moments he was back in his own room.

Picking up the bottle of Daugherty's as he passed the bureau, Longarm put it on the chair beside the bed. Lighting a cheroot, he took a swallow of the rye before stretching out on the bed to map the final moves that would bring his case to a close. He was still lying there a quarter hour later when a light tapping sounded at the door. Longarm swung his feet off the bed and kept his hand ready to reach for his Colt.

"Come in," he called.

Esteban entered. "*Buenos días, señor.* Eet weel be late this morning, the breakfast. Ees not for the half hour yet. I am help you to get ready, no? You like the shave today?"

"Why, I don't think I'll need any help, Esteban. I already got my clothes on, and you give me a good close shave last night."

Esteban bobbed his head in a half bow. "Then I go back to kitchen to do other work, eef you are sure."

"I'm sure. Thanks all the same, Esteban."

When Longarm entered the dining room a half hour later, Don Feliciano was seated in his usual place at the head of the narrow table. Even if Longarm had not known the reason, he would have noticed that the *hildalgo*'s morning had not been tranquil. His short-trimmed beard looked frowsy and uncombed, and in spite of his plump cheeks, his face looked drawn and haggard. When he turned to look at Longarm, dark smudges showed below his eyes. He acknowledged Longarm's arrival with a nod that was nearly no nod at all, so slight was the movement of his head.

Ellen sat on his right in the center of the long span, looking as fresh as though she'd spent the night alone, sleeping in her own bed. At the end of the table opposite Don Feliciano, a place was laid for Longarm. He did not wait to be invited, but went to it and sat down.

As though Longarm's arrival were a signal, Maldonado entered from the kitchen, followed at once by servants carrying platters of food. Maldonado took his place close to the wall and stood watching while the servants offered the platters around the table, then put the platters down and departed.

Don Feliciano filled his plate, but made no move to begin eating. He sat looking down at the food for a moment, then pushed it aside. Longarm and Ellen looked up, but he motioned them to continue eating. He watched them for a short while, then abruptly pushed his chair from the table and stood up.

"You will pardon me, I hope," he said. "Ordinarily I would not be so discourteous as to absent myself from my guests at a meal, but I ate quite early this morning. My stomach is somewhat uneasy, and the smell of the food is upsetting it still further. I ask you to excuse me. Maldonado will see that you are well served."

"I hope you ain't feeling so sick you'll have to go to bed, Mr. Aguierre," Longarm said. "I'd sort of like to set down and have a little talk with you after while."

"Maldonado will—" the *hacendado* began, but Longarm cut him short.

"I'm afraid this ain't something anybody but you can settle, Mr. Aguierre," he said firmly. "Of course, if you're real sick, I'll just wait around till you get better."

Aguierre gazed at Longarm for a moment, his eyes slitted. He opened his mouth to reply, but closed it and shook his head. Then, after a thoughtful pause, he said, "It is a small stomach qualm, no more. It will surely pass in a few moments. Come to the *sala* when you have finished your breakfast. We will talk there."

Chapter 20

Ellen watched Don Feliciano leave, a frown rippling across her brow. She said to Longarm, "I hope Mr. Aguierre being sick isn't going to keep us here another day. The more I think about Bob and Annie, and how they must feel, not knowing what's happened to me, the more anxious I am to start for the LX."

"Likely it won't hold us up," Longarm assured her. "What I got to talk about with him ain't going to take long."

"I'll go upstairs and get ready to leave when I've finished eating, then." Ellen smiled and added, "I forgot. I don't have anything to pack or any real getting ready to do."

"Go on up to your room and rest anyhow," Longarm told her. "Soon as I finish my business with Mr. Aguierre, I'll come up and get you."

They finished breakfast quickly and in silence. Ellen left to go upstairs. Longarm pushed his chair away from the table and lighted a cheroot. Maldonado still stood by the wall of the dining room. Longarm took a step toward him, and Maldonado came forward to meet him.

"There's a little matter I need to talk to you about," Longarm began.

"If it is the money for the job, I will see that you get it before you leave," the *mayordomo* said curtly.

"That wasn't exactly what I had in mind right this minute."

"What is it, then?"

Longarm studied Maldonado's lean scarred face while he took a puff on his cheroot before replying. He was still unsure of the amount of trust that he could place in the man. Finally he said casually, "I guess what your boss seen out in that shed by the stable sort of ruined his appetite. Can't say I blame him. It wasn't what I'd call a pretty thing to look at."

Maldonado's mouth fell open. His eyes slitted as he recovered from his surprise and asked, "How did you learn about what happened in the shed, Custis? I am sure that none of the house servants have yet heard about it yet."

"Oh, I got ways of finding out things I'm interested in. I don't expect you had anything to do with it, though. You don't strike me as the kind of man that'd go say prayers for his daddy and then set his corpse up for a show of that kind."

Maldonado shook his head. "I was as surprised as Don Feliciano when I saw the bodies, though looking at them did not shock me as greatly as it did him."

"You know, I give some thought to that business while I was waiting for breakfast," Longarm said. "And it strikes me as the kind of thing a real tough old man that's seen a lot of ugly things in his life might do. If he wasn't in such bad shape, I'd be mighty suspicious it was your grandpa done that."

Maldonado hesitated for a moment, then nodded slowly. "That thought occured to me also. I have heard him tell of the old rough days when he led the Comancheros of the plaza. *Abuelito* would not hesitate to use dead men as those were used, even if one of them was his own son."

"Just like after that fight with the Comanches," Longarm suggested. "When he seen everybody but him was killed, he was tough enough to get out of there and save his own skin, even if one of the dead men he had to leave was your daddy. But from what I seen last night, Magro's not in good enough shape to do a thing like that. Not unless he had some help."

"There are still two or three old men living here in the plaza who were Comancheros with my grandfather," Maldonado said thoughtfully. "They would do whatever he told them to."

"You got any idea why he'd do it?"

"As a warning to Don Feliciano, perhaps. That is the only reason I can think of."

"Well, I'll leave it to you to settle whatever there might be between you and your grandpa," Longarm said. "Now I got to tell you something, Maldonado. But before I do, I'll ask you a question or two, if you don't object."

"What sort of questions, Custis? I have already told you that I will see you are paid."

Longarm decided the time had come when he must trust Maldonado, no matter what the risk. He did not know how many men there were on the estate who were loyal to the Aguierre family, but he guessed that they'd outnumber him at least fifty to one. He wanted to be sure that after he arrested Don Feliciano he'd be able to take him to the nearest jail without having to fight his way out of the plaza against that sort of odds.

"I ain't got money on my mind right now," he told Maldonado. "Fact of the matter is, Custis ain't my full name." Longarm paused as a puzzled frown began taking shape on Maldonado's face.

"That does not surprise me," he said with a thin smile. "A man of your trade must use many names."

"Sometimes he does," Longarm agreed. He went on, "My full name's Custis Long, Maldonado. I'm a deputy United States marshal, and in about two minutes I'm going to walk across the hall and arrest your boss for breaking the federal homestead laws, because that's all I got the authority to arrest him for. But I'd guess after the whole story gets out, he's going to have a few murder charges to face too."

"You are saying—" Maldonado began.

Longarm did not let him finish. "I'm saying I intend to take Aguierre to jail when I leave here. And I want you to guarantee that I can get him out of here without any trouble."

Maldonado stood silent for such a long while that Longarm thought he did not intend to answer. Finally he said, "If you had told me this before, Custis—or Long, I should say—I would have fought to keep Don Feliciano free. But what has happened during these past days—" He shook his head sorrowingly. "Don Feliciano has changed in the past months. I have not let myself see how much until now, because in our way of life, *el patrón* can do nothing wrong. But it is I who have been wrong, I see that now. The killing and raiding of homesteads must stop. Arrest him, Long. I promise you, there will be no trouble from the people of the plaza."

Longarm nodded. "Thanks, Maldonado. Now if you'll just see that nobody busts in on us while I'm breaking the bad news to Mr. Aguierre, I'll appreciate it."

"I will stand outside the door of the *sala* myself to be sure none of the servants interrupts you."

Don Feliciano was sitting in front of one of the small corner fireplaces when Longarm went into the salon. On a small table beside him stood an earthenware jug. Longarm remembered the jug; it contained the potent Taos Lightning that he'd tasted on his first stop at Plaza Aguierre. In the *hacendado*'s hand there was an almost full glass of the liquor. His gaze was fixed on the crossed swords and ancient helmet that hung on the wall of the *sala*, and it was easy for Longarm to see that he'd been thinking over the days of his family's past glory. He took his eyes off the relics and stared at Longarm.

"What is this important matter about which you wish to speak to me?" he asked. "If you are looking for further employment, I thought I made it clear that Maldonado is the one you must speak to about such things."

"You expect to go on just like you been doing, then?"

"If you think I will be discouraged or will stop my raids because the one for which you were hired was badly handled, you have misjudged the determination of the Aguierres! I must have many thousand more acres of land before my plan can succeed!"

"I've found out a little bit about that plan too. Magro told me you've figured out how to get artesian wells started on almost all the little ponds and creeks on the Llano Estacado—"

Longarm did not have a chance to finish. His mention of artesian water had touched off a spark in Aguierre's mind, and the *hidalgo* leaned forward in his chair, his eyes glowing.

"That is true," he said. "And can you not see what the water will mean? I must have all of it for myself to make a new time of greatness for the Aguierres!" He refilled his glass from the jug and stared with glowing eyes at Longarm as he drained half the liquor in a single gulp. "Soon the world will speak in awe of Don Feliciano de Aguierre! My cattle, my sheep, my acres, will make the Aguierres the most important family between the two oceans! Here where my ancestors created only an estate, I will create a kingdom!"

"I'm afraid you ain't going to like what I got to tell you, Mr. Aguierre," Longarm said. He took the wallet containing his badge out of his pocket and flipped it open. "The fact is, I'm a deputy U.S. marshal, out of the Denver office. My whole name is Custis Long, like it says here on this badge."

Don Feliciano did not appear to understand. He gazed frowningly at the badge and began shaking his head.

Longarm went on, "I got to arrest you and take you to jail for breaking the federal homestead law."

Don Feliciano drained the liquor from his glass before he replied. The whiskey—together with what he must have consumed earlier, while waiting—seemed to give him courage.

"What kind of talk is this, this showing of false badges and threats of arrest?" he asked. "Do you take me for fool? You are a trickster, like all your kind! What is it you are after? A share of the wealth we Aguierres will have soon?"

"I ain't trying to trick you, Mr. Aguierre. And you can't buy me off. You're under arrest for breaking the federal homestead law by stealing deeds to file under a false name."

Don Feliciano stared indignantly at Longarm. "You—you have violated my hospitality, wormed your way by trickery into my house! Now you think to arrest me like some common criminal?" He laughed. "Oh no, my *pistolero* friend! Even if you are the federal officer you claim to be, I am too clever for you!"

"I don't see how you figure that," Longarm said. "I was on that raid, remember. I know you hired me and those men that you told to call themselves Comancheros, and I'll testify to that in court!" His anger mounting, he went on, "If I could do it, I'd arrest you for murder too, but there ain't no federal law that covers the kind of killing your men have been doing. I sort of guess Texas will bring some murder charges against you, though."

"Bah!" the *hacendado* snorted. "From the first I have seen that someone might discover my plan and because of their envy try to betray me. But I have taken care that this shall not happen!"

"I ain't betrayed nobody, Mr. Aguierre," Longarm replied. He could see that Don Feliciano was too drunk to accept reason, and wanted to get his job finished. He went on, "Now you'd best just decide to come along with me quiet and peaceful."

"A moment!" Don Feliciano seemed to be sobering up now. He looked at Longarm and smiled smugly. "To what can you testify in court? You were not employed by me, but by Maldonado. I have given you no orders of any kind!"

"Now as far as that goes, it's true enough," Longarm agreed

reluctantly. "But I was along with your Comancheros, I seen what they done to that homestead where two people was killed. I can sure as hell testify to that!"

"But you cannot swear of your own knowledge that men in my employment were responsible! Oh, yes! I have studied *Yanqui* law and know what you must do to prove me guilty of anything illegal! And there is no one else who can give such testimony! My half-brother, the bastard whom you knew as Zarzalo, is dead. So are the men who rode with him. Of course, there is Maldonado, but he will not talk. He is completely loyal to Plaza Aguierre, and to me, his *patrón*!"

"Not so!" Maldonado said loudly from the doorway. Longarm and Don Feliciano turned to face him. The *mayordomo* went on, "I helped you, Don Feliciano, because my father was also Aguierre."

"He was not Aguierre!" Don Feliciano broke in. "He was a bastard! He did not bear the Aguierre name!"

"He had as much Aguierre blood as you! The same blood that flows in the veins of your children flows in mine!" Maldonado retorted. "Evil man, do you not know why my father did as you wished? He began following your orders when I was a child, to get the money you denied him, to bring me up, to educate me like the *hidalgo* I am! To make me worthy of being Aguierre! You denied me this, as you denied it to him!"

"You are not true Aguierre!" Don Feliciano snapped angrily. "Your blood bears the taint of your bastard father and of the *peon* mother who bore you!"

"Do not speak so of my father and mother!" Maldonado shot back. "You make me ashamed of the very name itself, and of the Aguierre blood I carry!"

"Aguierre blood should be pure *hidalgo* blood!" Don Feliciano's voice rose to a shout.

Longarm started toward Don Feliciano to subdue him before the argument erupted into violence, but as he was taking the first step, the *hacendado* kicked the small table that separated them into Longarm's path. The move was so unexpected and the distance the table traveled was so short that Longarm could not dodge. The table struck his legs and sent him crashing to the hard tile floor.

Don Feliciano covered the distance to the wall in a single long stride and grabbed one of the crossed swords. While Longarm was still trying to untangle himself from the table, Don

Feliciano was running toward Maldonado, the heavy blade raised.

"Tainted blood deserves to be spilled!" he shouted.

Maldonado stood his ground. He had opened his coat and was reaching for the butt of a revolver that was tucked into the waistband of his trousers. Don Feliciano was less than two steps from him when Maldonado finally got the pistol out and leveled it. Then the glitter of steel cut through the air from the doorway beside him, and a knife suddenly appeared, stuck in Maldonado's forearm. His hand sagged as he triggered the revolver, and its bullet ricocheted off the floor to lodge harmlessly in the adobe wall.

"Aguierre!" Longarm shouted, "Drop the sword!"

Instead of obeying, Don Feliciano whirled at the sound of Longarm's voice and started running toward him, the sword still raised, ready to strike.

Longarm was not as clumsy in drawing as Maldonado had been. His Colt was in his hand spitting lead before Don Feliciano closed in on him. The slug from the Colt tore through the crazed *hidalgo*'s heart. Don Feliciano's body jerked at its impact, his knees buckled, and he dropped. The sword clattered to the floor as it fell from his lifeless hand.

From the doorway, Magro's voice rasped, "You are better with *la pistola* than I am think you to be, *Yanqui*." He stepped to Maldonado's side. "I am not like to hurt you, *nieto*, but is better I stop you to shoot Don Feliciano as to see *el mariscal Yanqui* take you to hang." He raised his hand and showed them the revolver he was holding. "If not the *Yanqui* have shoot him, I am to do it."

Longarm nodded. "I just bet you would've too."

By now the noise of the shots had drawn a gaggle of house servants from the kitchen. One of the women plucked Magro's knife from Maldonado's arm and quickly swathed it in strips torn from her apron. Maldonado was in a state of shock; he acted as men do in such a condition, staring blindly, ignoring his wound. At last the realization of what had taken place struck him.

"*Abuelo!*" he gasped. "*Es enfermo! Creo que sera a su casa!*"

"*Soy un gallo tosco, nieto. Un Comanchero viejo como yo no se que significa enfermo.*" He turned to Longarm. "I am hear what you say with Don Feliciano. If is somebody to take to *el carcel, tome mí!*"

"*Es tontería, abuelo*!" Maldonado said sharply. He said to Longarm, "If there is someone to be arrested, Marshal Long, it should be me, not my grandfather. He is an old man, and sick. I will go with you willingly, if you will spare him."

Longarm managed to keep his voice sober as he said, "As far as I'm concerned, there ain't anybody to arrest, now that Mr. Aguierre's dead. He was the one I was after, even if he was right about me maybe not being able to make a case against him. I'd 've sure took him to jail and tried to prove something on him. But now he's gone, and I guess my case is closed. Just as soon as you can get some of your men to saddle up my horse and Miss Briscoe's, we'll be riding north."

Sunset found Longarm and Ellen sitting their horses on the rim of Yellow Horse Canyon, near the headwaters of the creek that ran through it. The canyon was little more than a shallow slash in the ground at this point, and the creek little wider than a bandanna. Longarm looked down at the miniature gulch and lighted a cheroot. He passed the long slim cigar to Ellen and lighted another for himself.

"It ain't such a much of a place, right here," he said. "But it's big enough to accommodate the two of us tonight. It'll keep the wind off, and there's water to spare for us and the horses."

"We'd better make camp, then," Ellen said. "I'll just have time to cook supper before dark. And even a bed on the ground will feel good to me, with you sharing it."

"That's about the way I feel," Longarm agreed.

He twitched the piebald's reins and led the way down into the canyon.

SPECIAL PREVIEW

Here are the opening scenes
from

LONGARM AND THE DEVIL'S RAILROAD

thirty-ninth novel in the bold
LONGARM series from Jove

Chapter 1

His upper lip fully lathered, a straight-edged razor in his right hand, Longarm leaned his face close to the cracked mirror resting on top of the dresser—and cursed.

He didn't want to do it. The thought of shaving off his longhorn mustache filled him with dismay.

But then, abruptly, he shrugged and began scraping at his upper lip. It was too late to think this over now; he had already snipped off most of the mustache anyway, and besides, he told himself ruefully, it served him right for making his face so damn familiar to so many hardcases west of the Mississippi.

The operation completed, Longarm dipped his big hands into the pan of water sitting in front of the mirror and washed the lather off his face. Then he toweled himself dry and shrugged into his black cotton shirt, over which he pulled a buttonless, black leather vest. From the top of the dresser he plucked a black eye patch and tied it over his left eye. He didn't like the one-sided view it forced on him, but he had practiced shooting while wearing the patch for the past week, and he was confident it would not hinder his gunplay too much.

He clapped a black, flat-crowned Stetson on his head and began pacing back and forth across the cabin's rough-plank flooring, shooting an occasional glance at the mirror as he did so. Faking a limp, he was soon moving with a kind of sinister, dipping stride. At last, satisfied that his transformation was complete, Longarm pulled up and nodded grimly at his reflection. Deputy U.S. Marshal Custis Long was now the infamous Wolf Caulder, notorious as a one-man execution squad and, for the last few years, a ruthless but efficient robber of isolated banks and small trunk railroads.

Stopping before his cot, Longarm pulled it away from the wall, then snatched up the carpetbag resting on it. Inside the carpetbag were his brown suit, shirt, and cross-draw rig, including his Colt Model T .44-40, along with his Ingersoll watch and its deadly watchfob: the double-barreled .44 derringer that had pulled him out of so many deadly scrapes in the past. He would miss both weapons, he knew. But they too, it seemed, were almost as well known as that longhorn mustache of his.

He had already pried up the floorboards under the cot and hollowed out a small depression in the earth beneath them. Into this small grave he placed the carpetbag, with his snuff-brown Stetson alongside it, then replaced the floorboards. With a heavy rock he nailed the boards solidly back into place, pushed the cot back against the wall, turned, and left the cabin.

Longarm swung up into the saddle of his waiting mount, a broad-chested roan gelding. He had selected this mount carefully, then had ridden it flat-out for days through this rugged country. Only when he was certain that the big, handsome animal was equal to its appearance and had the endurance it would need, had he allowed himself to purchase it.

He would need such a mount if he was going to be able to pull off this desperate gamble.

It was close to noon when Longarm reached Ridge Town, Idaho. Before he rode in, he held up a moment in the shade of a cottonwood to look the town over. He knew the town well enough, having visited it twice within the past week. What he wanted now was to make sure there was no unusual activity. He had chosen midweek, a Wednesday, and as a result the town was just as quiet as Longarm had hoped it would be. The last thing he wanted was to find himself in the middle of another Northfield debacle.

He watched the nondescript town bake silently in the noonday sun for a while, then urged his horse on out from under the cottonwood, rode past the water tower, crossed the plank bridge, and continued on down Market Street to the First National Bank, a wood frame building with a high false front. Dismounting in front of the hitch rail, he dropped the roan's reins over the rail, ducked under it, and mounted the wooden sidewalk. He looked quickly up and down the street, patted the Smith & Wesson that rested on his right hip in its flapless army holster, then pushed into the bank.

The bank appeared to have no customers. There were two cashier's windows. At one of them Longarm saw a clerk with a green eyeshade counting out greenbacks. Drawing his revolver, Longarm walked up to the clerk and thrust its muzzle into his face. Then he pulled a pillowcase from his belt and slapped it down across the counter.

"Get that safe open, mister," Longarm told the clerk. "And fill this here pillowcase."

But the clerk was in no condition to cooperate. Wide-eyed, his mouth working in fear, he thrust both hands into the air and stumbled backward, the greenbacks he had been counting fluttering down about him to the floor. Another clerk—a small, round-faced individual coming out of a small office beside the vault—took one look at Longarm and flung his arms up also.

"Hurry up!" Longarm barked. "Get that safe open!"

At once the second clerk knelt before the huge vault and, with shaking fingers, spun the tumblers and pulled open the safe. Impatient, Longarm vaulted over the counter, snatched up the pillowcase, and thrust it at the clerk.

"Who—who the hell are you?" the round-faced clerk demanded as he took the pillowcase from Longarm.

"I ain't Jesse James," Longarm said, "if that'll make you feel any better. Name's Caulder, Wolf Caulder. But I like money just as much as Jesse does. So get in there and fill this up!"

The man swallowed unhappily and hurried into the vault. In a moment he returned with a bulging pillowcase and handed it to Longarm. Longarm took it, limped swiftly through the low gate, and hurried toward the door. Before he reached it, however, a gun roared behind him and a chunk of the door sill exploded in his face.

He looked back and saw that the clerk with the green eyeshade had a huge Colt in both his hands and was pulling it down to get off another shot. Longarm flung a bullet at the man, then ducked out of the bank, cursing. The shots had already roused the sleeping town. From a hardware store across the street, three men bolted, one of them carrying a rifle.

Longarm snatched up his mount's reins and vaulted into the saddle. Wheeling the roan about, he fired at the three men across the street, then clapped spurs to his roan and headed for the plank bridge at a full gallop, the deadly rattle of rifle fire erupting behind him.

He glanced back.

The three men had mounted up and were being joined by two others. As the five riders swept down the street after Longarm, two more joined them, throwing lead as they came. Longarm clattered over the wooden bridge, swept past the cottonwood, and let his mount have its head. At once he felt the animal's powerful legs increase their stride.

Once more he looked back at his pursuers. The small posse had not yet reached the water tower. Even as he watched, he saw other riders joining up, causing a momentary milling about as the posse decided on its leadership. Longarm smiled, turned back around, and patted his mount's neck, urging him on with soft words of encouragement. The animal responded with a second powerful surge as Longarm glanced ahead of him at the dim, spectacular ramparts of the Bitterroots. He was certain, now, that he would reach them safely.

Two hours later, his horse cropping the meadow grass behind him, Longarm watched the posse winding its way up the narrow valley toward him. When he judged that it was time, he returned to his horse, led it over to a small sapling, then tied its reins securely to the sapling's trunk. He did not want the firing of his Sharps to spook the horse. He could not afford to lose it now.

Withdrawing the Sharps from its saddle scabbard, he clambered up onto the shelf he had selected a week before. Sitting down crosslegged, he unbuckled his cartridge belt and set it down on the grass beside him. Half the cartridges on the belt were .50 caliber, center-fire. He brought up the Sharps, levered the trigger guard, which opened the chamber, and slipped one of the .50-caliber slugs into it. Pulling shut the trigger guard, he wedged the rifle's stock into his left shoulder and sighted carefully down the barrel at the lead rider. He judged the distance at just under six hundred yards.

He had already cut himself a shooting stick. He now put the rifle down and stuck the stick into the ground. The stick was not very steady, however, and he had some difficulty finding a spot able to accept the stick deep enough—but at last he was ready. He rested the barrel of the Sharps in the crotch of the stick and began to track the lead rider once again.

The distance was close to five hundred yards by this time. He pulled the hammer of the Sharps back gently, tucked the stock securely into his shoulder, aimed, took a deep breath—and squeezed the trigger.

The stock dug into his shoulder as the Sharps recoiled, its detonation filling the narrow valley with a reverberation that seemed to increase in intensity with each echo. Longarm saw the lead rider pull up suddenly as a chunk of granite from the wall over his head splintered down upon him.

Chuckling, Longarm reloaded, sighted carefully a second time, and fired. This time the turf in front of the second horse-man exploded. In a moment the posse was milling in the narrow valley, trying to decide where the shots were coming from. Longarm reloaded rapidly and fired a third time. A branch just above a posse member galloping up to the leader snapped off and crashed down before the rider. The horse reared almost straight back, flinging the rider to the ground.

So far, so good, Longarm told himself. It had been a long time since he had used a Sharps, but it had never failed him before, and it sure as hell was doing the job at this moment. Figuring one more shot would do it, Longarm reloaded, aimed carefully, and fired again. He cut it pretty close this time, and saw the lead rider grab for his hat a split second after the slug ripped it off his head.

Cold sweat stood out on Longarm's forehead. He swore softly, reverently. He had not intended to cut it *that* close!

But that last one did the job. The riders whirled about and galloped back down the narrow valley. Before long they were well out of range, and a moment later they were out of sight. A broad smile on his face, Longarm picked up his cartridge belt and slipped down off the shelf and headed for his mount.

It was close to sundown and Longarm, astride his mount, watched the cabin far below him carefully for signs of life. He had been waiting on this ridge for close to an hour and was beginning to lose hope. But the indolence of the more slothful members of the human race was something that never failed to amaze Longarm; he kept his vigil and waited patiently.

At last his patience was rewarded. A lone figure left the cabin carrying something—it looked like a slops jar—and emptied it off the lip of the ridge on which the cabin had been built. Then, scratching his untidy mop of gray hair, the fellow returned to the cabin and disappeared inside.

Longarm knew the man.

His name was Cal Short. He used to rob banks, stagecoaches, and anything else handy, and had, as a result, served time in a few of the more notorious prisons of the West. But since his last term he had not raised a bit of dust, and yet was quietly and rapidly getting wealthy as he lazed away his days and nights swilling whiskey in this mean little cabin he had found in the middle of the Bitterroot Mountains.

Satisfied that Short was in the cabin, Longarm relaxed and eased himself out of his saddle and took a long, lazy stretch. So far everything had gone just as he had planned. Wolf Caulder had just robbed another bank, confirming the fact that he was still at large.

Only Longarm and Marshal Billy Vail knew the truth—that Wolf Caulder had been gunned down by a young Mexican gunslinger in a cantina somewhere south of Chihuahua, Mexico, six months ago. It was only by chance that Vail had discovered this fact, and when he had reported it to Longarm, both men saw in it the chance they had been waiting for all these months.

The moon was up, a ghostly silver dollar sitting on the peaks behind him, when the sound came of many riders galloping up the narrow draw leading to the ridge below. In a moment the posse appeared. Before the horsemen arrived at the cabin, Cal Short appeared in his littered front yard, cradling what looked like a shotgun in his arms.

The posse halted before him. Not a single rider dismounted. Longarm could not hear what was being said, but he could imagine the dialogue. Since everyone in the county knew of Cal Short's past and of his recently acquired affluence, he was naturally the first person they would seek out in their attempt to find Wolf Caulder. After a moment of dickering, Longarm saw two men dismount and move past Cal Short into his cabin.

The search did not take long. The two men left the cabin and mounted up. After a few more words with Short, the posse turned about and rode off, moving this time in the direction of Ridge Town. Longarm waited a decent interval, then mounted up and set his horse walking down the slope toward the cabin.

He did not dismount when he reached the ridge, and made no effort to quiet his approach to the cabin. As expected, the lantern within the cabin winked out suddenly, and a moment later the door opened and a white-haired figure appeared in the doorway. In the cold light of the moon, Longarm caught the gleam of his shotgun's two barrels.

"Okay, mister," Short called out. "Hold it right there. And don't make no moves sudden-like."

"Hadn't intended to."

"Who are you?"

"Wolf Caulder."

The man squinted up at Longarm in the dim light, then moved closer for a better look. Longarm sat his mount quietly and let Short get as close as he wanted.

"Hell, sure enough. You're Wolf Caulder, all right. Eyepatch and all. There was a few men on horseback up here not too long ago, lookin' for you. Seems you robbed the First National Bank in Ridge Town. You must be a rich man all of a sudden. That so?"

"It's getting chilly out here and I could use a cup of coffee."

Short chuckled. "Guess you could at that," he said. "Light and set a spell. A man with your reputation is always welcome."

"That's what I heard," Longarm said, dismounting.

"You can leave your mount go loose," Short told Longarm. "He can run with my animal in the meadow below. There's always fresh graze and plenty of water."

Longarm nodded and set to work unsaddling the roan. As he busied himself with the cinch, Short told him he would put the coffee on, and walked back into his cabin. Longarm smiled with satisfaction as he lifted the saddle off the roan, then peeled off the sweat-stained saddle blanket.

The plan was working. He had reached the first station on the Devil's Railroad—and he had his ticket already. It was inside that pillowcase he had filled at the bank.

A moment later, after watching the horse kick up its heels as it disappeared into the meadow below, he lugged his saddle toward the cabin's open door, smelling with anticipation the aroma of fresh coffee heavy on the air.

But as he started through the doorway he heard quick, light footsteps behind him and felt the mean bite of a gun barrel prodding him cruelly in his back. Before he could turn, there came a sharp, clear woman's voice whispering to him to keep going without uttering a sound, or she would be forced to shoot him in the back.

Longarm hesitated only a moment, then moved into the cabin. His back to the door, Short was placing a coffeepot on the table. The man suspected nothing, either. With an inward groan, Longarm dropped his saddle on the floor and turned about to face the girl. The big Colt in her right hand did not waver.

He was startled by her beauty and by the icy anger he saw in her dark eyes. All this planning, Longarm thought wearily, and a fool woman mucks it up.

LONGARM

He's a man's man, a ladies' man—the fastest lawman around. Follow Longarm through all his shoot-'em-up adventures as he takes on the outlaws—and the ladies—of the Wild, Wild West!

_____	05983-8	LONGARM #1	$1.95
_____	05984-6	LONGARM ON THE BORDER #2	$1.95
_____	05899-8	LONGARM AND THE AVENGING ANGELS #3	$1.95
_____	05972-2	LONGARM AND THE WENDIGO #4	$1.95
_____	06063-1	LONGARM IN THE INDIAN NATION #5	$1.95
_____	05900-5	LONGARM AND THE LOGGERS #6	$1.95
_____	05901-3	LONGARM AND THE HIGHGRADERS #7	$1.95
_____	05985-4	LONGARM AND THE NESTERS #8	$1.95
_____	05973-0	LONGARM AND THE HATCHET MAN #9	$1.95
_____	06064-X	LONGARM AND THE MOLLY MAGUIRES #10	$1.95
_____	05902-1	LONGARM AND THE TEXAS RANGERS #11	$1.95
_____	05903-X	LONGARM IN LINCOLN COUNTY #12	$1.95
_____	06153-0	LONGARM IN THE SAND HILLS #13	$1.95
_____	06070-4	LONGARM IN LEADVILLE #14	$1.95
_____	05904-8	LONGARM ON THE DEVIL'S TRAIL #15	$1.95
_____	06104-2	LONGARM AND THE MOUNTIES #16	$1.95
_____	06154-9	LONGARM AND THE BANDIT QUEEN #17	$1.95
_____	06155-7	LONGARM ON THE YELLOWSTONE #18	$1.95